Praise for

The Sun in Your Eyes

A *New York Times Book Review* Editors' Choice

The *Wall Street Journal* calls *The Sun in Your Eyes*
one of "the season's most exciting fiction reads"

One of *Vulture*'s "7 Books You Need to Read This July"

Harper's Bazaar picked it as one of
"Spring's Hottest Breakout Novels"

One of *Chicago Tribune*'s "30 Books
You Should Read This Summer"

"Marital torpor, love triangles, adultery: big themes that Deborah
Shapiro touches on in her debut novel about female friendship . . .
[but] Shapiro's quarry is rarer. She's after a subtle emotional mix . . .
a subset of nostalgia reserved for intense, unresolved relationships
we're trying to outgrow. . . . Shapiro adroitly conveys the women's
complicated intimacy, their shared history and private jokes. . . .
Lee's erotic pull, inherited from her father, is a rich loam feeding
the women's friendship. Shapiro turns over just enough of this to
satisfy our curiosity. Viv and Lee were never lovers, but they did,
for a time, complete each other. What happened to that closeness—
and how to move beyond it—is as much a mystery as Jesse Parrish's
long-lost tapes." —*New York Times Book Review*

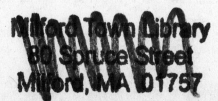

"A novel that shines darkly, like literary glitter. Deborah Shapiro has created a glamorous world of irresistible, erudite narcissists and perfectly tousled sociopaths—the people we commonly call 'artists.' She's given that world gravitas by zeroing on the casualties of these personalities—their children. Lee and Viv, for all their efforts at collecting the trappings of adulthood, are still trying to make sense of their intimate, stifling friendship, and the tragedy that has haunted Lee all her life. Two women on a road trip—through romantic, exclusive enclaves on the East and West coasts—trying to untangle the mystery, not only of Jesse Parrish's death, but also of how to let go of the damages of their youth; in short, they're two women who are trying to grow up. Shapiro's prose is elegant, effortless, but it's her characters that will keep you up late into the night, making you hope you can save them, while knowing you can't."

—Stephanie Danler, *New York Times* bestselling author of *Sweetbitter*

"The novel is grounded in the richness of its characters. . . . Shapiro's writing is light and lovely, evoking the sun of her title. . . . The scene, of the sort once presided over by Ellen Willis, Lester Bangs and Joan Didion, is . . . an evocative setting, but the main action remains in the space between Viv and Lee, in their closeness and distance."   —*Washington Post*

"*The Sun in Your Eyes* is a wise, funny and original road novel about female friendship, rock worship, and life in all of its odd turn-offs and detours. Deborah Shapiro's keen wit and deep compassion give her a dazzling grasp of her complex, passionate characters. This fantastic debut always surprises, always rewards."

—Sam Lipsyte, *New York Times* bestselling author of *The Ask*

"Deborah Shapiro's sharp, funny and engrossing debut novel, *The Sun in Your Eyes,* appears at a glance to be an examination of female friendship. It's that, sure; through the juxtaposition of the women's college days and their present-day road trip, Shapiro delves into her characters' psyche and reveals how they shaped one another. But the novel goes deeper still, as Lee and Viv are forced to examine their relationships with everyone close to them. As they uncover the truth about the past, the friends are left to decide whom they trust and how to move forward."
—*BookPage*

"Put down everything and pick up *The Sun in Your Eyes*! It's beguiling, funny, bighearted, and true—the perfect summer book. You're welcome."
—Ann Hood, bestselling author of *The Knitting Circle*

"Realistically complex, defined by moments of betrayal, loyalty, and closeness. . . . This novel unravels the competing nature of affection and jealousy in friendship, illuminating the stickier facets of emotional dependency between friends."
—*Kirkus Reviews*

"Deborah Shapiro is ferociously smart and ferociously funny. So is her novel. If Evelyn Waugh, Eve Babitz, Elaine Dundy, and Elaine Benes got together to tell a story about lost legends and lost friendship, it might read just like this: sensitive but unsentimental, lacerating but amused by the louche, poignant, and (often) lunatic. It's inescapably right about both our culture and the ways people need and then don't need each other, and it's full of existentially fraught one-liners that I couldn't help reading aloud to anyone who would listen. Says one of her characters about the alchemy of affinity: 'She only knew that it felt a lot like this: sitting with someone and wanting to keep sitting with them, to keep hearing what they said.' Open this book and you'll feel the same way."
—Carlene Bauer, author of *Frances and Bernard* and *Not That Kind of Girl*

"Often flat-out funny . . . with a skewering wit and keen attention to the outer details . . . that shape the characters, particularly the late 1970s. . . . A complex journey, but one a reader will want to make."
—*Washington Independent Review of Books*

"The nuances and subtleties of female friendship are highlighted in Shapiro's candid and humorous story. Viv and Lee are distinctive, each singing in their individuality. Through a well-crafted plot, Shapiro expresses clearly Viv and Lee's contrasting and conflicting thoughts, along with the indelible marks they leave on each other."
—*RT Book Reviews*

The Sun in Your Eyes

The Sun in Your Eyes

DEBORAH SHAPIRO

wm

WILLIAM MORROW
An Imprint of HarperCollins*Publishers*

P.S.™ is a trademark of HarperCollins Publishers.

HarperCollins books may be purchased for educational, business, or sales promotional use. For information please e-mail the Special Markets Department at SPsales@harpercollins.com.

A hardcover edition of this book was published in 2016 by William Morrow, an imprint of HarperCollins Publishers.

FIRST WILLIAM MORROW PAPERBACK EDITION PUBLISHED 2017.

Designed by Claire Naylon Vaccaro

Library of Congress Cataloging-in-Publication Data has been applied for.

ISBN 978-0-06-243559-0

17 18 19 20 21   OV/LSC   10 9 8 7 6 5 4 3 2 1

For Lewis and Callum

Remember it happy; the sun in your eyes.

—NICHOLAS MOSLEY, *ACCIDENT*

Did You Hear That?

Annie Davis

The Village Voice, March 3, 1975

I'll admit it: Jesse Parrish used to make me feel bad. Uptight. Not very rock and roll. Like the angry, anxious (ethnic?) New Yorker that I am. He always seemed to be asking, in his easy L.A. way: *Why are you trying so hard?* He made me question what I was seeking. Communion? Transcendence? Freedom? A revolution? He couldn't be bothered with your politics and their complications, he was too busy sustaining eye contact. Too busy, essentially, *being* sex. He was always so distractingly good-looking and sang with such aching need that you forgot to want anything else and what was my point?

Oh, yes. His one-off show at the Academy of Music last Saturday night. It's been less than a year since he released his latest album, *The Garden of Allah,* and then disappeared from view amid rumors he was getting clean or

seeking psychiatric help. I wasn't so sure I cared for that troubling record. Stark. Cryptic. Mercurial. It struck me as a fuck-you much more than a fuck-them and I couldn't find a way in. I struggled with just about every song and called it quits at the end of "Goodnight" when he repeats the line "Tell me you care" (I didn't). I heard it as taunting and cold, directed at someone he was ready to be done with. And it was as if he had to voice the line a few times merely to keep himself from falling asleep. The final word in bored detachment. But when he sang it on stage last weekend—tell me *you* care— it turned into a plea, an urgent, compulsive mantra. It was sad, searching, and sublime. I've sometimes thought of Jesse as a lesser, slightly campier Neil Young, and did I need a lesser, campier Neil Young? Maybe I did and never knew it. Maybe I never took him seriously enough. I don't think I could have before this.

Something has changed. Gone are the form-fitting, flamboyant outfits he used to slink around in. Gone, too, the flab and that mustache that followed, a kind of bizarro overcorrection. Let's never speak of it again. Except to say that for a short while there Jesse looked the way so much rock music sounds these days. Bloated. Lumbering. Blah.

I caught an echo at his show of what I used to hear, what it used to mean to me, what I wanted. What, deep down, I still do. Communion, transcendence, freedom. Revolution? I don't know. Call it rebellion. That spirit that never really goes away. It only goes underground if it has to, until it finds a new form, alive again. In the meantime, I'll be patient. I'll wait it out with Jesse Parrish. I'll tell you I care.

Jesse Parrish Dead in Car Crash
By Reuters, June 24, 1978

New York—Jesse Parrish, the singer-songwriter and guitarist, died on the night of June 22nd. He was 31 years old. Police said Mr. Parrish was killed when the car he was driving veered off the road and into a ravine in the Catskill Mountains. His girlfriend, Marion Washington, was in the passenger seat. Ms. Washington suffered severe injuries and has been transferred to the intensive care unit of a Manhattan hospital, where she remains unconscious. Mr. Parrish was pronounced dead at the scene. The county coroner's office has ruled it an accident.

Mr. Parrish, who is perhaps best known for his 1970 album *Motel Television,* had been separated from his wife, fashion designer Linda West, for nearly a year. He had struggled in the past with drug addiction. In recent months, however, he had temporarily left his home in Los Angeles and was staying at the upstate New York studio of producer Charlie Flintwick in order to record a new album and mount a comeback. "He was in great shape and in good spirits," said Mr. Flintwick. "He'd surfaced. He was up."

Fans have already flocked to the roadside where the accident occurred, creating a makeshift memorial. They expressed further dismay over reports that the recordings Mr. Parrish was making have disappeared from Mr. Flintwick's property. "Your guess is as good as mine," said Mr. Flintwick. "Jesse was something of a myth when he was alive. I suppose he's going to be a legend now."

Mr. Parrish is survived by his wife, Ms. West, and their four-year-old daughter, Lee.

some sort

of alchemy

Lee, 1996

There were many ways Lee tried to obscure the fact that she came from money, but flying coach wasn't one of them. She'd done it, once, in a kind of defiance of her mother, only to realize that her small act of rebellion meant little to anyone but herself and wasn't worth the lack of leg room. She took for granted luxuries like this, but she saw how they excited Viv. How her new—newish—friend took to the spacious first-class window seat like a just-crowned queen, poised but nervous.

"The good thing about being a catastrophist," Viv was saying, "is that it makes me get everything in order, in case anything happens."

"You mean, like, if we crashed?"

"Right, or if the house gets broken into while we're away. Or, you know, if there's an earthquake when we get to California."

"What do you even need to get in order?"

"Things."

"Things?"

Viv frowned, though she loved being drawn out.

"My journal. I have to make sure it's in a safe yet accessible place. Not like anyone would want to read it."

But you write in it as though you imagine someone will, thought Lee, who didn't exercise any preflight precautions—didn't plan for the worst, didn't unplug toaster ovens or check the stove and the faucets. She simply got on planes. Viv at nineteen was already thinking in posthumous terms. Lee, twenty-one, was thinking in terms of . . . what? Lee suspected Viv had what amounted to ambition, something she either didn't have, or more likely, couldn't admit to, for reasons she didn't want to dwell on. They were going to Los Angeles.

"Have you ever been in an earthquake?" she asked Viv. When Lee had come east for college, she'd fielded countless variations on that question. What was it like to live in a place with fault lines, no seasons, just sun? She would come up with something to say but she could never explain exactly what it meant, to grow up in L.A.

"Once," said Viv. "At a seafood restaurant in Maine, this place my family would go every summer. Checkered red-and-white oilcloths on the tables, buoys and lobster trawls on the walls, that kind of thing. My dad starts getting annoyed and tells my brother to stop shaking the table but then you could see, on the wall, this swordfish. Its nose had been pointed up and now was pointed down. Anyway, it turned out the epicenter had been in Quebec, and the seismic waves were weak by the time they reached New England, so it was basically just a quick ripple." That look again on Viv's face: *Why do I say these idiotic things to you?* But really it was a look within a look: *You want to hear these things.* And Lee did. She wanted to hear how Viv had parents who took her on vacations where they stayed at tidy motels, walked through paths of brambles to get to a rocky beach, and ate oyster crackers out of cellophane packets while waiting for their dinner to arrive in shallow plastic baskets. Viv could tell her the most mundane stories and Lee would find a point in them. *I know this about you and you know that about me.*

Viv had laid her winter coat across her lap, twisting her hands into it.

"You know there's a closet where we can put that."

"Oh, right. Of course."

"Sorry. That sounded really condescending."

"No, it's okay."

Viv handed over the large wool blazer, in black watch plaid, a dingy menswear label sewn by the collar. Lee had made her try it on at the thrift store. When they'd gone shopping, Lee had taken an armful of prospects off the rack while Viv had seemed at a loss, holding on to a seventies ski parka that looked a lot like the one she came in with. Lee insisted on the blazer. It didn't completely hide, as most of Viv's clothes did, her hourglass figure, and the deep blue and green flattered her complexion, bringing out the auburn notes in her hair. She looked instantly more grown up. Lee wasn't going to encourage her to start smoking, but this she could get behind. A way for Viv to present as a little less plain, even as Lee understood that plainness was Viv's cover, in a sense. Part of a deflecting modesty that downplayed her quiet but firm sense of self. What Lee wouldn't have minded having a little more of.

"I don't know how warm it'll be," said Viv.

"Wear a sweater under it. You'll be fine."

"Won't it clash with things? It's not very practical."

"It's great on you!"

"You think?"

"Get the fucking coat."

Viv had found a way to wear it just about every day since.

Lee passed it to the flight attendant with a theatrically underplayed smile and nod that she immediately regretted as something her mother would do. When she told Viv about Linda, Lee was never sure if she was trying to impress her or warn her, or both.

Former model, famous widow, Linda used to arrive at airports to a handful of photographers waiting for a glimpse of her at the gate: dark hair, bangs to her eyelashes, gauzy white tops or tight black knits, braless on occasion. Men and women alike were drawn to her. Women wanted to look like her, and so began the Linda West label: slinky dresses and high-waisted trousers in the seventies, bodysuits and blazers in the boxy eighties, and now the baggy, deconstructed pieces of the nineties. More than one magazine profile had used the word "timeless" to describe Linda's allure. An extremely expensive French handbag had been named for her, inspired by her *je ne sais quoi*. She had once been in a commercial that showed her prepping for a photo shoot, carrying her namesake satchel to a lunch meeting, assessing fabric samples in her office, and then coming back to an empty foyer a little lonely and forlorn, until she heard a girl's voice calling out "Mom!" Lee couldn't remember what the ad was for. It wasn't her voice and it wasn't their house.

Out Viv's window: a gray sky, slush on the tarmac. Lee watched luggage get tossed into the cargo hold as other passengers pressed their way into the plane. One of them stopped short to take the seat across the aisle. A youngish man who did a subtle double take as if he knew her from somewhere. He carried a just-beat-up-enough leather bag. His hair looked as if he hadn't washed it in a day or two, likely courtesy of some expensive product, to make you wonder what might be keeping him from shampoo. He glanced at his seat and then back at Lee. For a second, she thought he might ask if Viv wouldn't mind trading places and she wished Viv were a stranger who would get up and move. And then she felt terrible for thinking that. But he just said, "How's it going?" and sat down.

"Good," she said. "How're you?"

"Not bad. Can't say I'm the biggest fan of flying, though."

"No?"

"I'll be all right."

"You sure?"

He smiled as if he found her naïveté refreshing. Viv didn't kick her foot or anything, but Lee could sense her observing the interaction intently. Journal material.

"What?" Lee said, turning back to her.

"Nothing."

Seeing the slight hurt on her friend's face, Lee leaned her head on Viv's shoulder in a show of apology and affection. Something of a show for the man across the aisle, too.

Sometimes it felt to Lee that Viv had been standing in a crowded room, looking around and waiting, and Lee had come up and taken her hand and off they went. It looked as if one was leading the other, but when you take someone by the hand, you're also holding on.

"Let's get drinks," said Lee.

"Is that a thing we should do?" Viv was taken with the novelty of it.

"It's definitely a thing we should do."

"White Russians?"

A joke, but not. Who orders a White Russian? Viv did when Lee took her to a dank place in downtown Providence, not too far from College Hill but far enough. Students, mostly, and the occasional thirty-something nodding solemnly in the back. The bartender, a woman just a few years older, had looked askance at Lee—*Who is this girl in your charge and wouldn't she rather be at an ice cream parlor?* So Lee asked for one too, though Kahlúa made her ill. The club's owner, a local fixture, meaty, pushing sixty, Hawaiian shirt over a black tee, told them he liked their style. "Nobody ever comes to this shithole for cocktails!" They came for a sweaty assault of noise. "Not my kind of music," he said. "But you kids need a place to play."

The man across the aisle had now taken out a book, but he wasn't really reading. Lee didn't recognize the title or the author, but Viv did. Viv started talking, leaning across, saying how *devastating* the book was, but, like, in the *best* way.

"Yeah, it is pretty bleak," he said. "But funny. At least, that's what it says here on the back." Eyeing Viv, but not saying it for Viv. So Lee laughed a little and he gave her another smile, not *How young you are,* but one that said, *We're in the same place at the same time.*

"Well, I read it for a class last semester actually," said Viv, "so I don't know, maybe it's one of those, like, texts that you can get into analytically and endlessly interpret so you wind up thinking it's more than it is? You know what I mean?"

"I'm not sure I do," he said. "But I think my ex thought the same thing about me."

Speaking to Viv again while waiting for Lee to laugh. And she did. She burst out with it, an uncorking, and Viv caught it. The pair of them, not even sure what they were laughing about, to the point of losing their breath, finally containing themselves when the captain came on, ordering seatbelts fastened. Had it become obnoxious? Lee turned to the man. "I'm sorry. I don't know what that was."

"No, you have a great laugh. You laugh with your whole body."

Lee had heard versions of that line before, but they had never had such an effect on her, had never left her like this, blushing, feeling exposed. Alive. It wasn't really because of him, she knew. It had more to do with Viv sitting there next to her, hearing it. Some sort of alchemy happened when they were together. Everything was transformed.

someone

new

∽

Viv, 2010

I used to be so diligent. Growing up, I kept a record of everything. Notebooks full of impressions, wishes, words. For what? There's an inscription in the façade of the Central Library at Grand Army Plaza in Brooklyn—that inside that fortress of a building is "enshrined the longing of great hearts." I looked up at that when I was twenty-two and thought, *What a perfect way to describe what a book is.* I wanted the longings of my own heart to be recognized and enshrined somewhere. Somewhere other than a shelf in my closet. Along the way, though, it became hard to think about—let alone talk about—that aspiration without resorting to self-deprecation, a mode that really works only for the self-assured. Without that assurance, you just deprecate and deprecate until there's not much left. I stopped trying to understand things by setting them down. I started *doing* things, whether I understood or not. But even then, I was aware that was something of an act, an imitation of how I thought Lee lived life. Closer to the core, somehow, and therefore better. I always secretly suspected her heart was greater than mine.

There are so many places I could begin, but I'll start here: a message from her, after three years of no contact, suggesting we get together at a diner just off Broadway that occupied the first floor of a shabby hotel whose art deco exterior shrank into the blinking spectacle of Times Square. It had, at one time, been our meet-in-the-middle spot. Cream-colored walls with ornate white and gold scrollwork rose to a high, chandeliered ceiling, a baroque confection interrupted—bluntly, commercially—by the movable-letter menu board and mirrored panels above the Formica counter. This place had never been legendary enough to be haunted. The effect of being there was less akin to stirring up a ghost than discovering a likable layer of old wallpaper. Safe to say the food was the culinary equivalent of that wallpaper. So why had we kept coming here even after we moved to different neighborhoods and got new jobs? It was a remnant of another, long-gone New York. We never wondered who we might see or want to impress, never worried whether we were getting the best of the best. We knew we weren't.

I showed up first, of course. Sitting in a booth, staring at my phone as if it had important things to tell me. But I was much more interested in the door. Then, through slanting May sunlight, I caught her before she could see me. First thought: *You can duck down and hide, there's still time!* Second thought: *She looks good, objectively, as always, better than you, but you know, she doesn't look* that *much better than you. God, this really* is *like meeting an old lover.* And then she saw me and there was nothing to do but wave.

She wore a black T-shirt and jeans, her light brown hair pulled up in a pile, a few lanky pieces framing her face. No makeup, no jewelry except for that agate slice ring of her father's, which she never took off. Faint circles around her eyes alluded to light vices like coffee and cigarettes. Or no, nicotine gum. From the distance of a few yards, there might be nothing distinctive about Lee Parrish, nothing you could put your finger on, and yet, if she were to walk into a room, you would notice her. And if you were with her, I'd always thought, you could walk into any room.

"Hey," she said.

"Hi-eeee!" That extra syllable of mine should have squealed itself into a hug. I almost got up, she almost leaned in, but we settled instead for uncertain smiles. She sat and didn't say much and though I didn't want to be the one to keep talking, on I went. What a beautiful morning it was. How good she looked. How long had it been? I knew very well how long it had been.

"I'm sorry I was so out of touch," she said.

I had reminded myself on the way here that I had a spine and that I should straighten it. Don't be so conciliatory, don't jump on the first apology.

"A lot can happen in three years."

Lee nodded but didn't ask me to elaborate, the assumption being that while a lot *could* happen in three years, not all that much probably *had*. It irked me, mostly because it felt true. I'd been anticipating this moment ever since I opened the email she'd sent two weeks earlier (to an account now primarily collecting shipping notifications and offers to connect with local Christians). I had often wondered about Lee. There were women who looked like her from the back, on the subway, on the street, tall and slender, with her long hair, her self-possession, but none of them was ever her. I believed that if something momentous or terrible had happened to her, I would have felt it telepathically somehow. There would have been a sign—a stopped clock, a big black bird falling to the sidewalk right in front of me. Nothing like this ever happened, though. She had moved back to New York, she wrote, from Los Angeles, and was working, if I could believe it, for her mother. She would love to see me.

"I brought you something." She handed me a Linda West gift bag. "For the summer. Totally shapeless but kind of exactly what you want to wear when the air is sticking to you."

"Not very body con."

"No, body uncon."

She seemed to be waiting for a clever rejoinder, a quickness we used to have. I wasn't coming up with anything though. I was out of practice. Would I earn a laugh? Why did I have to earn anything? I just thanked her.

Linda West, Lee's mother, designed expensive, loose-fitting, expertly draped separates for women in search of some strategic coverage, a category of clothing that once belonged to my future and increasingly to my now. Linda West had a flagship in each major metropolis, and in any quaint town populated by sometime-city-dwellers who placed a premium on homemade jam, there was always a shop, often run by a woman in hammered silver jewelry, that carried the Linda West line.

"If I ask you how you feel about gauchos, we can expense this."

"How is Linda? Do you like working for her?"

"Linda would say I'm not working for her, I'm working for myself. But you know, she also likes to trot out the idle hands are the devil's workshop line and tell you how she basically lived in the devil's workshop one summer in the south of France and if you've seen one orgy you've seen them all."

"Sure."

"But, honestly, I do like working for her. Odd as it sounds. I've got a head for business apparently."

Our waitress appeared and took our omelet orders. I thought about getting French toast, a bowl of borscht—something that said:

You can't disappear, stop getting back to me, then turn up and expect every-thing to be exactly the same. The thing is, I wanted an omelet.

"I've got some time off, actually," Lee continued. "I'm planning on taking a road trip. I'm going upstate for a few days."

"Sounds nice."

She picked up the little tin pitcher of milk on our table but didn't pour any into her coffee.

"Would you want to come with me?"

"Just like that?" My voice rose an octave and I hated it. "Like I can just pick up and go. Like I've just been sitting around waiting for you to drop back into my utterly uneventful life." Her gaze fell to her scalloped paper placemat, perhaps to hide the question in her eyes: *Haven't you?* I'd been thinking she must have had some news to tell me. I hadn't expected this invitation and I wanted to be some-one who was more angry than curious. Someone who wasn't simply flattered to be asked. Not someone who saw that *Haven't you?* and mostly thought *Yes.* But when Lee looked up, that question had van-ished, if it had been there at all. In its place was regret.

"No, not just like that. I didn't mean—I'm sorry." She paused. "I'm going upstate because Charlie Flintwick lives there. I got in touch with him because I'm trying to find the tapes. I was hoping you would help me."

The tapes. The last, lost tapes of Jesse Parrish. One of the mys-teries attendant to her father's puzzling and premature death, only enhancing his cult status. The legend that illuminated Lee and en-shrouded her. It was one of the first things you knew about her, be-cause someone always whispered, *That's Jesse Parrish's daughter.* Lee's father had been only thirty-one years old—four years younger than Lee now—when he was killed in a car crash. Already at that age he'd been famous, then washed up, then on the verge of new success. Every few years, the publication of a Jesse Parrish biography, the release of a documentary, a tribute album, or, most recently, a remastered box set with a bonus live performance disc caused renewed speculation about the fate of his final recording sessions. A number of theories had been put forth over the years. Maybe the tapes had been in the trunk and were destroyed, perhaps intentionally, along with the totaled car. Maybe his girlfriend—Marion Washington, generally painted as the fucked-up groupie who did nothing to stop his deterioration—was furious with Jesse over something trivial and had trashed the tapes. Maybe Marion told him this while they were arguing in the car just before he drove them both off the road, leaving her in a three-week coma and with no memory of the accident. Maybe the tapes, secure in their cases, were simply swiped from the recording studio—but by whom? If the recordings had survived, they should have surfaced by now.

"I know," Lee continued. "It probably sounds very Harriet the Spy or something. But I've been thinking about my father a lot lately. Listening to all his old stuff. And I want more, to have more of his voice, to hear something I've never heard. I started tracking down some people, got in touch with Flintwick, and he said he would be happy to see me if I thought he could be useful. It may be a total fool's errand, but I don't really want to do it alone and you're the only person who would understand. Andy, too—maybe Andy the most, in a way, but . . ."

She couldn't ask Andy. Because that would have been too weird, to ask that of your friend's husband, especially when you had a history with him. She twisted the ring on her right hand, working it over her knuckle then slipping it back.

"How is Andy?" she asked.

"He's good. He's really good."

"That's good."

It was right after Andy and I got married that Lee really pulled away. Weeks would pass before she would return my call and then she would somehow always reach me when I couldn't pick up, leaving a short message. We had been drifting for a while. She had already left New York at that point, and I could guess at the reason for her distance, though she never explicitly told me. A long time ago, before either of them met me, Andy had been Lee's more-than-a-friend friend, in that he had feelings for her. I turned the configuration into something of a triangle, and then I chose Andy over Lee. That was one version of the story. Another version, one that I never much liked to think about, is that the triangle wasn't a stable one, that its sides shifted, and while it might seem like that's where all the action was, the movement only distracted you from the base, the line connecting the two original points, Lee and Andy, a line that remained fixed and unbroken.

Andy and I had taken the subway together that morning and said goodbye on the corner of Forty-Seventh Street.

"How is it that you, we, always owe her something?" he asked. "What do we owe her for? At this point."

I could think of many things, but I also didn't see it as debt. I did my best to hide my hope that she wanted something, *anything,* from me.

"We're just catching up," I said. "Not that big a deal." But if it was nothing, then why had he gotten off the train with me when it wasn't his stop and he would only have to get back on? I looked at him on my way down the block. Was he standing there watching me walk away or waiting to catch a glimpse of Lee?

"So, Charlie Flintwick."

"He still has his studio up in Ulster County."

I mostly knew Flintwick, the long-time producer, as the deep-voiced issuer of grandiose and louche statements in documentaries about Lee's father. "We'll be forever touched by the influence of Jesse Parrish. Now, where we'll be touched, and how, I will leave to your imagination. The question is, how pliant are you? Hmmmm?" He was disgusting and yet charming; it wasn't quite a put-on, nor was it straight-faced.

Put it this way: I couldn't actually imagine Charlie Flintwick having sex with anyone, I could only envision him sprawled on his side, naked and Rubenesque, suspending a bunch of grapes over his own head.

"He wasn't gross," Lee insisted. "Just open to meeting me. I think he sees me like a daughter."

"That's supposed to be reassuring?"

"Well, I'm going to talk to him and see where it goes. I have to at least try before it's too late. He's had two heart attacks already."

She picked up the little pitcher again and this time added milk to her coffee, completing thoughts out of sequence.

"It's funny—not funny—but it's like I think I'm supposed to have moved beyond it. But if anything, at this point in my life, the older I get, the more strongly I feel it—that loss of my father. I still don't even really know what it was I lost. What was going on with him in that time, before he died? What was he thinking? Feeling? It would be there, wouldn't it, in the record he was making?"

If it were possible to have an ongoing conversation with a dam, it might have been a little like talking to Lee. She could be almost opaque and unbreachable in her circumspection and then she would let out a sluice of talk. She barely noticed when our meals arrived. Then she was on to her mother and Linda's immunity to the past.

"Linda can dine out on the same old stories for years but it's just dinner party talk. Interview patter. She's not nostalgic for much of anything. She's surprisingly forward-looking in a lot of ways. I was in this meeting the other day with her and a couple of our designers. And one of them had this mood board with a picture of Talitha Getty on it?"

I shook my head; the name didn't register.

"Socialite–actress–drug addict in swinging sixties London. She also had a home in Marrakesh. She OD'd and died and then became a style icon for the aristo-boho set."

"I see."

"So Linda goes, 'If I hear one more word about Talitha Getty and Moroccan fucking chic—Talitha fucking Getty! You know what you need to do? You need to *Getty* a new idea!' If I told her what I wanted, where I was going—and I haven't told her anything—I'm sure she'd tell me it's time to Getty over it."

I laughed, finally, and so did Lee.

"I'M NOT SAYING that she's that callous. Though maybe I am. It's just that almost everything I know about my father has come through Linda. Not that she's been keeping something from me or denying me something, but these recordings would be something that hasn't been filtered through her. Through anybody. One thing of his that was never public."

She was nervous. It was new.

"So. What do you think? Will you come with me? To see Flintwick?"

It did seem kid-detective, Lee lighting out on a well-worn trail that had never led anywhere, as far as I knew. But she was also the femme fatale—the one who shows up with a story full of holes and you, the cynic and the sap, still follow her. And the old friend whose powers of persuasion still held sway because those powers had once persuaded you of so, so much. I thought of a time a couple of years out of college when we'd sat at these exact spots. I was coming from a grad school workshop where something I'd written was met with a resounding "eh." Nobody in the class could pinpoint what was wrong with it, they simply didn't find it all that compelling. And instead of getting angrily energized, developing a thicker skin, it was like I had no skin at all. On the subway afterward I stood looking at my reflection in the dark window of the doors as the train car tunneled along, thinking, *There's nothing really wrong with you, you're just not all that compelling.* I got off, walked to this restaurant, and there was Lee. Whatever we talked about wasn't that important. But it was like listening to a radio, having been stuck on static and then finding a channel that came through strong and played songs you loved. It was always like that with Lee. Sometimes it seemed we were tuned to a phantom frequency, something only we could hear. I won't belabor the metaphor. Lee said she would read the story and mark it up, double underlining everything she liked. She gave it back to me with pages full of railroad tracks.

My doubts were never much of a match for my tendency to say yes to her. If I thought that had changed, my difficulty in meeting her gaze now proved otherwise. She had this look—*You* have *to. You have to or you'll be missing out on a real adventure. I'm giving you this chance and all you have to do is take it.*

"Work is super busy at the moment, you know? There's a lot going on there. Jason and Justine—Jastine—are finally going to get married, only to honeymoon in a newly unstable island country.

They've survived cancer, kidnapping, and Count Andre, but it remains to be seen if they can they survive a coup."

"Who is Count Andre?"

"The Slavic financier who almost split them up. I guess you're not watching the show."

"Oh. Well, no. I wasn't sure you were still writing for it."

"I am. And I don't think I can take off right now."

"Sure. I understand."

"But I don't know. Maybe I could get away?"

I suggested she come over to our apartment for dinner that night to discuss further. I hoped Andy being there, between us, would help me get my priorities straight. I also wouldn't have minded Lee seeing Andy and me in our cozy home. We could make her a meal, tend to her for a couple of hours, then send her on her way, maybe a little jealous of our life together.

Dinner would be great, she said, but she'd already made a plan to see another friend of hers tonight.

"What other friend?" I asked.

ANDY AND I once mused about one of the unexpected benefits of our marriage: how it made flirting with other people easier. Because flirting became less a means to an end and more of an end in itself. Taking someone to that slightly charged but relatively innocent level of desire and not needing it to lead to anything more. Paradoxically, this works only if you have a relationship typically characterized as "good"—a solid foundation from which to venture forth and to which you can return, emboldened but never really shaken. Though Andy and I never said it, we smugly assumed that having this very conversation spoke to what a good relationship we had.

Going off with Lee for a while wasn't flirting. It was something more, though I tried to make it look to Andy as if it weren't. At breakfast the next morning I read the junk mail, the catalogs featuring adult-sized footed pajamas designed for a demographic that a marketing service had determined I now belonged to. From the windows in our front room, I could see the 7 train snaking above Queens Boulevard. Before we moved here, all I had known of Sunnyside was that Richard Yates referenced the neighborhood in a short story about an out-of-step World War II veteran, confounded by the fifties and his own masculinity. Now it was home to pockets of Irish immigrants, Eastern Europeans, Colombians, and the young professionals whose presence justified a *Times* article every six months or so declaring this borough the "next frontier." Andy had found us a top-floor apartment with a distant view of the Empire State Building. A Versailles sitting room met cut-rate nursing home in the powder blue lobby with its complicated molding, oxidized mirrors, and fluorescent tube lighting. It was more space than I'd ever had in the city. The muffled rumble on the elevated tracks had become a sound I didn't hear anymore, until the silence of this morning. Finally I spoke:

"It's just a few days."

"A few days can feel like an eternity." I think he was quoting an early-results home pregnancy test commercial. It would have been an opportune time to tell him that I had, three days ago, taken one of those tests and that it had been positive. Instead I let the moment pass and sat there trying not to look conflicted.

"You want to go. That's fine. I just hope you know what to expect."

"I don't know what to expect. I don't think Lee knows what to expect."

"Lee and her spontaneity."

"She wants one last thing of her father's."

"She wants attention."

"I can give her attention. I have enough to go around. And I'll be back before you even miss me."

I didn't register the false cheer in my voice until Andy spoke again.

"I've *been* missing you."

He leveled his gaze at me, but I couldn't meet it for more than a second or two, which incited him to keep going. "It's like you haven't been here for a while. So, really, what's the difference? You should go."

Andy had tried to fight with me about how I didn't know how to fight. I could argue, meet logic with logic. I could write fights for the show, fangs out, one bitchy line after the next, but that was a circus act. It was engagement with a performance, not with another person. I had wanted to improve, to engage with Andy, for him, and I had gotten incrementally better. Still, I tended to meet confrontation with a full system shutdown.

"You don't have anything to say?"

"I don't know. You're right?"

"That's just it. It's not about me being right or wrong. Or you being right or wrong. It's what the fuck are you feeling and why can't you talk to me about it?"

"Okay, I guess I'm feeling angry at you right now for telling me what it is and isn't about."

"You guess? Be angry then. But don't act like there's nothing going on and like you just want to help out a friend. Or whatever Lee is."

It wasn't *acting,* though. Acting suggests you can turn it on and off. This was a reflex—a turtle going into its shell. And I was only beginning to see this as a problem. My problem. One that was related to but distinct from a more generalized marital malaise. I wanted the malaise to be generalized, part of some matrimonial bargain you strike that involves using phrases like "date night." I had willed myself to believe that over time two people simply reach a point where they harness the electrical current between them for something like the smooth functioning of an efficient refrigerator—this is just what happens and maybe this even meant it was time to have a child. I told myself the closeness we had, a brain-centered intimacy, more than compensated for what I missed. But what was the closeness if we weren't close enough to talk about what was missing? If I couldn't bring myself to talk about it? I didn't know how to tell him that the choices I'd made with him—to get married, to go off the pill—had started to make me feel that I no longer knew who I was and that I wasn't ready to become someone new.

Lee, who didn't need me to be someone new, had appeared at just the right time. I wasn't entirely sure why she had come back when she did, but I knew that what propelled her was longing—an almost physical tug.

I'd like to think I would have gathered some courage, looked up, and tried to get all of this across to Andy if he'd stayed at the table for one minute more instead of going to the kitchen sink and wordlessly rinsing his dishes before getting in the shower.

Luxelovah, Massachusetts: I heart Jastine! I haaaaated Jason when he was with Lillian. They were the most boring couple ever (lol!). Justine brings out his fun, verbal side. But don't tell me Justine is carrying Count Andre's baby.

Debbysmom, Michigan: Why did they kill off Liza if there just gonna bring her back??!! I hurt she lost weight but shes not even pretty. She looks like a wrinkled raisin!

CaseyP, Florida: If I wanted left-wing politics, I'd watch network news. Enough with the Afghanistan veteran story line. NOT. BUYING. IT. Writers, you are running the show into the ground. Hel-LO? You are driving away your fan base!!

I had seen CaseyP before, though I hadn't noticed until now that she (he?) had a black-and-white image of Ayn Rand for an online icon. Debbysmom had a kitten, Luxelovah a hot-pink handbag. CaseyP vented with a prune-consuming regularity and I had tried to stop taking the remarks personally because it only led to a reflexive antipathy (*Who takes the time to write these things?*) that turned in on itself (*Who takes the time to read these things?*). The dignified reaction was to see this as proof that viewers still cared enough about *To Have and to Hold* to get worked up and post in forums. Proof that we still had viewers, despite the constant, dispiriting reports of dwindling ratings. *To Have and to Hold* (THATH to its devoted audience) belonged to a dying breed: daytime, English-language soap operas. And its few surviving New York kin had decamped to Los Angeles to cut costs.

It was time to stop procrastinating and head to my boss's office to discuss Samantha Trudeau, who had come to Mill River, a fictional town located somewhere between Manhattan and Philadelphia, as a conniving call girl and blackmailed her way to becoming a cosmetics executive at Blythe Beauty. We were in the process of revealing that she was the long-lost daughter of district attorney Saul Rappaport.

The news would not only rock the town, it would start Samantha on a path of transformation, which would involve her discovering her Jewish heritage.

"If you are now or have ever been a whore, do you have to go through a special cleansing ritual?" Frank asked as I came in and took the chrome-and-leather chair facing his desk.

"I'll have to check my handbook and get back to you."

"I didn't know they still made handbooks. That's why I count on you, young person. You keep me up to date."

Frank Sussman: mid-fifties, tailored khakis, V-neck sweaters, and the driest delivery of anyone I have ever known. His first day, he'd gathered us around and said, without breaking stride: "I'm not into posturing, but we do need to pump some virility into the shriveled men of Mill River. I think the last time Rick Howard's dick saw the light of day, or even the crepuscular half-light, was 1985. I know we love us some divas around here but—" He sighed then plaintively sang the words "vagina dentata" to the tune of "Hakuna Matata."

"Special cleansing ritual. You mean like a mikvah?"

"Yes. Do we need to go there?" Frank shifted his chin in rumination. "How about we wait a few months, back-burner it for the summer, then have her atone on Yom Kippur and apologize to all the people she's hurt clawing her way to the top. We could do for Yom Kippur what we do for Christmas." Christmas on the soaps was an expertly sentimentalized snowy time of hearth and home. Frank stopped himself. "On second thought, no. We'd have to keep this somber. Have Samantha really struggle with who she is. For a day or two."

"What if we gave her a friend? A woman she could talk to, confide in?"

"Humanize her in a realistic way? It's worth exploring." He jotted down a note, or pretended to, and then handed me a sheaf of marked-up pages. "Moving on. Let's talk about these Jastine scenes, shall we? I can tell you've been doing some research. Reading up on Latin American juntas."

"I have, actually."

"That's the problem. Jason and Justine get schooled in rural poverty and state-sanctioned violence by Miguel, the hotel proprietor? His daughter relates the secret history of CIA involvement over a plate of *arroz con pollo*? Admirable, but we're not trying to be NPR here. Look, it's like in *Anna Karenina*. Levin starts going on about farming and peasants and you're like, dear Lord, can we please get back to Anna and the Vron? You need to think of this coup not as a sociopolitical event but as an obstacle for Jason and Justine—how are *they* going to make it through? It's also an excuse for Justine to interact with a few hot, if sinister, men in uniform. You can do better."

"I can?"

"You're going to have to. Don't be so conscientious. Think hammocks and coconuts, colonial shutters and crumbling stucco, Jastine cavorting on a beach, sitting in a hotel lounge with a Graham Greene vibe or however Graham Greene–y we can get within budget. Maybe they're at the bar, talking to Miguel.

"*Jason: 'Miguel, I used to think love was the greatest con of all. But if it is, I want to go right on being a sucker.'*

"*Justine: 'Ahem?!'*

"*Miguel: 'I'll drink to that, my friend.'*

"Something like that. End of the day, okay, Pro?"

I could never quite tell if Frank was being ironic when he called me Pro, since it sounded like something he'd gleaned from a manual on effective team leadership. But I was heartened to hear it. In the six years I had reported to Frank, he had always seen potential in me. It made me want to never let him down.

"I'm on it. But, Frank, then I need to take a few days off."

"What? No. Not now you don't. What you need to do is this rewrite and then you need to get started on the Romola Dougherty custody case. Did sweeps suddenly slip your mind?"

"I'll check in as often as I can. I'm really sorry, but you know I wouldn't do this if it weren't important."

"What is it?"

"It's personal." He looked a little offended.

"Vivian, this is just such terrible timing."

Vivian. Like a parent.

"I know. I know."

Frank's anger resided in his jaw. The arteries in his neck thickened into tree roots.

"Do what you have to do." No Pro. He just raised his hands, as if surrendering to my free will as a human being while questioning my longevity as his protégé. But Frank's disappointment couldn't suppress the wave of freedom and escape that carried me down the hall.

"I WAS LISTENING to some Jesse songs on my way home," said Andy. Standing in the doorway of our bedroom after we'd eaten dinner in front of the TV and I had started to pack my bag. "I realized I hadn't, in a long time. And it was weird. I felt like I was inside a giant brain scan or something, walking through a gray area I lost use of and now it was all lit up again."

"Sounds psychedelic."

"Kind of, yeah. It was this really physical sensation."

I wanted him to keep talking about Jesse Parrish as I packed.

To feel his anger yielding to something closer to interest in what I had decided to do. He was no longer in the mood for a fight, which was a relief. And yet, it made me sad to think that he had given in. Given up.

You are being impossible, I thought. *What more do you want from him?*

"I'm gonna sound like I'm high if I try to explain it more."

"I don't mind."

"It just brings up so many associations that used to hold everything together, in a way, and all of those associations are still there, but they don't have the same meaning for me anymore. I think there are things you have to come to at exactly the right age to really fall in love with them. If you're too young, you don't quite get it. And if you're too old, you get it, you appreciate it, but it doesn't necessarily move you so much. You don't identify in the same way."

"You don't think the music changes with you? That you can experience it differently over time?"

The look on his face: *I didn't mean to make this a metaphor for our relationship.*

I held his look, long enough to feel that something between us would crack wide open if neither of us averted our eyes. But he did. I pulled more things from drawers. If he'd noticed that I was reaching for the best versions I had—my most flattering jeans, the T-shirt that hangs just so, my "good" underwear, as opposed to the tattered yet still functional pairs I wore around the house all the time, around him—he didn't say anything. And whatever might have combusted between us under slightly more pressure merely dissipated. The rest of the night passed like so many other recent ones, ending with the two of us in bed, reading. Andy turning off the lamp on his side and rolling over. Me turning off my lamp and doing the same.

THE NEXT DAY was Saturday and I realized I should have chosen a spot to meet Lee instead of having her pick me up at my apartment. Leaving Andy would have been tense but not nearly as complicated as it was now. Because now he was home with nowhere in particular to be. If he'd come up with something to do, it would have been a signal: I must take my strong feelings elsewhere. I still *have* strong feelings when it comes to Lee. No, he would have to stay and be here when she arrived. They would have to interact, I would have to watch them interact, and then he would watch me go with her. I was the one who had put us all in this position. I didn't want to ask myself why.

Lee rang the buzzer as I was getting a few toiletries together. Andy let her up, and part of me wanted to stay in the bathroom forever and just listen to them.

"Andy," I heard her say by the door. And it was so much at once: greeting, apology, request, demand, past, and present.

"It's good to see you, Lee."

I gave them time for what might have been an intense hug before calling out, "I'll be right there!" and heading into the hallway, ready to go.

"This is such a nice place you guys have," she said.

I thanked her but didn't ask if she wanted to look around. Something had already shifted since I saw her at the diner, when I'd wanted to have her over, to show off to her. But Andy offered her a tour. He took her from the kitchen into the living room, and she complimented the ways we'd filled the space. The teak sideboard Andy's parents had passed down to us, a marble and brass lamp we'd bought one weekend in Cold Spring, an old framed mirror. Furnishings that conveyed intentions, building a life together.

Through her eyes, though, I saw them as an arrangement of props. Staged domesticity.

Andy didn't ask her about the last few years, and she didn't offer him details. Maybe it was understood that I'd already let him know. Maybe neither of them cared, in the sense that it didn't matter to them; they would always just pick up wherever they had left off. Or maybe I was reading too much into it and each of them wanted to get this over with and get moving. Andy asked Lee if she'd like a cup of coffee and she said no thanks, she'd had one earlier and didn't want to get overcaffeinated. Everything was smooth, polite, and strange. The way Lee and Andy said goodbye. Even the way Andy and I said goodbye. A quick kiss before he pulled away.

"Call me from the road?"

I nodded.

"Good luck."

And then Lee and I were in the elevator. An old contraption, with a door you had to pull, walls thick with decades of paint. Taking it always seemed like a bit of a risk, and maybe we should've used the stairs, I said to Lee. It was all I could think of to talk about just then. She went along with it—trying to read a name someone had etched into the latest coat of taupe—until we got to the lobby.

"So the car's a few blocks away. Street parking isn't easy around here."

"I should've said so. You could've called me and I could've come down."

"Oh, but that wouldn't have been half as awkward."

Her flashing eyes. Her smile. I wanted to forget everything. I wanted to link my arm in hers. To walk down the block like that, leaning together, the camera behind us, watching us go.

I MET LEE the summer after my freshman year of college and nothing before that seemed to matter much, despite my having scribbled down all the details. I know I had opinions, reactions, beliefs that had guided me to where I was. I'd had what I thought were formative suburban high-school experiences. Slept with a boy who was fixated on a friend of mine, a willowy, emotionally unstable cross-country runner. His infatuation with her baffled me—her taste in and knowledge of just about everything except athletic shoes was far less discerning than his. I thought, *If only I could lift the scrim and make him see!* But see what? I knew exactly what he liked about her: she ran long distances through forested paths with determination and agility. It didn't matter what she was thinking, whether she had ever seen *My Own Private Idaho* or *Stranger Than Paradise.* Heard of Sonic Youth or Cocteau Twins. To watch her run along the perimeter of the school fields at practice was to want whatever it was she had. That, and she was incredibly moody. When her parents committed her to an in-patient psychiatric program, he asked me how she was doing. I used our mutual concern to get closer to him and I didn't really see anything wrong with that until I was sitting on his bed, putting my sturdy beige bra back on, wishing I were a better friend. Wishing I were more willowy, more emotionally unstable, so that he would fall in love with me. He offered to drive me home and while the day before I would have jumped at the opportunity to sit in the black bucket passenger seat of his dusk-blue Chevy Nova, I decided to walk. And then I started running, halfway across town back home. As if I could outrun my shame. But what really powered me was pride. I'd done it. With him. I remember thinking I couldn't have run like that in less supportive underthings.

I had some measure of personality and direction, a solid enough core to resist no less than three offers to join cults my first semester freshman year. By the third time I realized the joke: I was one of those people who was waiting to be approached, to be tapped and told, "Your life is going to start now." And those people who wait for life to come to them, they do get approached, only they get told something like: "Your life is going to start now and it's going to be a series of communal breakfasts and questionable sexual encounters with a messianic father-figure."

By the third time, as soon as the girl sat down next to me on the broad steps of the humanities library, I knew what she was after. The thick paperback she pulled out—Earth on the cover against a glossy black background with a flaming red lozenge hurtling toward the blue planet—confirmed it. But she was striking without trying too hard in her sundress and gray sweatshirt and her sunglasses, which made me think she was part of a group I should *want* to belong to.

"This is a good spot for reading." Her manner was laid-back and content. She possessed a secret knowledge.

"Yeah, it's nice."

"Not that anyone aside from us students reads much of anything anymore. All people do now is shop, right?" The hitch in her delivery, the narc falseness of "us students" belied her tranquil conviction. "As if rampant consumerism is going to fill the void created by modern society. It fills the void in the way a candy bar does, satisfying your craving but rotting your teeth."

"Right."

"I'm not saying we should go live in the woods, survive on berries, and make our own clothes. It's not that simple, obviously, but I do think there's a better way." She opened her big book and I looked at her shoes—a pair of latticed plastic skimmers you could buy in drugstores, the sartorial line between a certain stripe of style-conscious girl and diabetic septuagenarian. It could have gone either way, but we both knew those shoes, on her, were cooler than mine on me.

On a stained and highlighted page of her tome, an elaborate mathematical formula hovered above an illustration of a wormhole and the bolded words "Sentries of Perception." She started to explain but her rising enthusiasm muddled her clarity. She apologized. "I know it probably seems like nonsense or bullshit. But I swear, it's not. It's complicated, but in the way that, like, breathing is complicated. If you think about everything that goes into your taking a breath, well, it's obviously incredibly complex. But"—she exhaled—"most people don't think about it."

"Right."

"Listen, there's this study group I belong to—study group makes it sound like work—it's more like we have get-togethers over dinner. Maybe you'd want to check it out sometime? I think you'd really like it."

"Why do you think I would like it?"

"It's just a really good group of people, trying to live better. Figuring out how to live better, together."

"Why me? I mean, why out of everyone here, why single me out?" Hostility rose in my tone. "Do you know this is the third time someone like you has come up to me?"

"Someone like me?"

"I'm sure the Sentries of Perception stand at the gateway to a wonderful world of peace and happiness and freedom from the shackles of consumerism. I'm happy that you have a belief system and you have dinners, but I just don't feel like being brainwashed today."

Students on the steps turned toward our commotion or deliberately looked the other way, embarrassed for me.

"I just thought you looked friendly, and yeah, to be honest, a little sad. That's all. I didn't mean to upset you."

Whisking my book into my bag, I walked quickly away, hoping to God I wouldn't trip, and when I'd made it around the corner, out of sight, a sob escaped. Just one sob, then I caught my breath and thought about the complexity of breathing.

After that, nothing much happened for the duration of my freshman year, except for the diminishment of my expectations. I busied myself with schoolwork. Somewhere in that time, I had applied for and received a research assistantship with a comparative literature professor writing a book on sentimentalism from *Clarissa* to *E.T.* Landing the position and the small stipend attached to it was the type of goal I knew how to achieve through hard work and conscientiousness—fine abilities to have, except they didn't help me do the thing I most longed to do, which was fall in love. My unimaginative plan to stay in the dorms over the summer started to seem like a bad haircut, an unnecessary handicap. When I saw the flyer—*Roommate needed to share apt. with one M and one F (not a couple). Own large room, close to campus. $250/month. Call Andy/Lee*—I made myself call. It was tacked to the wall in the coffee shop that I would hesitate to go into if I wasn't dressed right. There was another coffee shop nearby, fine for coffee, where nobody cared how you were dressed, but there was no point in sitting in that one. Nothing interesting was going to happen to you there.

In the three hours between phoning, speaking to Andy, and showing up, some fantasy had already taken shape in my mind. The slight halting in his voice conveyed an intensity that made it hard for him to speak smoothly, and though he might initially think of me as a little sister, the sexual tension between us would be too strong to deny, possibly leading to some complications with Lee, but we would cross that bridge when we got there. When he came to the door of the drooping Victorian, I silently scolded myself for being disappointed.

My first impression: Andy had a friendly face and a soft body. He wore clothes meant for a more effete, leaner man and they fit him snugly. In a vintage bowling shirt with the name Tom embroidered on it, he looked a bit like Tom, the suburban recreationalist who self-medicated with muffins, whose butt cheeks had grooved the vinyl driver's seat of his '86 Cutlass Ciera into a cradle. I detected no sexual tension between us as he led me up the narrowing stairs to the third floor. My disappointment set me at ease. I didn't have to be afraid of saying something stupid, I only had to judge whether he said the wrong thing or decide to be generous and suspend judgment altogether. Only he wasn't saying the wrong things; he was saying straightforward and sociable things ("I'm Andy"; "Nice to meet you"; "How's it going?") that betrayed no subtext whatsoever. My self-assurance withered into humility (*He doesn't find me attractive enough for subtext?*), which then briefly descended into desperation (*Why doesn't he find me attractive?*), which then picked itself up, dusted itself off, and morphed into resentment (*Who is* he *not to find* me *attractive?*) and a renewed superiority (*If I wanted to, I could make this happen . . . if I wanted to*). Did I say there was no sexual tension?

"Sometimes I wish we had a stair lift," he said.

"Sometimes I want a motorized scooter," I said.

He looked back and smiled. For a moment, on the landing, I forgot there was a third person in this equation. Then Andy opened the door onto a few feet of hallway and a living room where a girl in a red shirt sat on a white sofa. Light slanted on her from a bay window, and it made me think of when you face the sun and close your eyes.

I thought, at first glance, that this girl had no use for enthusiasm.

But that was how she was so disarming. She simply smiled, getting up and putting out her hand, saying "Hi." She seemed familiar, but I couldn't place her.

There was no incense in their apartment, not a tapestry in sight and no dorm-room door dry-erase boards. Instead there were drawings tacked to the wall, piles of books, Salvation Army furniture covered in bed sheets. A vase of flowers on the mantle of a disused fireplace. I never thought to bother with flowers. To buy them would have been an extravagance, but I wouldn't have even considered picking flowers like these purple and yellow ones that grew in untended curb grass; probably because my mother never bothered with flowers. She preferred hearty plants: ficus trees, decorative yet practical arrangements of branches or an earthy bowl of pinecones. My mother would have said that flowers were lovely but ultimately frivolous. She wouldn't have considered them lovely *because* they were frivolous.

Aligned in their attitudes, my parents had instructed me to be noncommittal when looking for an apartment, even a summer sublet. Weigh your options, do your homework, don't fall in love with anything, as though you could choose not to fall in love. But I had been doing my homework my whole life. How bad a mistake could I make here, on these wide floorboards in the room they led me to, under this sloping ceiling with the maple tree outside the dormer window?

In the kitchen—wood-paneled walls, linoleum—drinking beer that Andy bought legally, I learned a few more particulars. Andy had a job at the computer science center. Lee was taking summer classes. Andy would be a senior come September and Lee would have been except she'd taken time off. She didn't go into detail, which made it so mysterious.

0

It hit me, then, where I recognized Lee from. Not because she looked the same as she had that day on the library steps—her hair, now a dull blue-black, fell in a jagged bob—but because I had the same feeling I did the first time I'd encountered her: standing in the ocean, close enough to shore to resist a riptide, but wanting, deep down, to see where the pull would take me.

"I DON'T KNOW if you remember this," I said, "but I think you once tried to talk to me about something having to do with the Sentries of Perception."

Her laugh was throaty and layered. It reminded me of a science museum exhibit that charted sound as waves of light along a dark wall.

"Oh! Holy shit." She began to chew one of her nails then drew her hand away from her mouth. "You were my first and last Reach Out. That's what Bruce called them."

"Who's Bruce?"

"Who isn't Bruce?" Andy interrupted, his voice increasingly booming. "He's a seeker and a prophet. A desert bloom! A brave soul caught between the astral plane and the check-out lane."

"Bruce was an adjunct anthropology professor," Lee said, a little irritated. "But now he works at the Stop and Shop and heads up a local chapter of Mind Faith. This spiritual community? They have these intensive workshops and their own vocabulary. It's a lot of reconstituted Castaneda and Huxley."

I nodded as if I knew what she was talking about.

"They also have potlucks," Andy added.

"I met Bruce about a year ago. I was troubled. He was really good-looking. It was a low point in my life. Blah, blah, blah. I put you on the spot, didn't I?"

"I just felt like I had a sign on me or something that said 'loser.' I'm sorry I ran off."

"Actually, you power-walked off. I remember thinking you needed, like, a fanny pack." Andy laughed. I laughed too, as if it didn't sting. "*I'm* sorry. I'm just pretty embarrassed by the whole thing now. It was getting so skeevy. You were right to run off. I was glad you yelled at me that day. I must have seemed predatory and weird."

"No, you didn't."

"Well, I'm totally done with it, so please don't let that worry you about moving in here. If you think you want to?"

My dad's voice in my head said, "Tell them you'll give it some thought and be in touch." I wondered if Andy and Lee consulted their fathers before moving into this place. Did they even have fathers? They seemed beyond parents. At least, Lee did. They were only two years older than me but I felt exponentially younger. The house was no more than a ten-minute walk from the main campus, but I had never come this way.

Three days later I moved in.

I quickly grasped the existing dynamic of my new household: Andy had feelings for Lee and Lee knew it and they both went about being sibling-like to each other.

If it wasn't my first night there, it was my second or third that Lee went to meet up with Noah Stone.

"As in chiseled from," she said.

"Just like the Mount Rushmore presidents," said Andy, saliva flying out of his mouth.

Lee wiped her face.

"Sorry," said Andy.

"It's okay, I liked it." She gave him a lewd look and the lovelorn part of him no doubt wished she were serious. "Bye, Viv. Hey, are you sure you don't want to come with me?"

I noticed that she didn't "get ready" to see Noah Stone, she just wore what she'd been wearing the whole day, black cutoffs and a gray T-shirt, an outfit that seemed to be the result of a) feminist principles, b) laziness, c) self-assurance, or d) all of the above.

"I don't want to intrude on your date."

"It's not a *date* date. There are always like ten other people over at Noah's. Always."

"Thanks, really, but I don't have a bike."

"Okay. See you guys later, then." Before she left she fixed me with her eyes, transmitting a message: *Fair enough. But we're going to work on this. We'll get you a bike or whatever it is you need not to make excuses. You've gotten this far, don't back down now. It's going to be great. You'll see.*

From folding aluminum lawn chairs on a little porch off the kitchen, Andy and I watched her ride away for the evening. There was a gallantry about her.

"You don't like Noah Stone?" I asked Andy.

"I like him. Everybody likes him. He's perfect. He's like a ten-year-old. How can you not like a ten-year-old? He's pre-analytical. He's so fucking full of childlike wonder. You know what it is? He's so literal about everything more cerebral types have covered in layers of abstraction and meaning that he seems, in his simplicity, like a revelation. Like, he would maybe make a giant cigar out of Hamburger Helper and everybody would clamor to find all the meaning in it and they'd ask him and he'd just say something like 'I don't know, I was wondering how much Hamburger Helper it would take to make a ten-foot-long cigar.' People eat that shit up. There's no intellectual remove for Noah. That's what gets him laid. I'm sure that's what'll make him successful."

"It's your intellectual remove that keeps you from getting laid?"

"It must be. I mean, I think girls look at me and they're like, damn, I want a piece of that fine man-flesh, and I'm like, okay, take it easy, there's plenty to go around, and then, you know, things progress, as they will, and I'm about to get with her and she's like, Andy, I don't just want your supremely hot body I want your mind but I can sense this, like, *intellectual remove* or something—what's *that* about?"

He had taken my hand and placed it against his chest to demonstrate what the girls were like with his man-flesh. He let it drop. When he let go, I didn't know quite what to do with it.

"Noah's artsy without being pretentious. Which makes it hard to despise him. So, I get it. I can see why Lee is into that. He's guileless. Like, I'm sure Noah has no idea who her father is and she likes that."

"Who's her father?"

"Jesse Parrish."

I knew enough about Jesse Parrish to know I should be impressed by this but nothing else. You know who knew about Jesse Parrish? The boy who loved the willowy cross-country runner. He'd put on a Jesse Parrish record that afternoon in his room but I couldn't get past the fact that it was the same one my parents had in their meager collection, alongside their Anne Murray and the soundtrack to *A Star Is Born.* I suppose I was afraid, if one thing led to another musically, I would have had to admit to liking it when my parents turned up the hi-fi and swayed in each other's arms to "Could I Have This Dance?"

A lot of people owned that album, according to Andy. The one with the cow on the back cover. *Motel Television,* his first solo record.

It should have established him as one of the major talents of his era. Only it didn't. To own Jesse Parrish records now, especially his subsequent ones, required curiosity and effort, knowledge of a secret handshake.

I followed Andy into his room, where he pulled out several records from a crate and proceeded to play "Always Lately," the first track on *Motel Television*. Melancholy strumming of an acoustic guitar and a voice: boyish and bell-like but one that easily slipped into a gritty, growling lower register, occasionally within the same phrasing. The song, about the empty space between two lovers, made you feel you were somewhere just off the highway on a rainy morning, after driving most of the night, with nothing to do but contemplate the flat landscape outside your motel room window. The last line, "Remember this?" seemed less of a question than a request made by someone who had already come to a decision, who was already gone. The stripped-down opener gave way to a string arrangement and an echo-y second track; it sounded romantic and sweeping but the lyrics were about ice buckets, vending machines, and a lie.

The album's sleeve, when opened flat, showed Jesse standing alone in a field one misty dawn, looking downright foxy, his mouth slightly open, about to break into a rakish smile, and to the right of the fold, in the distance, the random Holstein.

"Brian Reiger produced it," Andy was saying, "and he was just— you hear the guitar? How it just *rings*? You don't hear that on the CD or other versions of the album. You have to listen to the first pressing, which is what this is, and then you really understand how great of a role Reiger played in the sound. He could hear things nobody else could, which eventually drove him crazy. Like, certifiably. Jesse never went that far off the deep end, but he kind of had his own breakdown. This is what it sounded like."

Andy put on *The Garden of Allah,* underappreciated and even alienating when it came out in 1974, he said, but now hailed as a masterpiece. The first song was harder, struttier. The yearning melodic voice had a raw, sarcastic leer in it. For a song or two. Then the sound was all over the place, berserk, plunking piano, sloppy vocals, a gospel choir at one point. Courtly strings, orchestral arrangements, a celestial Mellotron, steel drums, and bongos. A glockenspiel. At the end of the LP's closer, you can hear Jesse snarl, "Stick a fork in me."

"Basically he got loaded on Quaaludes, went into the studio, recorded some stuff, and then abandoned it in disgust. But there was enough there for Reiger to come in at the end and work his magic."

"Was it like a Cat Stevens thing?"

"No, the Garden of Allah was the home of a silent film star. Alla Nazimova. She built this lavish place in Hollywood with a pool supposedly shaped like the Black Sea, and when she ran out of money, she turned the estate into a hotel. A lot of actors would stay there. F. Scott Fitzgerald lived there for a while. A lot of legendary debauchery went on and then it got kind of seedy, but not high-end seedy. Eventually all the famous people started staying across the street at the Chateau Marmont. So it was torn down and turned into a bank. Jesse Parrish knew his history."

As did Andy.

Jesse's label dropped him. He got fat. He got strung out. He got thin. At some point Lee was born. He left Linda or did Linda leave him? He took up with a groupie. He wrote songs other people made famous. He was going back to the studio. He died. Lee was four.

It all seemed removed from the girl who had just biked away. But it also explained her, and my instant fascination with her. People obsessed over Jesse Parrish, worked his life into legend, and Lee was part of that. She was part of a level of society I was only beginning to see. I'd never met anyone famous, unless you counted Michael Dukakis, with whom I shook hands once in sixth grade on a class trip to the State House. The affluence I'd grown up around had exposed me, at its upper boundary, to remodeled kitchens and glitzy Bar Mitzvahs. Lee's father's fame was not the most lucrative kind—it generated more cultural capital than actual capital. But, as I learned from Andy, Jesse came from a family whose mini-empire of supermarkets had been dismantled and dissolved. But not before certain trusts had been established and, in Lee's case, well-maintained, thanks to her mother. On top of that, Linda West, former model, muse, and party girl, had turned out to be a remarkably savvy businesswoman.

The more I looked at Jesse's picture, the more I saw the resemblance to Lee. The sleepy, wide deep-blue eyes that darkened to violet at the edges, the fullness of her mouth, softening the sharpness and structure of her other features. They had *faces*—made for cameras and stages, made to be looked at. Lee shared with her father (and her mother, I would come to find out) a powerful, preoccupying magnetism. So that, in a group photograph, you're always drawn to them first. When you can't look at them anymore because you know you'll never get to the bottom of them, then you start seeing the other people in the frame and wondering where the picture was taken.

"Does Lee talk about him at all?"

"Sometimes. Yeah. Last year some guy was writing part of a dissertation on him and wanted to talk to Lee. She agreed to, but in the end it just weirded her out. Like he was projecting all this stuff onto her father. But I think what really upset her is that she didn't know if it was a projection or not. I mean, she never really knew her father."

I hardly knew Lee then, but I already wanted to protect her. I was at the beginning of something, something I didn't want to disappear.

THERE WAS A girl we knew in college named Kirsten. She and Lee could both be impetuous and headlong. Kirsten was ultimately more successful at it, I think because she was more shallow. She treated our women's studies class to a graphic video of her girlfriend in bed and then got married not two years out of school to a guy she met while knitting in Prospect Park. We understood sexuality could be fluid. But we barely recognized her at the wedding without her dark eye makeup and bulky boots. What threw us was the realization that that had merely been a look in the same way that the letterpress place cards, the tea lights twinkling in the trees, the greenery in mason jars, her reworked vintage bridal gown, was all a look. Her ardor for performance seemed to exceed rather than express a passion for her groom. As though she were getting married largely for the pictures and a license to throw dinner parties. Lee and I scoffed. But it also made us insecure about who we were and what we should want.

"I envy her tolerance for being embarrassed," I said to Lee. We were sitting on a stone bench on the grounds of an old estate, drinking champagne, not too far from the guests on the patio but out of earshot. "No, but I do. She doesn't care. She's not cowed by self-consciousness."

"I think the word you're looking for is shameless," said Lee.

"Yeah, but we say that like it's a bad thing. Where does shame ever get us?"

"Kirsten's a nutbag, okay? She throws a nice party though."

Late into that night, music continued to drift out of the open French doors of a ballroom to the sloping lawn where a group of revelers kept going. In the early but still dark hour when dew starts to settle over everything, Lee and Kirsten and I found ourselves alone down by a boathouse. In my mind's eye we are sleepily draped across various surfaces, women in a pre-Raphaelite painting.

"I'm knitting him a pair of socks," said Kirsten, apropos of nothing but the digressive course of the conversation we'd been having. We nodded in an indication of listening.

"No, like, I'm knitting my *husband* a fucking pair of fucking *socks*. I have the yarn and the needles and everything all packed up in my bag for our fucking *honeymoon*."

We murmured some indistinct acknowledgments.

"God. You two. You guys are like a fucking *planet* together. You make me feel like a little ant or something. Do you know I almost didn't invite either of you? But I wanted to be generous. I wanted you to share this with me. But you know what? You don't really share anything with anyone but each other. So, like, fuck that!" She laughed and took another drag on the joint between her fingers. I looked to Lee, but she wouldn't return my gaze. She just stared up at the rafters, as though what Kirsten said was, for once, well-reasoned and true, and it disturbed her.

Within a year, Kirsten left her husband, moved across the country, and became an apprentice to a marketing guru. She was forecasting trends on daytime talk shows, wearing wrap dresses and stilettos, discussing happiness as it related to various colors. She and the guru renovated a San Francisco townhouse. They spoke of their love, for their home and for each other, in the pages of a shelter magazine. It wasn't Kirsten's fault that the guru soon began an affair with his new assistant, but hadn't I turned on the

TV one morning and heard her say, "You are your choices"? It was back to New York, where she lived with an advertising executive–turned–rooftop farmer, incorporated antlers into the design of several downtown hotels, and acquired a new wardrobe of structurally challenging clothes you may have at first suspected weren't particularly flattering before concluding that your eye simply wasn't avant-garde enough to appreciate them. Kirsten moved through life in a series of clean breaks. Perhaps, in some parallel reality, a landfill of her past messes grew more and more massive. But unless this world collided with that one, she'd never contend with the garbage heap of her existence. I could try to heave myself up onto a ledge of superiority, tell myself that Kirsten didn't really know herself. But was knowing yourself worth more than all the life she had lived? How well did I know myself anyway?

About a year ago, I happened to be downtown for a doctor's appointment in the middle of the afternoon and I ran into her. She was leaving a showroom and looked like a celebrity dressed to avoid the paparazzi: sunglasses, flats, leather jacket, of-the-moment bag.

"Viv fucking Feld!" She insisted we go get a coffee right then. Sometimes I felt I alone had maintained a life that left room for unscheduled coffees and it was like being the last house standing on an otherwise razed block. Where had everybody gone? But here was Kirsten, and though I knew her impromptu availability wasn't the same as mine, I couldn't say no. I hadn't seen her since Andy and I got married.

We covered the preliminaries: she told me about jetting to Peru recently for inspiration. I said there was good Peruvian food in Queens. She told me how funny I was.

"Are you still with—I'm sorry, I've forgotten his name—the guy you were with at our wedding?" I asked.

"Russell. No. God, no! That seems so long ago. *Men.*" She sighed, as though that were the definitive word on the subject. But then she continued. "You and Andy are very lucky. Some of us just aren't built for marriage. We always want something more."

"Right. I think there's a song about that."

"Speaking of which, how's Lee?"

"I don't really know. We've kind of lost touch. I think she's in L.A."

"Oh, yeah? What is she doing?"

"I'm not really sure. I think she was trying to figure that out."

"Well, I hope she does. You only get one life. I just hope she's happy."

I wanted to ask Kirsten if *she* was happy, but happiness (and what it had to with various colors) was merely a topic to discuss in front of a studio audience. And I suspected she was only capable of caring about Lee's well-being because she believed she had finally eclipsed her. I had never spent much time with Kirsten alone. I hadn't realized how much Lee's presence had kept her in check. Kirsten had acquired a triumphant yet breezy authority that, like a gas, filled the space where Lee would have been.

What Kirsten had meant as a slight—how fortunate Andy and I were to be so easily satisfied with each other—resonated strongly. Listening to her talk, I *did* feel lucky to be with Andy. Still, I remained awed by Kirsten's restless momentum. Lee's too. But if Kirsten, out of nowhere, had asked me to drop everything and hit the road with her, I would have said no without even blinking.

෬෧

What would you say to those detractors or critics who've said your work can be repetitive? That perhaps—and I'm not saying I feel this way—that too many of your songs sound the same?

Well, I guess I would say it's all the same song. They're right. In the wrong way.

That's quite a koan.

Yeah, I should get it printed up, make some fortune cookies.

That would be an interesting sideline for you.

Put it on some T-shirts. A real merchandising opportunity.

Does that bother you? That maybe it's becoming more about the marketing than the music?

It's always been about the marketing. As long as there's been a market. You're setting me up for these, I swear. [Laughter from the audience]

Okay. Different subject. Is it true you believe in flying saucers?

Flying saucers?

I've read that you've been to a flying saucer convention.

Oh. Yes. My wife took me there.

It's your wife, then, who believes in aliens?

Oh, I think the aliens believe in her. [More laughter from the audience]

Do you get a lot of ideas from your wife?

I get a lot of ideas from a lot of places. I'm easily influenced. I'm very, uh, I'm very permeable. [Laughter, cheers] But, yes, Linda. She's right there. She can tell you. [Applause and shuffling, as a microphone is brought to Linda]

Hi, Jesse.

Hi, Linda.

Well, I think I understand those aliens now! Linda West, everybody.
{Applause from the audience}

Aren't you gonna ask me how we met?

Sure. How did you two meet?

At a party. In the kitchen. At her boyfriend's house.

Whoa there, this is national television. You're scandalizing us, Jesse.

You and the kitchen, man.

This interview used to be hard to find, bonus material at the end of a Jesse Parrish import box set. Now you could download it in seconds. You could be anywhere. You could be driving up the Hutchinson River Parkway, through Westchester, in 2010, listening to Jesse in 1970. How transporting it was. I needed it in order to feel involved in this world and justified in leaving my own. And to not feel quite so guilty for being excited about it. And I was glad Lee put this on because it gave us a focus, a distraction from the fact that here we were in a car, back in each other's lives.

So now what?

"I don't know if I remember it or I just think I do," said Lee. "But he had such a nice voice, the way he talked."

"He did."

I had heard snippets of interviews with him here and there, but I had never listened at length. I tended to think wit had to be surgical, swift, and a bit cruel, but Jesse's was lingering, it had warmth.

I have to say, you don't seem particularly interested in playing a
game with journalists, the way some of your, well, peers {chuckle} do.

There are some notoriously prickly recording artists out there, and one or two of them have even deigned to come on this show. But you're very open and I don't feel like you're putting me on.

Why would I put you on? [Laughter again] It's like this. If I said something in a song, I needed a song to say it. So I get how it's a drag to be asked to explain yourself beyond the song. But that doesn't mean I can't sit here and have a perfectly fine conversation with you about extraterrestrials.

Your fans certainly feel they understand your songs. They're extremely devoted to you.

Yes. Yeah.

You seem to inspire a great deal of fantasy, of fantasizing.

They're very imaginative, the fans. Very creative. They do like to imprint me into their fantasies.

I want to read an excerpt of this—it's from a fan letter that was sent to our show. This woman—I say woman though I don't know how old she is—this woman writes: "In the dream, Jesse is waiting in line behind me at the airport and the line isn't moving so he leans over my shoulder and suggests we get out of there. He takes my hand and all of a sudden there's a moving sidewalk that brings us all the way to this beautiful old palace with loads of rooms and I get lost. It's also a little like the White House. I pass a lot of people wearing suits and ID badges. They are looking at me because I am running down this marble hallway and I can't find Jesse anywhere. Then he pulls me through a secret door and he says he has disguises for us, the disguises that we're going to need. He asks me to help him take off his clothes." I'll stop there. It gets considerably more detailed. Does it ever shock you?

Uh, it doesn't shock me. I think that's what, uh, performance does. What it can do, when it's good. It creates a space for the imagination. I love that I can do that for people. It can get a little heavy, though. Sometimes. Sure.

Does it ever leave you feeling, well, I imagine it might leave you feeling rather blank?

Uh, depleted, sometimes. I don't know about blank. You know, that's interesting about the disguises. I'd like to know what they were!

Jesse Parrish, ladies and gentlemen. I want to thank you again for coming on the show this evening. It's been, well, what would you say it's been?

It's been a pleasure.

That one moment when Linda came on—*Hi, Jesse. Hi, Linda.* You could hear how coupled up they were at that time, inside a world of two, looking out. I said as much to Lee.

"I know. I kind of resent it. Their twoness. It reminds me I'm essentially back where I was at twenty-five, only now I'm ten years older."

"I doubt that's true."

"You're right. At twenty-five I had higher hopes. Basically the only thing I remember about the last guy I went out with was that he told me he liked to fantasize about Patricia Arquette."

"*Lost Highway* Patricia Arquette ? Or *Medium* Patricia Arquette?"

"Both, I think."

The more recent events of Lee's love life, or the photographic record of what looked like events, hadn't escaped me during the time that we'd been out of touch. Lee's level of celebrity didn't make her a target of tabloid gossip, but from time to time she would appear in the coverage of a party or a premiere, be snapped by a street photographer. I asked her if it was true that she'd been "linked" again to Jack Caprico, the actor who had managed to remain relevant and frequently cast twenty years after his breakout role as a Gen-Xer who read Beat poetry during his downtime on the McJob. She had been seeing him before, and brought him to my wedding, but I'd heard they'd broken up. Rather, I'd read they'd broken up.

"Yes, we were linked," she said. "Like breakfast sausage."

"Sounds hot."

"It was always pretty hot with him. That was never the problem."

"So what happened?"

"We're friends now. Friends who don't talk much or see each other. But you know. I got kind of depressed when we were together this last time, and he said it reminded him of his mother and his sister and he couldn't deal."

I expected her to change the subject, turn it to me, but she continued, as though a vein had been opened. Depression may not have been the clinical term for it, but she'd been low. She got herself to work, but the rest of the time she was too low to do little more than watch TV or lie in bed thinking about how much effort it would take to do anything but lie in bed. Low in a way that felt like a habit or an addiction; her lowness made her want more unstructured and unaccountable time in which to be low. Social engagements—any kind of *engagement*—encroached on that time and were therefore a source of resentment. The lowness was like an addiction, too, in that she was compelled to hide it. She would keep the remote in her hand, ready to turn off the TV as soon as she heard Jack's key in the front door. She would quickly get out of bed. "What are you doing?" he would ask. "Oh, just tidying up." Along the depression spectrum, there must be a point at which one is no longer able to be furtive, when you're too depressed to care about appearances. She hadn't reached that point. But how many times can you center a pile of books on a night table? Stand over your coffee table looking slightly lost? Was paranoia part of it too? Jack could, if it occurred to him, determine whether the TV was warm and just-watched. He could detect the recent impression of her body on the quilt and sheets, the indent in the pillow. Even the TV and the bed—her greatest comforts— were against her. She reached what she thought was a nadir at the supermarket when she found herself crying in the aisle to a soft-rock standard. She began to worry that she was disappearing, that she'd never really been there at all. (*Me too!* I half wanted to interject. *Can we run off and read Emily Dickinson poems to each other for the rest of our days?*) She woke once from a dream in which she could fly, and Jack said flying in dreams was good. Freedom, power. She said she was inside a big house, and she was flying from room to room. Well, more like floating. Floating speedily. So nobody would see her. *Like a ghost,* Jack said. How obvious. How sad. But what she didn't tell him, what she couldn't tell him, is that she had loved her ghostly advantages. Moving around undetected, the superiority of it, being slightly above everyone.

"These kind of dreams, they were pretty much the only color in my life. Anyway, it was Linda who finally made me see a therapist."

"What does your therapist think of all this? What we're doing."

"I haven't talked to her about it. Which is something I should talk to her about. She's great, really. It's, um, therapeutic to talk to her. But sometimes things will happen and I'll think, Viv's the person I want to talk to about that."

She was often still the one I wanted to talk to, not simply out of habit, but because if she were listening, if she knew about it, whatever it was would be more interesting, more significant. I wavered between believing she felt the same way—how could she not?—and sensing that I was deceiving myself. If she'd really wanted or needed to talk to me, she would have. But it couldn't be that simple, I thought. Our relationship wasn't that simple. No, she must have wanted to talk to me but couldn't bring herself to do so precisely because it wasn't that simple and she trusted me to understand that. Unless our relationship really *was* that simple for her? She had left me with a mystery I tried to solve with circuitous thinking. It was a way to keep her present. It pleased me no end to hear her confirm now that I hadn't merely invented the complexity between us and that I wasn't the only one still holding on to it.

"I know."

"I know I'm the one who stopped returning your phone calls. It became hard for me to talk to you. But it was also hard not to talk to you."

"I know what you mean."

"You do?"

Say it. Tell her.

"Lee, I'm pregnant."

"What?"

"You're the first person I've told."

"What—oh. Oh my god. That's—that's wonderful!" she said, her pause giving the lie to her words, as though I had been there a minute ago and was now lost to a world of architecturally significant strollers and bamboo-fiber baby carriers. Lee had once told me that she worried she was never as excited as she was supposed to be when friends told her this news. To mask insensitivity, she said, and perhaps that lonely, quiet panic that the world is leaving you and your aging reproductive system behind, you learn to ask certain questions. *How far along are you?! How are you feeling?!* Legitimate questions, sincere ones even, but what did it mean if she asked them of me, now? "It's wonderful. I mean, it's good, right?"

"Yes, it's good. Andy and I were planning this. We're on the same page. When did I start saying things like *we're on the same page?*"

"I know. You hear yourself saying stuff and it's just—I used to think you could divide the world into things that were cool and things that you held in contempt. But as you get older, there's this other category of things that you value just because they're comforting and easy."

"Like when you find yourself watching a commercial for chocolate—take a break and treat yourself right!—and you think yeah, I do need to take a break and treat myself."

"Right. Women and chocolate. In the eighties it was all 'Chocolate is like an orgasm!' Now it's like chocolate is a respite. Going to the spa without leaving your kitchen. It's 'you time.' Which I guess means women used to want sexual satisfaction and now they just want a minute alone."

"What was chocolate in the nineties?"

"Good question." She thought about it. "How far along are you? How are you feeling?"

"About a month."

"And I'm the only person who knows? "

"I haven't even been to the doctor. I mean, I called them and they said to come in a couple weeks, that if the home test confirmed it, that's a yes. I already have to pee all the time. But I haven't told Andy."

"I thought you were on the same page."

"We are. In general. As far as pages go."

"Are you thinking you don't—"

"I don't know why I haven't told him. It's like I'm scared it will make it real. Even though it already is real. But it's not like I don't want it to be real. I do."

A flicker, a darkening across Lee's eyes, led me to think she was on the verge of telling me something before she switched modes.

"You've got that glow."

"You can see it?"

"Yes, like a phosphorescence."

"Like I'm a glow stick."

"I've missed you, Viv."

"I've missed you, too."

TWO HOURS NORTH of the city, at the end of a wooded, secluded drive, lay Charlie Flintwick's compound: two small, squat buildings, a sagging multicar garage, what looked like a camp cabin, and a dark brown A-frame house overlooking a pond. Bird trills and fallen brush underfoot were the only sounds as we walked from our parked car to the front porch, and then we heard faint strains of elevator jazz. A shriek, then another one, splashing, a dock creaking. Lee advanced around the corner of the house as if it didn't matter if we found a party or a crime scene. But then she stopped and we hung back, watching.

"Flintwick, you fat fuck, you've outdone yourself!" A guy in red swim shorts, lead-singer looks, shook a bag of kettle-cooked potato chips into a bowl.

"It's just a grilled cheese, man. But, hey, I'll take the hyperbole." *Fat fuck,* I now saw, was a holdover from heftier times. Flintwick had the look of a picked-apart scarecrow. Lee had told me he maintained a blog about his recent gastric bypass surgery, with posts titled "Saggin'" and "New Pants." But even in his shrunken state, his aura remained rotund and kingly. He could have been wearing an ermine-trimmed robe.

"But this cheese! Is it artisanal?"

"Yes. It was made by the artisans at a processing plant in Illinois."

"Fucking delicious." Without noticing us, he took his plate down a path to the Adirondack chairs by the water's edge, occupied by a tattooed lot, two men and a woman, who all looked to be around his tender age.

Flintwick then turned the music up via remote and stuck the corner of an unpackaged cheese slice on his tongue so the rest of it flapped against his chin. He proceeded to hoist it into his mouth while eyeing the group at the shore with contempt or lust or both. I read once that Flintwick wasn't his given name. He had changed it from something chewier, of eastern European extraction. But Flintwick, with its Dickensian and pervy echo, did him justice.

"Well, hello!" He turned. We advanced. "Miss Parrish, I presume. You've made it."

"I hope we're not interrupting."

"Please, I've been expecting you. This is just"—gesturing toward the whole scene—"this is business. They're using the studio."

"Who are they?"

"The Episcopal School Experience. The Horse Fluffers. The Fuck-wads. Something like that. I don't know. I forget. Would you like something to eat? She's fired up and ready to go." Pointing to the charcoal grill, and then to me. "Sorry, I didn't catch your name."

"This is my dear friend Viv." *Dear friend*—the affected, beau monde construction we reserved for Elena Sterling Rappoport, socialite-businesswoman-matriarch, on THATH. Flintwick responded with a compressed bob and weave of his large head, as if to say, *So that's how you want to play it? Well, okay, we can save the vulgarities till we know each other a little better.*

"Why don't we go inside to talk." Flintwick grabbed a platter of grilled kabobs and slid open a glass door to a musty interior. "After you." He motioned to a massive L-shaped sectional, upholstered in black velvet, positioned around a squat jade table on which sat two heavy brass candelabra. On the wall behind him was a gun rack loaded with antique rifles and a bayonet. The fine layer of dust on the lamp shades and their ornate bases, resting on end tables, did little to dispel an actively carnal atmosphere. The room of a country squire who sidelined in pornography. It must have looked about the same the last time Jesse Parrish saw it.

"I used to think all this kept me young," he said. "But now it's the opposite. I feel preserved. Jellied. The world is Dorian Gray and I'm its grotesque, aging portrait." He took up a kabob in each hand, like antennae, pointing the skewers toward us. "What can I get you to drink?"

I was coming to understand that I was in the awkward stage of the first trimester, when, if you don't want to announce it, you need an excuse for not drinking socially. Antibiotics sounds like you've just come from a round of swab work at your ob/gyn. A polite refusal, much like fainting, only incites suspicion. If there was a tactful dodge, I didn't know it. I was relieved when Lee asked for a seltzer. Flintwick pulled back a lacquered door to a wet bar, fixed glasses for us, then sat down across from Lee, staring at her with pleasure and fondness.

"Forgive me. I'm ogling. I didn't anticipate how vividly you would resemble your parents. I can remember your father sitting in that very spot. It's like time stopped. Or folded back in on itself. Like my old abdomen."

Lee laughed and then sank into the sofa, granting him the favor of looking at her. You could write Flintwick off as a buffoonish slob, but that would be to ignore the fact that he cultivated his buffoonery. Flintwick was like a land mass that had seen whole populations come and go. He had provided for certain tribes who knew how to tend him. If you recognized his gifts, he would yield something.

"I'd like to help, but I don't know what I can tell you that I haven't said already, about that time or those recordings."

"I thought if you could tell me about those last days in a new light maybe some detail would emerge. Or maybe I'd just get to know my father a little better."

"Well, it's hard to know why certain people take hold of you. Jesse wasn't alone in what he did. He wasn't exactly a pioneer or one of a kind. Yet here we are. When you called me, I thought, Why not? Let's see how Jesse and Linda's girl turned out."

"Did you know my mother well?"

"Everybody knew Linda. But I knew Linda from way back in New York. Before she'd even finished high school. Before she moved to L.A. and changed her name. I knew Linda Weinstein."

Flintwick had known the fast girl for whom New York was too slow. It gave you the impression that life was long, that one can have many incarnations. I found myself, for the first time, laying my hand on my lower abdomen. As inconspicuously as I could.

"Back then," Flintwick was saying, "I was something of an impresario. Promoting parties, promoting bands, promoting myself. Linda was always hanging around in those days and, oddly, when I looked at her I didn't see a *girl* who I could take to bed. I saw *myself*. I should have gone into business with her. She was all of eighteen. But I pitied the guys who just wanted her for sex because they had no idea what they were getting into. I'm sorry. You don't want to hear these things about your mother. You came here to talk about your father, after all."

"He spent his last days here," said Lee. "I thought I would feel his presence or something, being here."

"And you don't?"

"I don't know. Not really."

"A lot of people have passed through here. If these walls could talk, they would probably say they'd like to take a shower." He didn't smile. "I've told those stories. It gets old. Look, people are people, and they don't lose their personalities when they happen to be in a relatively debauched state. Jesse came here with a goal and he worked hard. He was very in control, and rather controlling, when we were in the studio. He didn't want to just make music. He wanted to be a *star,* to be adored by people he didn't know, but there's a certain drive and pathological self-absorption that comes with that territory. I always felt Jesse looked at me with a mix of respect and scorn. He valued the function I served, but it was beneath him. He would never stoop to my level. See, we all hung out with some unsavory people—some of us still do—but it was a question of getting your hands dirty. Calculating how to capitalize on something or someone, how to profit from a situation, how to exploit— these weren't virtues, not with that crowd. Jesse could have been strung out, sleeping with God knows who, disgracing himself in any number of more creative ways, but that wouldn't have compromised him. He could quietly pull some old family strings to get out of going to Vietnam, and still, his hands would never have been dirty in the way that mine were. There was always something untouchable about him. Like he appreciated the low life, but he would never get that low. Put it this way: I was his Falstaff for a few months."

"You're saying my father liked to slum it, but he was really a snob?"

"Not a snob. Just different from me. Some part of him found me distasteful, and I wonder if that part didn't feel similarly toward Linda, as taken with her as he was."

With this, Flintwick seemed less Falstaff, more Iago, sowing seeds of doubt. But Lee nodded, and I wondered if this was exactly what she'd wanted to hear. A way in which she was like her father and could identify with him, against her mother. She too found her mother distasteful.

"When Jesse was here, he had some fun—Marion was on the scene then—but mostly he was very focused. Actually, Marion sang backup sometimes. He brought a bunch of people out to work with him. Chris Valenti. They always had that thing between them, when they played together, that rowdy partnership with homoerotic over-tones. Valenti was an extraordinarily talented guy, more talented than Jesse for sure, but he didn't have half the charisma. Wound up recording insects or some shit and died about ten years ago out-side of Minneapolis. But I digress. Jesse was totally lucid about what he wanted in the studio. He was going in a really melodic direction, but playing around a lot with feedback. I can't say it was super-innovative technically, but it was classic in an out-of-its-time way. He made some gorgeous noise. Think about what was going on then. You had your disco, your funk, your stadium rock. Your let-me-get-coked-up-so-I can-write-a-song-about-the-evils-of-coke genre and its Californian twin, the pass-me-a-bottle-of-Beaujolais-I wanna-get-mellow music. You had *Songs in the Key of Life.* You had *Rumours.* You had Iggy Pop over there in Berlin getting the Henry Higgins treatment from David Bowie. Remember, you had punk by then. The beginnings of hip-hop. New wave. Looking back, I don't know quite where Jesse's album would have fit in, but I would love to be able to listen to it now, give it the old retrospective spin. See if it would blow me away. Some of the tracks he was working on never got to be more than demos, but they were just dazzling. He had ac-cess to that rare combination of bravado and melancholy."

"Marion," said Lee, interrupting Flintwick's oration.

"Was a distraction. A beautiful distraction," he said. "B
a kid, a child, and children need a lot of attention."

Lee may not have felt her father's presence, but I could s
a corner of the room, spotlit, Jesse sitting in the wingchair
right ankle resting on left knee, a bowl of fruit and a beer
ble in front of him. He plays his guitar, and Marion come
behind, placing her hands over his eyes.

"Still," Flintwick continued, "I think Linda was threa
Marion. Maybe not Marion herself, but the fear that Je
leave her for good. That he would get back on his feet, bec
success again, and leave her behind."

"And me. He would leave me behind, too," said Lee.

"Oh, I don't know about that. But Linda was upset e
come out here from California. I believe she went to Ma
to see her family and she must have brought you because
already here. You were both already out here in New York
accident happened."

"That's a blur for me. I remember being at my gran
house with Linda, but I don't know if that was then or if it
other trip."

"Does Linda never talk about it?"

"Not really."

"Flintfuck!" A voice bellowed from outside. The front
tered with a towel around his waist, pine needles clinging t
feet. "Who do we have here?"

"Lee, Viv, this is Ethan Warren of the, uh—"

"Of Sticker Shock."

"That's right. Sticker Shock. Currently taking a certain
the Internet by storm."

Ethan shook our hands and I couldn't tell whether he was embarrassed or proud.

"Lee's parents and I are old friends," said Flintwick.

"That's rad. You guys should come down to the lake to chill. I
just came up to get more beer."

Lee gave him her easygoing smile. I felt tired, old, and slightly
above it all. I imagine Lee did, too, but she was so used to giving
that easy smile. Like a mask she'd forgotten to take off.

"Oh hey, man, do you have any more of those figs-in-blankets?"

"No. Your fucking vegan drummer ate all of them."

"Shit. Those things were tasty."

Flintwick met Ethan's open simplemindedness with a blank stare,
daring him to disappear. Which he did, heading back down to the
water.

"Where were we? The accident. Perhaps I should just say the crash.
There was the typical collective mourning. The rush to judge poor
Marion. Some of them—the fans, the critics—wanted to crucify her.
There was always something foul about the way they would refer to
her as his 'black' girlfriend. Then, of course, there were the missing
tapes. I was out of town for a couple of days when it happened, but
I came back as soon as I heard. I was here when your mother came
to sort through your father's things. She was still his wife. She came
alone and she looked terrible. It was just the two of us—everyone
else had cleared out—and I insisted she stay the night. I didn't have
any ulterior motives. Well, I *always* had an ulterior motive, but I
wasn't going to act on it. Like I said, I didn't see Linda that way. I
could have *convinced* myself to see her that way, it wouldn't have been
too hard, and I was getting the unmistakable vibe that she wanted
me to see her that way. I chalked it up to her vulnerable emotional
state. She wanted to go for a swim so we went down to the lake and

she undressed and stood there like she wanted me to judge her. If she'd slept with me, it would have been out of disgust and normally, hey, I'd be all for that. But she was clearly wrapped up in something and I was outside of it. I remember she just said 'fine' and walked into the water. Kind of spooky. She started swimming out past the dock, and I thought, *Well, shit, I better go in after her now 'cause if she drowns?* I huffed and puffed and eventually caught up to her and we're both naked and treading water and she thanked me for going after her. After that we just swam, in figure eights, like some weird synchronized routine. Nothing like my Esther Williams fantasies, though. She got all sentimental and reflective and started telling me how strange it was for her to be back here in the Catskills, near Hirschman's.

"Hirschman's?" asked Lee.

"The resort. Her family spent summers there. It's just a few miles away, abandoned now. Used to be a jewel of the Borscht Belt. Very *Dirty Dancing.* Nobody puts Linda in a corner! She was experiencing some kind of freaky frisson, the Then overlapping with the Now. She was a spooky, spooky chick that night. But she was gone by the time I woke up, and I couldn't shake the distinct impression that I'd been had."

"How so?"

"I don't know. I still don't. It was just a feeling. She'd cleaned the place of any trace of Jesse. Her right, of course. But it felt like a theft."

"You think she took the tapes?" Lee asked. "She didn't want them out in the world for some reason?"

"There's not much I would put past Linda," he said. "Hold on"— he rose like a judge and exited the room, leaving us with that troubling implication.

"I've asked Linda before, you know," Lee said to me. "She's always said she has no clue." We sat in silence, listening to the hooting sounds down by the lake. Flintwick came back holding a cardboard sleeve from which he pulled a photograph: Jesse on a stool in the studio, a hank of hair over his face but his laconic smile still visible.

"There was one thing Linda didn't get a hold of. A box of negatives and contact sheets from a photographer I'd brought here to shoot your father the day he died. Talk about spooky. I held on to them for a long time but sold them all to a collector in the city a couple of years ago. Cash-flow problems, I'm sorry to say."

"Can I contact him? The photographer?"

"He's no longer with us either. David Haseltine. I'm sure you've heard of him. Relatively obscure and relatively impoverished until he passed away relatively young. Had to die to make a living, that old story. But you could talk to the collector. Bill Carnahan. He's a thoroughgoing prick though. I think I've been a complete dead end, huh?"

"Not at all," said Lee. "You've been very generous with your time."

"Would you like to have this?" Flintwick handed the photograph to her.

"Oh, I couldn't."

"Yes you could. I'm sure it's worth more to you than it is to me. I insist. It does beat, you know, my schlub-aesthete heart. Why don't you stay? Hear Sticker Shock. They rock the party that rocks the body."

"That's a very tempting offer."

"I know."

"But I don't want to impose. We should get going. Thank you for this," she said, the picture in her hands. Her face didn't have enough artifice to hide the emotions that had taken hold during Flintwick's reminiscence. At least, I wanted to think she couldn't hide it from me.

"Please give Linda my best." He'd started to walk us down a hall when a crash and some yelps from the lake demanded his attention. "I used to think of myself as a general of sorts, taking foot soldiers and turning them into samurai. Now I feel like a babysitter. Apologies. I'm afraid you'll have to see yourselves out."

I MET LINDA for the first time when I went home with Lee for winter break my sophomore year of college. Her khaki-colored, paper-bag pants and tangerine hoodie over a tight black tank top were Charlie Chaplin's tramp meets yoga instructor. But it was a look. She was one of those women who could make almost anything stylish, a gift she'd given her daughter. She had the same bangs and long hair she had in old pictures, only salt and pepper now, piled on her head. I didn't have the vocabulary to define the clean yet eclectic way Linda had decorated her 1930s home in the Hollywood hills, I only understood she had an eye, a way of organizing her environment that was at once homey and sophisticated. Persian rugs. Actual paintings, not prints from museum gift shops, hanging on the wall. Vases of peonies and potted dark-leaved plants. Issues of French *Vogue* in an upstairs bathroom with slightly peeling wallpaper. She must have read the magazines, wrinkled and curled from steam, while bathing. The house, as Linda lived in it, was a play of light and shadow. And I was a child, walking past glass and crystal displays in a department store, my mother cautioning me not to touch anything. Linda's house was part of a mysterious adult world to which I didn't yet belong. I expected a wave of inadequacy to wash over me, but instead, it was privilege. Being let in on some-thing special.

THE NIGHT WE arrived, Lee went to bed early, jet-lagged, but I was too keyed up to sleep. Linda took me to the kitchen and brought out a half-eaten chocolate cake, setting it down on the counter. No plates, just forks, and we stood there digging in, as though it were a ritual we'd performed many times before. I never did this with my mother. We never just had a cake standing by, as if for this very purpose. Our forks were utensils, not shapely design objects. No fragrant breezes such as these came through an open window in our house.

"What is that?"

"Winter-blooming jasmine. I love that this is what passes for winter here. I still haven't gotten over it."

"You grew up on the East Coast?"

"Sure did. Linda Weinstein, nice Jewish girl from Mamaroneck. Right?"

"Right," I said, not sure where she was going with this, where I was supposed to go.

"Well, that certainly wasn't going to cut it. Weinstein? And *Mamaroneck? Blech.* So I decided, at the ripe old age of eighteen, to flee. I changed my name to Linda West. Because I was going West, young woman! Later, when I met Jesse, he asked me if it was West like Na-thanael, and I had no idea who that was. He bought me *The Day of the Locust* and said, 'Here you go, honey.' I read it and I was horrified and I decided that I would be West like Nathanael. He would be my spiritual father. Because my real father? Mort Weinstein of Mort's Discount Clothing Mart? *Please.* But deep down I was always Big

Mort's daughter. A New Yorker. Sharp. I had uncles who ran numbers. I wasn't going to be that girl getting high all day and baking pies for my old man. Or I *would* be that, but I would have a secret self all the while."

"Weren't you"—I didn't want to finish the question, but she was waiting—"weren't you scared? At all?"

"Of course I was scared. I think that's what drove me. But I look back on it now and I was also so cocky. And why shouldn't I have been? I was hot shit, Viv. I had that beanpole look. It would have ruined me a decade earlier, but I was born at just the right time. So I came out here with my girlfriend Karen and I don't think we had a plan other than *let's just go!* Let's go be where it's at, right? I was barely eighteen and I was gonna sleep with whoever I wanted and write poems and take pictures and maybe get famous. We knew a bunch of people who'd come from New York and it was *easy*. I was a secretary for a few months and then I found modeling work and then I was just in it. In the scene or whatever. But I got tired of rock and roll early. Those boys."

It was the women who interested her. The girls and what they wore and what they meant by what they wore. A costume designer she knew asked her to outfit the ingénue in a movie—her "Edith Head moment" as she put it—and it led to more work of that sort. She took courses in pattern making, met with manufacturing contacts and other associates of Big Mort's. In 1972, with a bank loan she could only secure with the co-signature of her husband or father, she opened a small shop on Sunset, the first Linda West boutique.

"You know what the big cosmic joke is, though? Here I am, Mort Weinstein's prodigal daughter, back in the *schmatte* business, after all."

She made it sound so easy. I filed away all of the names to look up later, names that might help me make sense of it all. *Nathanael West, Edith Head, Mamaroneck.*

"So, what about you? Lee tells me she's bringing a friend home and that's pretty much it. She doesn't say a word about how lovely you are."

I had been primed by Lee to see all of this as part of Linda's shtick. But it didn't matter. I was hers.

The next evening Linda had guests for dinner, a movie director and his girlfriend, a British actress in a witchy black dress. We sat out on Linda's redwood porch, under eucalyptus trees strung with lanterns, overlooking a dark blue tiled pool. To my surprise, I didn't feel abandoned and clingy when Lee and the actress, who had hit it off to the point of giggles, went for a swim, leaving me with Linda and the director. Maybe it was the wine I had been drinking all night. Maybe it was that I kept telling myself that the director, whose last movie I had gone to see twice because it beguiled me even though I didn't really get it, couldn't possibly be looking at me like he wanted to keep looking at me, in a filmic way, because that just wouldn't happen, but *wasn't* he? And when I allowed myself to ask him something about the Jungian aspect of a scene in one of his movies, he looked charmed. "Viv here is pretty brilliant, isn't she?" he said to Linda, and she winked at me and I wasn't a precocious child they had decided to patronize and laugh about later. I was brilliant. Bewitched.

The guests spent the night and in the morning, Linda told us all about the dream she'd had in which she slept with her father. Which sounds like the kind of thing you say to shock someone, but Linda spoke with unfiltered openness and a complete lack of self-consciousness. "The thing is," she said, "it was really good!" I didn't think she was aware of the effect it might have on her daughter. But that right there was Lee's problem with her. Whether it was blithe lack of forethought or knowing disregard, it hurt. I was the only one who saw Lee's face when Linda said that: like finding out a secret note of yours had fallen into the wrong hands. What must it have been like to have a father whom women recollected with yearning and faintly dirty smiles, a man whose seductive qualities never ever diminished? If he's your father and yet you never knew him, really, does he seduce you, too?

"Was it really your father or was it a stand-in?" the British actress asked.

"It was really my father. He called me Lindy. He smelled like Aqua Velva and Chock Full O'Nuts."

Linda's candor and freedom, the space she luxuriously floated in, amazed me. My own parents seemed so contained in comparison. They had done such an excellent job of shielding from me their inner lives that I had naturally concluded they didn't have very rich or complicated ones.

Some months later, when Linda asked us all out to dinner one Parents' Weekend, I excitedly anticipated introducing my mother and father to Linda. She would dazzle them, would make them see life didn't have to be so small.

Would the Felds—Jonathan, a dermatologist, and Natalie, a middle-school language arts teacher—have been able to command the most inviting table in the restaurant or would they have had to wait for two hours like everyone else only to be seated by the bathroom? When it came to appetizers, my mother ordered the simple mixed-greens salad while Linda ordered several plates of the "exquisite" zucchini blossoms she'd had here the last time she was in town, along with something involving fennel and a citrus drizzle.

"The zucchini blossoms actually are really good here," Lee said to my mother, as though apologizing.

"They sound delicious," said my mother, warming to Lee.

"I've read about this place," said my father. "People say it's top notch. I've always meant to make a reservation."

"Really?" I said. My father either didn't hear or pretended not to as he focused on the wine list, choosing a bottle that cost three times what he typically spent on the special occasions when he drank wine. When it arrived, he deferred to Linda, who raised her glass and said, "To our daughters, our incandescent girls."

"Hear! Hear!" said my father, and he clinked Linda's glass first while my mother and Lee exchanged a look: *yes, okay, sometimes Linda gets it right.*

The talk turned to what we'd done with our respective days. Linda and Lee had gone to lunch with an old friend of Linda's who now happened to be the dean of alumni relations. "She used to handle PR for me when I was just starting out with the line," said Linda. "And she was perfect because she thinks in sound bites. Half the time she made me feel like a rambling old loon, but that's what I was paying her for." My parents and I had been to a panel discussion, "Illness and Creativity," led by Patricia Driggs, who had joined the faculty that semester and had just come out with her latest book, a memoir about living with fibromyalgia.

"I thought she was remarkable," said my mother. "So smart. And off the cuff like that—I've always admired how, in her writing, she can distill very complex ideas into such elegant sentences. But she *speaks* that way. You were talking about sound bites—it's the opposite of that. The deep complement to that."

"Oh God, I'm sorry, but *eeecch,* Patti Driggs?"

Prompted by their inquiring looks, Linda elaborated. Patti was her nemesis. They had come of age around the same time, in the same place, circling each other at parties in the canyons of Los Angeles, accepting dinner invitations from the same hosts, turning up at the same clubs. They were friendly and Linda even felt a bit sisterly toward Patti. Thin and birdlike Patti, her nerves as vibratory as a tuning fork. She once told Linda she often found herself compulsively counting headlights on cars at night. To not count them would open her up to an unnamable terror. And yet, Patti was steely. It was Patti who made the most acute, withering comments, or she would listen more intently than empathically, like an aural snare trap. Linda liked having tense and pitiless Patti around. Or so she thought.

Patti was writing sharp essays and journalistic reports about life in Los Angeles that would eventually be compiled into a much-lauded, much-imitated volume. It was Linda who helped facilitate Patti's profile of Jesse Parrish, persuading Jesse that Patti wouldn't lazily paint him as the country boy who couldn't resist the glittering temptations of the city. She might, as others had, contrast his sweetness with his swagger, describe his music in terms of purity and corruption. Write about how polite he was, as if that were exotic. But Linda convinced Jesse that Patti would somehow get it *just right*. Imagine Linda's reaction, then, when she read Patti's piece, which contained (blessedly, perhaps) only one reference to her: "His wife, a model from Mamaroneck, appears by the pool and asks if Jesse would like to wear the blue caftan this evening or the gold and if he wants the gold caftan, he should really wear the purple velvet pants, oh, but wait, the purple velvets are at the cleaners. She pauses, corrects herself: *aubergine*, not purple. The mood is very serious."

Patti went on to write novels (*Dispatches from the End,* which established her voice as that of a generation, followed by *Managing by Walking Around*) and two plays—one a "vital, scabrous take on sexual harassment in academia" and the other a "hilarious descent into the dark heart of a deteriorating marriage" according to the introductory leaflet I'd been handed at the lecture hall. She also wrote an indispensable book on photography.

Linda never forgave Patti for the early betrayal. What rankled Linda most was Patti's duplicity. Patti would be duplicitous even in her insanity. If Patti were to really lose it one day, as she feared she would, she would only go crazy enough to write about it in a best-selling fashion; she would literally be of two minds, never batshit enough not to be intelligible, shrewd, and marketable.

"You'd like her to have a complete and total breakdown?" my mother asked.

"I'm not wishing it on her. But it would finally be honest. I just get so tired of her moral authority. She writes a book called *Dispatches from the End* and everyone goes on about how significant it is, how powerful a portrait of anomie in our apocalyptic times. And I'm thinking, it sounds like a book about taking a shit. But even after all this time, it hasn't changed. It's not just that she made me look like an idiot all those years ago. She didn't even really get Jesse, who, by the way, never owned a pair of purple velvet pants. Excuse me, *aubergine*. Patti *loved* him, no doubting that, and I'm not going to get catty, but it was like she wanted to instruct him on how to be a better person. He didn't need her instruction. Other people criticized him for being out of it, for not being political enough, like he only cared about himself. But you know how young men write those songs and sometimes you can't tell if they're about a girl or Jesus or heroin? Well, Jesse would cover a protest song, and it would come out sounding like it was about love, about getting your heart broken. He had this vulnerability, this really aching feminine quality, which is just, my God, so sexy in a man. And it was all there when he sang. *Right there.* He's with you, you're with him. I think that's what makes him timeless. What's that T. S. Eliot line about news that stays news?"

"Pound," said my mother, who often grew doctrinaire in the face of social unease. "I believe it's Ezra Pound. On literature."

God. You couldn't have just let that go?

"Oh, you're right. Pound, Eliot. I'm always, like, whoever it was who didn't like the Jews. But then, neither of them did? It gets confusing. That's what Jesse wrote, though. News that stays news."

"I know I had his first record," said my father. "But I'm afraid I never really delved into the Jesse Parrish oeuvre. I liked that first one, though. With that cow on the cover? I never understood what that cow was doing there."

"It was a field, Dad. The cow was just in the field."

"I know, but was there supposed to be some kind of significance to it?"

"Like what?" I asked.

"Some biblical allusion? Something about sacred cows? I'm free-associating here, but I wonder."

Stop free-associating. Stop wondering. Just stop.

Linda jumped in. "Well, Jesse and I were staying at a place in the country and we went out walking and we walked and walked and we reached this pasture and there was this lonely cow just grazing and I always had my camera around my neck in those days and Jesse said, 'Take a picture.' So I did. It's as simple as that. People have asked me about it for years, though, because if you look closely, it looks like the cow is kind of smiling."

"A bovine Mona Lisa," said my father.

"Yes! I got so lucky with that cow."

"Mom," said Lee.

"Mom? I got a 'Mom'? I can't remember the last time you called me Mom. It's always Linda with you."

"Can we talk about something other than you getting lucky with a cow?"

"Oh, my dear, sometimes I regret that I never went in for all that Emily Post stuff. I think I did us both a disservice."

"I know what you mean," said my mother. "I wasn't very good about making my kids write thank-you notes and it haunts us to this day." A lie. I'd never witnessed my mother lie like that, and it threw me. Not just because she was lying (she was on me about thank-you notes as soon as I could properly hold a pen), but because the lie effectively did so much work, expressing sympathy for Linda but ultimately defending Lee, and at my expense. I couldn't immediately name the feeling that crept up on me, but on reflection, it seemed a lot like jealousy. I wanted my mother's affection for myself.

"Lee is her father's daughter," said Linda. "She's gonna do what she's gonna do." Ostensibly celebrating something irrepressible in Lee, Linda's comment had an ugly undertone that seemed aimed at the table, a warning to all of us when it came to taking sides.

"Yes," said Lee, "and right now I'm gonna get that waiter back here and order another bottle of wine."

UNDER A CANOPY of trees the dirt lane from Flintwick's compound led to a paved, sleepy road. We passed a barn and yellow and green fields that soon dipped down into a darker, cooler valley, shaded from the disappearing sun by the tall, dense pines of the Catskill preserve. Brown signs etched with yellow paint marked turnoffs for a campground, a waterfall, the trail head for a hike, until the forest cover thinned out again and we came to the two-lane route we'd taken in. Instead of turning right, which would take us back the way we came, Lee went left along the winding mountain road. Some scenic detour, I figured, to keep things going before we headed back to the city. She'd promised me a road trip, and I didn't want to go home yet.

In the passenger seat, I leafed through a scrapbook Lee had been given by her aunt Delia, whom she'd gone to see in North Carolina a few months earlier on a fact-finding mission. Press clippings from a local paper and a copy of a page from his 1965 high-school year-book picturing Jesse perched on a stool with his guitar, clean-cut in permanent-press pants and a crisp-collared, button-down shirt under a sport coat, his hair still short enough to be corralled into a stiff side sweep off his forehead. The caption beneath the photo: *Jesse Parrish never fails to entertain!*

"Delia told me that in his first band at boarding school, they played a dance at the girls' academy nearby. His guitar went missing afterward and the headmistress found it a week later in one of the girl's beds. He drove her to theft."

"But he stole her heart."

"It's possible Delia made that story up. She's sort of lucid and sort of bonkers. But I don't know. Have you read the letter yet?"

Tucked in there was an envelope postmarked Los Angeles, May 27, 1970, containing this:

Dear Sis,

I hope this finds you as well as can be. I won't go on with a thousand apologies for being out of touch, because you know how it goes. You're as bad as I am. But I wanted to let you know that Linda and I got married. No society page announcements. A few of us on a beach down in Mexico. Tumbling surf and a light breeze and all that. Do you know it was the first time I've ever seen Linda nervous? Not that she said so. It was in her eyes. Just a flicker of a flash. I probably should have been nervous, too. It's only right to be nervous in the face of something so cosmic. I can see you making a face, but it's no joke. With Linda, it's completely cosmic. It just fucking is.

When we got back to L.A., my wife (mah wife, yessir) set this writer friend of hers on me. I talked a whole lot to this lady and now I think I'm going to regret it. She reminds me of a matchstick. A twig, flat, flat, flat, and then up there at the top is her ignitable mind. I liked her intensity at first. Sort of clarifying, the appeal of someone who has your number. But then it got exhausting. She's going to make a fool of me. She's got this bright disdain. That's her lens, and Linda and I are soft and ridiculous through it. Well, fine. We are soft and ridiculous. But not where it counts. I know where it counts. Here's what I wonder. Does Patti Driggs ever feel anything when she listens to music? Anything other than a drive to explain it away? I don't think she needs music to show her who she is. I don't think she needs it to get through. I don't think, for her, it's like fucking, or even like a fucking cigarette. Gosh, you know there's this health-nut drug dealer my manager is pals with and he's always on me to quit smoking. He'll come over with a loaf of yeast-free bread, some bottle of weird juice, and a bag of psilocybin mushrooms. But oh, those cigarettes have got to go, man! All right, now you can make your face.

Please take it easy, Del. Call or write when you can.

Yrs for yrs,

Jesse

I had never seen a letter of Jesse's and I didn't know why but out of all of it—the description of his wedding to Linda, his acute, knowing read of Patti Driggs—it was that "Gosh" of his that really brought him to life for me.

"Oh, I know," said Lee. "You should hear Aunt Delia talk. It's all 'Gosh!' and 'Golly!' It's like no matter how fucked up things got, she never stopped being a well-mannered Southern belle. Maybe that's what's fucked up about her."

"How is she fucked up, exactly?"

"Pretty much like the rest of the Parrishes were. In and out of places since she was seventeen. Substance abuse. Depression. Manic depression. They were all alcoholics, you know, on Jesse's mother's side. It's kind of unbelievable. Like it's almost too on the nose or something. I knew my father's father shot himself when my dad was a kid. But I didn't know how Southern Gothic it all was. Do you know what the family did? They had a party. Every year his mother's mother threw herself a lavish birthday celebration at their home. But by home I mean mansion. This big white house on a lake among the pine trees. They would put up a tent for the evening—all elegant. So my grandfather kills himself and my great-grandmother just goes ahead and has her party as planned. Jesse and Delia were out there in their finest, watching everyone, their mother included, get progressively more hammered, until one of the servants came to take them inside to get ready for bed. Delia told me she and my dad didn't know it was suicide until they were grown. Hunting accident, they were told. Delia is the only one left now. I never met any of the others. It doesn't even seem real to me. But sometimes my father barely seems real to me. Which I guess is the whole point of this, right?"

She pulled over and though no official signage marked the spot where we'd stopped, it was obvious where we were.

"How did you know where this was?" I asked.

"Educated guess."

The shoulder began again after dropping off precipitously. To the right, the road bordered a high wall of blasted rock. To the left and behind us, a guardrail curved along a steep ravine above the stream into which Jesse Parrish's car had fallen. Over the years his fans had consecrated the site with flowers and plaques and a bulletin board erected between two trees on which were affixed poems, letters, and laminated drawings. Among the least weather-beaten additions were an original sketch of Jesse ascending to heaven on a rainbow, and a charcoal drawing of Jesse snuggling two kittens, signed "with love from Angie," a passport-size picture of the artist attached. Angie looked to be about forty-five.

The shrine was both touching and embarrassing. People had loved him so much, and still did, but it was an adolescent love, narcissistic and showy. It was hard not think that the love reduced and diminished its object, and the object of worship wasn't magnificent enough to withstand kittens and middle age.

"I've seen this place in pictures and I never thought I'd care to see it in person," said Lee. "In Paris once, I was walking through the Montparnasse cemetery, just to walk through it, and I saw Serge Gainsbourg's grave. It had all these metro tickets on it and packs of Gitanes that people brought. A couple of heads of cabbage because of that song he wrote. It was kind of lively, celebratory. But this place always just seemed mawkish. Why do people do this? Maybe it's because my dad doesn't have a grave. But people go out to the desert, too, where Linda scattered his ashes. It's strange. I feel like there's this character Linda West, and then there's my mother, the real person I know. As real as you can get. With my father, though, I have only what everyone else has. These people, Angie or whoever, these people know him better than I do."

"That's not true."

"I have a few memories. I have 'Yours.' But even that's not really mine." The waltz-like song Jesse had written for Lee had become a commonplace father-daughter dance at a certain kind of wedding—the wedding that didn't want to be a wedding but was a wedding nonetheless. I always figured Lee had her own interpretation of the lyrics "you and the sun and the sun in your eyes." But here it was, represented rather literally—a big sun in place of a pupil in a folk-arty painting embellished with glitter glue and coated in shellac. Craning for a closer look, I lost my balance and started to slip down the incline before scrambling up. The patch of ground was precarious, falling off sharply, a testament of devotion on the part of the memorial pilgrims.

Lee saw me stumble and quickly moved to help me to my feet. We stood there, gazing down. There's no good ravine to accidentally take a header into, but this one was especially dicey and unforgiving. If you were looking for an out, it would likely get the job done. Lee had never told me what she thought about the crash, if she believed it was an accident or if she thought her father had purposefully pulled the steering wheel hard to the left and accelerated. Like his father, in spirit, before him. In any case, there was no question he was intoxicated.

Maybe we were thinking the same thing.

"I do have his genes, though. It's encoded in me."

"You can't think that way. You aren't your father."

"I'm not saying I'm going to kill myself, Viv. If that's even what he did. The tapes are like a big hole. I don't know what they would fill in, but something. In all the shit you can read about my dad, they talk about his breakdown like it was this isolated thing. They never really talk about him struggling with an undiagnosed illness. But you can't meet Delia and come away thinking he was fine, fine, fine, then lost it one day, and then was fine again. I don't want to romanticize it, but I want to feel closer to his experience of it, to know if my experience is anything like his. Because those tendencies certainly don't come from Linda. I doubt she's ever been down—like, really down—a day in her life."

"You're okay now though, right?"

"I can fucking get up in the morning. But then I wonder what I'm doing with my life. It sucks when you've aged out of the time when it's still socially acceptable not to have things figured out."

"And you haven't yet reached the age when it's socially acceptable that whatever you thought you had figured out starts to unravel." I thought I should have at least another ten years before it was time for a midlife crisis, though it seemed to me that "midlife" and "crisis" were increasingly slippery terms.

"I just have this sense that I've squandered my legacy. That I should have been a lot more than I am. But what was my inheritance? Beauty? Sex appeal? That doesn't promise much. Maybe my dad had it right. Like, burning out is better than fading away or whatever."

"Lee."

"What?"

"I don't think those are the only options."

"Maybe not," she trailed off, laced her fingers together on the crown of her head, her elbows wide, as if to survey her domain, and then picked up again. "Don't get grossed out."

"About?"

"I had this dream once. One of those strange, long-finish dreams that cast a shadow on the whole day when you wake up. I was at a house by a lake and there were people there that I seemed to know. I walked down this carpeted hall and there was this row of doors made of plywood and I opened one to a room with a bed. It was all pink and gold. This young guy, in jeans and one of those three-quarter-length baseball shirts, hair like my father, came in and I knew something was going to happen and I was excited but I also had a sense of doom. I wanted something from him. I wanted him to be interested in me. We were on the bed and our actions started to look like a slow series of photographs. I held his head in my hands. He lifted my shirt and pressed his face to my stomach. Then like a slide show our position would change. I felt so close to him. He said he had to tell me something, and I knew what it was, and also that it didn't matter, that I wanted to stay in that room with him. So yeah, I woke up and I was like, fuck, I'm just like Linda, dreaming about my father."

"I guess everyone has dreams like that."

"Have you?"

"Well, no, not with my own dad." Lee ground her gaze into a leaf pile and I tried to keep myself from fully registering the awkwardness of the moment. "But I once had a dream about Michael Landon. As Pa from *Little House on the Prairie*. Does that count?"

"Yes, I'll accept it." She sighed. "Let's get out of here."

"Where do you want to go? With this." Gesturing down at the ravine.

She wanted to find a place for the night, talk to Bill Carnahan in the morning. But she didn't want me to feel obligated to help, in my condition and all. I told her it wasn't much of a condition yet. Then I texted Andy: *Here for the night. Will check back soon.* No immediate response. Was he away from his phone? Or was it a calculated silence? What was the calculation?

In the car, in search of a motel, we passed the rusted but still-standing L-shaped sign heralding, in a pointy, peaked font, Hirschman's. The deteriorating resort of Linda's youth. Lee pulled off the road again and onto an overgrown drive that met with a high chain-link fence through which we could see the falling-in red roofs of three large buildings, the vestiges of an extinct way of vacationing.

I imagined Linda there, in a taffeta dress and dyed-to-match heels, in the banquet hall at the end of the season. How many turns one life could take. We agreed it was odd that Linda, who "practically invented the overshare," didn't talk to her daughter about that time, rarely discussed Flintwick, and had never once mentioned Hirschman's.

"She must have her reasons," I said.

"I'm sure she does," said Lee.

YELLOW COUNTERPANES WITH blue flowers, a crosshatch weave on the heavy drapes, a low ceiling you could palm when standing, as Lee was, on one of the double beds, pink tile in the bathroom: our room for the night.

"You know who lives around here? Besides Charlie Flintwick?" She flopped down on the lumpy mattress and rolled over next to me.

"Who?"

"Rodgers Colston."

Rodgers Colston. It was a name that should have made me stop and think *Who? Oh! I haven't thought of him in years.* But no. Like Lee showing up out of the blue, but not really out of the blue—some people are with you all along, even when they're not.

"Yeah?" I tried to modulate my voice, not to betray too much curiosity.

"He has a place up around here and an apartment in the city."

I still thought of us, of my cohort, as being too young and not established enough to have more than one place of residence. I lagged behind the reality of my peer group.

"Let's call him and see what he's doing. I need a break from all this dad stuff."

"You're in touch with him?"

"I see him around now and then. I went to his last opening."

She said it so casually but I couldn't help hearing a cutting subtext: *There is a whole world you are not a part of.* When I first met Lee, I'm ashamed to say, I thought of her as "my famous friend," that some social boundary had been made permeable and that I had been allowed to cross it. I wondered if I was merely an opportunist and Lee presented me with opportunities. Eventually that boundary disappeared and I hadn't recognized it again until now, hearing her talk about Rodgers. But it wasn't just that Lee was friendly with Rodgers. It was that they had been in touch when Lee and I weren't. I had wanted to believe she had dropped out of the world for a while, when apparently, she had just dropped me.

Rodgers Colston belonged to that lazy, golden summer when Lee and Andy and I first became friends. That summer of long afternoons and warm dreamlike nights. Time worked differently. It blurred. There was a party once, a show, a thing, and I don't know why but we decided to dress up. Lee fashioned herself an outfit involving a shiny bathing suit and a black slip she found at Savers. She stuck a few pieces of tinfoil in my hair and let me borrow a short purple shirtdress that looked a bit like a uniform. Loose on her, the dress pulled at my chest and hips. I was still learning how to cultivate an appeal, figuring out what clothes to wear. Lee had introduced me to the subtle and transformative power of blush. That bright-eyed, Lizzy-Bennettramping-across-the-countryside glow. That *I know my sister is prettier but with my radiant complexion am I not irresistibly spirited, Mr. Darcy?* effect you could get, even though we barely needed it then. I took Lee's word for it that I looked good. Andy wore a blue T-shirt with a large satin seahorse sewn on the front. We went to the old brick textile mill where Noah Stone and his friends lived, where silk-screening tables and a mountain of salvaged junk (bed springs, a washing machine, a carburetor, a pair of gigantic plush slippers in the shape of pigs) had been pushed to a wall to make room for a stage on which four guys in masks methodically generated discordant dance music. The smell of sweat and beer permeated the space.

Lee and I found ourselves in a room they called "the study," where there were two torn-up sofas and shelves of mildewed books. I pulled down a pre-Fonda exercise manual featuring pictures of women in navy blue leotards demonstrating poses in a gauzily lit living room. I had opened to a page where a woman stretched her legs in a V, feet in the air.

"Maybe it's because she reminds me of my mother, but that one does it for me." The voice came from over my shoulder. Male, with a mildly Southern lilt to it. I became aware of my back, my spine, my bare collarbone as areas that could be touched by whoever that voice belonged to. I turned to see him. Sharp features, dark hair. Heeled boots that made him Abraham Lincoln tall. Slim-fitting brown corduroys secured by a leather belt with an ornate buckle. He also had on a black blazer and under that a pink T-shirt, which said Camp Young Judea across the front. I wondered if there wasn't something vaguely anti-Semitic about him wearing this shirt, in the same way I'd puzzled, as a kid, over the bumper stickers that said "My Boss Is a Jewish Carpenter." It was at these times that I most felt my Jewishness, if only because I became aware of it as something to be appropriated. I'd had a T-shirt just like that which I'd adorned with glitter paint one summer at a Jewish girls' camp where we sang easy-listening hits and used shampoos that smelled like apricot. Another art school student somewhere probably had my old shirt in rotation.

But if his outfit confused me, it also made me less self-conscious in my blushing-alien-stewardess get up, which might have been sexy on Lee. Andy had envied Noah Stone for all the girls who wanted him, but I began to wonder what kind of way Noah had with women. These guys, these boys, made me feel like the young woman I was, but also like an aging and impotent dandy. Their bodies amazed and frustrated me. Then this walking pastiche came along and made an inappropriate joke about his mother.

"RODGERS COLSTON," SAID Lee, as though they had a history. I half expected her to add, "So we meet again."

"In the fleisch," he said. To distract from whatever was passing between them, Lee introduced me.

"This is Miss X." Was she trying to make me seem mysterious? Was there some reason I shouldn't want Rodgers Colston to know my name?

"I like your tin foil, Miss X."

"Thank you."

"Miss X-Files." He pronounced it X-falls, which sounded so much looser and better than the pinchy way I would say it: X-fiy-uls. I realized I was still holding the book of calisthenics. He seemed to be waiting for me to say something. Topics of conversation popped up in my mind like Whac-A-Moles: David Duchovny, squat thrusts, the Civil War. Everything got the mallet. I wondered if he could somehow read my thoughts because he just stood there, stooped over me, his mouth a little open and on the verge of a smile. Finally he said, "I'll see y'round."

I turned to Lee but she had gone. Out in the main room I spotted Andy on the sidelines of a throng by the stage. He raised his arms and gave me a "please save me" look, and I felt a huge surge of affection for him for being pudgy and wearing an ill-fitting shirt with a big satin seahorse on it. The performance ended and the sound system came on; the music grew progressively dronier as the crowd thinned. Still no sign of Lee. Andy and I found a disgusting mattress in a back room, and I was so tired all I wanted to do was lie down on it. It was disgusting in a way that I romanticized as arty.

I didn't remember falling asleep, but a murmur woke me up. By then the place was silent. Lee knelt by Andy's head, her mouth close to his ear. What she was saying I couldn't make out, but something tender-seeming as her fingers brushed the side of his face. She kissed his temple, his forehead, and then she kissed him on the mouth. He sat up and pulled her closer, his hand in her hair. Through a triangle of space, my arm crossed over my face, I could watch without their knowing. Or so I thought. When Lee drew back for a moment, I shut my eyes but not before a flicker of contact had been made. She moaned a little, but the kissing continued until it was replaced by shifting and creaking. "Mmm," I heard her say. "C'mon." The springs in the mattress rose. Footsteps. I opened my eyes and they were gone.

I wanted so badly to be someone who didn't care. I wanted to go find Noah Stone or Rodgers Colston and sleep with one of them in a desultory way. I wanted to be someone who didn't think to use the word "desultory" in relation to sex. I wanted to be lost and to surrender the way Andy just had. But I took Lee's seduction of Andy personally, feeling somehow that she was making fun of me, of my ability to draw lines and my inability to cross them. The worst part is that I just lay there, believing Andy would come back, that we'd log a few more hours of sleep and then go home.

But I was on my own. I tossed and turned, scratched at what I assumed were fleas, and waited for the sky to lighten to a deep blue. When it finally did, I headed out to a parking lot, a near-treeless vista of abandoned warehouses and disused railroad tracks. Vacancy. A quiet morning. The rush of highway traffic faintly audible. Lee likely would have known how to orient herself by the sun's low position in the eastern sky or something like that. Sometimes we would go to a park by the water—a strip of green between the interstate and the harbor—and sit on a bench in the sun, not doing much of anything beyond looking out and watching shore birds land on wooden pilings. Lee knew what the birds were—cormorants, great blue herons. It was incongruous. Who taught her these things? Was she one of those children who develops an interest and clandestinely pursues it? Had she kept a field guide under her bed and studied at night while Linda entertained in the hills above Los Angeles? Her ability to name a bird, or a tree, or a constellation, her knowledge of the natural world, conflicted with the idea she had of herself—as a bright enough but not particularly bookish girl who didn't fully merit whatever academic success she'd achieved. It wasn't her intelligence, she seemed to suggest, that had gotten her here, to the school that Andy and I had worked hard to get into. And maybe it wasn't. Still, she would have known what to do here, standing at the edge of this rusting postindustrial plain. The childish part of me said it didn't matter, that I might as well walk myself into a situation so terrible that Lee and Andy, but especially Lee, would feel, for the rest of their lives, the guilt of leaving me alone. Some other part of me, the underutilized, bootstrapping part, said, *Buck the fuck up, you're on your own and the day is mild and you have a city at your feet, so just go*. I saw a Dunkin' Donuts in the distance. To each his own lodestar.

Two patrons sat at small tables and a third leaned against a counter by the window while an employee in an orange and pink smock attended to a tray of crullers behind the register. I took my coffee and glazed donut to my own little table and sat there, feeling existential. I hadn't noticed, until he'd moved and was standing over me, that the customer by the window was Rodgers Colston.

"Miss X."

It sounded like Miss Sex. I tried hard not to drop the cup in my hand.

"Mister Colston."

"Did you have a good time last night?"

"Yeah. It was great. Right?"

It didn't matter what the words were, only that we had established a rhythm and kept it going. He sat down and we said more basic things while his eyes flashed with something like wry amusement. I remember focusing mine on his upper lip and wondering what it would feel like against my neck, the back of my thigh. He caught me staring.

"I still don't know your name."

"Viv. Vivian."

"That suits you."

"Does it?" Like a stylist. It reminded me of the hairdresser at the upscale salon my mother took me to when I was fifteen and going through a homely phase. He had thick swoopy hair, he could pull off a red buffalo plaid work shirt with white jeans, he was from Vermont, and I would have believed anything he said. I believed him when he told me I was pretty and that he was sure I'd have a boyfriend soon, if I wanted one. That I didn't soon have a boyfriend, that I didn't even really like the haircut he gave me, somehow didn't make me question the first part of the statement. I never, for instance, wondered if my mother had tipped him to say such a thing, I just took heart in his compliment. It got me through sophomore year.

"I just mean it's a nice name."

"I like Rodgers."

"It's a family name."

"Do people ever call you Rod?" I became very conscious of how I was swallowing my coffee.

"No." Finally he full-on smiled. Crooked teeth. Pointy teeth. Back woods? Or so upper class as to be beyond orthodontia? "No one calls me Rod."

We took our donuts and started walking past the deserted factories and down blocks of two-story houses with siding, beige, light blue, pale green, the main avenue of the city's Little Italy, where two or three bakeries were raising their gates. We walked across the highway overpass, past the old stone office buildings downtown, the bus hub, the new river promenade, up the hill toward campus. The quiet of the early morning still hung over the city. At some point I realized he was walking me home.

"I don't really see it," said Rodgers, when Lee and Noah came up like celebrity gossip. "Why Noah?"

"Andy says it's because he has no intellectual remove."

"Could be." He shook his head at Andy and intellectual remove. "Andy, I mean, he's all right. He's that guy, you know that guy, that kind of sexually ambiguous guy who is basically dating the record store and, you know, if he could only meet someone who likes Bedhead as much as he does, everything would be fine."

I nodded and told myself to find out who Bedhead was. Also, *Andy* was sexually ambiguous?

"You nod a lot," he said.

"Do I?"

"You do." Like he was noticing details about me. But also like everyone knew what that was good for. There was some buoyant thrill at being taken for a sexual object.

"But I know what Andy means," I said. "Noah's so good-looking, and everything he does is just so *awesome* and so *rad.*"

"And you hate that."

"I don't hate it. I just hate feeling like I don't know what to do with it."

"You're jealous."

"Of what? Are you going to tell me I wish *I* was fucking Lee?"

"Heh. No. I think *you* want to do something awesome and rad. It's easier to not try to do anything than to admit you have any kind of ambition."

"I'm not putting myself out there?"

"I don't know. Are you?"

"I don't know. I think it's like Flaubert said, you should be ordinary and regular in your life, like a bourgeois, so you can be violent and original in your art." *Wow, you really know how to flirt. Flaubert. Jesus.*

"Okay. But that easily turns into an excuse for not really living. Especially if you're a bad artist. Then all you are is a . . . *bourgeois.*" This was the first time I'd come close to experiencing what I'd seen in movies—the romance of walking and talking.

We'd reached my front steps. I was supposed to do something unbourgeois. Something Lee might do. But another voice in my head said

Lee wouldn't approve. Twenty bucks says Lee will tell you something about him that will leave you feeling humiliated. Fifty bucks says those are the real terms of your friendship: her judgment, your humiliation. And, in the scheme of things, what small, petty sums! Where was this even coming from? When had Lee ever judged me, other than to think I looked a little lonely and sad on those library steps?

I tried to give Rodgers a meaningful look that probably came off as constipated. He took my hand and I had no idea what he was going to do with it and maybe he didn't either because he just held it for an incredibly long ten seconds.

"I'm missing my chance," he said.

"No, you're not."

We kissed in the street and kept kissing until I could no longer stand on my tiptoes. In a way, it was my first kiss. The first one that ever made me feel the way I'd heard kissing described. Not merely something you did as a prelude to sex, but a key reason for having a body. So your breath could be taken away, so you could go weak in the knees.

It was almost too much for me and I pulled back.

"What?" he asked.

"I don't know." Then, because I couldn't think: "My calves are cramping."

"Is that your way of asking me in?"

I just stared at him. I was missing my chance.

"I'm glad you went to that party," he said.

"Me too."

"All right."

"Okay."

"I'll see y'round, Miss X."

He looked back at me and then turned the corner as I fished my keys out of my bag. Our neighbors—Lee and Andy called them Moose and Chipmunk—were on their porch, stretching for their morning run. Lee had lived on their hall freshman year and she regarded them with something less than scorn but more than indifference. Moose had a long face, knobby features, and a prominent chin. Globally, she seemed sweet and dull. Chipmunk, with her round cheeks, ski-slope nose, and darting eyes, looked meaner and capable of crossing you. Sometimes, on the sidewalk, Chipmunk would bare her white, white teeth and let out a sustained shriek. She called this laughing. Moose and Chipmunk played tennis. They wore preppy shirts with thin stripes and driving moccasins. The closest we came to real feeling for either of them was the time Lee read an article about plastic surgery in *Vogue*. "I wonder what Chipmunk thinks when these doctors talk about aesthetic improvements in the field, how today's look is more natural, less cookie-cutter, how they'd *never* do a ski-slope nose now. What does Chipmunk do with that?"

"Late night?" said Chipmunk.

It took me a second to realize she was talking to me.

"Yeah. Sort of."

"Nice dress," said Moose in the friendliest tone.

"Thanks," I said morosely and ducked inside. What was my problem? Why did I have to be such an asshole?

Nobody else was home and I found myself stopping in the hall, tipping my face upward at the angle it had made while I was kissing Rodgers, opening my mouth, moving my lips. I replayed moments from that morning, in the shower, over a bowl of cereal, on the couch as I tried and failed to read a post-structuralist essay on *Terms of Endearment*.

"Where *were* you?" Lee and Andy asked when they finally came back.

"Where were *you*?"

"We looked all over for you."

"It's fine. Rodgers Colston took me home."

"Rodgers. How about that."

"What do you mean, how about that?"

"Nothing."

Then the three of us acted as though we had shrugged the whole thing off, but a change in mood came over our little household after that day. Several years later, in a grad school seminar, I would come across a passage in Kafka's diaries, a fragment of what he would eventually publish as "In the Penal Colony." A man compares himself to a dog: "With his hand on his heart, he said 'I am a cur if I allow that to happen.' But then he took his own words literally and began to run around on all fours." That seemed about right when it came to Lee and Andy and that time. I spent the rest of the summer trying to prove to them (but mostly to myself) that not only was I not their pet, but I didn't *want* to be. Which was hard, because I had liked making myself into their responsibility. I was Sal Mineo in *Rebel Without a Cause*—Lee was James Dean, of course, which made Andy Natalie Wood. Lee spent more and more time off with Noah Stone. I got to know Andy better, hanging out together enough so that we each forgot the other was the next best thing.

I ran into Rodgers Colston on the street and he told me about another party and wondered if I would be there. I thought I should be blasé, so I said maybe. But then we high-fived and he held on to my hand for a long moment. A curling began in my stomach and unfurled throughout my body. I couldn't stop smiling the rest of the day.

I mentioned the party to Lee, thinking for once I might know about something she didn't.

"Yeah. You want to go? Is this, like, a thing? You and Rodgers?"

"No. I don't know. What do you know about him?"

"Not too much. But I have this feeling he's the kind of guy who wakes you up the next morning wanting to jerk off on your face."

"That's a *kind* of guy?"

"And he's *old*."

"He's, like, twenty-four. He's in grad school. And wasn't Bruce old? Older?"

"Bruce. God. Yeah, well, that's my point."

If old Rodgers had woken me up that way, I don't think I would have minded. It was the fact that Lee thought it was objectionable. My interest in Rodgers couldn't stand up to her judgment.

I went to the party with Lee. We were drunk, on a roof, lying in plastic lounge chairs. Firecrackers went off over our heads. Rodgers sat by me, moving his hand up and down my calf, then behind my knee and up under my skirt. Lee couldn't see, or pretended not to. I had two thoughts: *What is he doing?* And *Please, don't stop.* But I couldn't leave Lee and go with him when he suggested we get out of there. So he left and I didn't see him again that night.

Soon enough, he had a girlfriend and on the occasions I ran into him he would just say hello and give me a slanted smile.

It shouldn't have meant anything to me, the prospect of seeing him now. It shouldn't have made me nervous.

"I don't know why you never went out with Rodgers." Lee had her phone in hand now, scrolling through her contacts.

"Maybe because you told me he would masturbate on my face?"

"What did I know?"

"I thought you knew everything."

"Viv, I was dating a guy who wouldn't fuck me."

"Noah Stone?"

"Yeah."

"*Really?*"

"He couldn't get it up."

"But he had such a reputation."

"He said it was his meds. He was good at other stuff."

"You and Noah, you were together for a *while*."

"I figured I would eventually be the one to help him out of it. Typical."

She acted as though she weren't rearranging the entire past as I'd understood it, but merely picking up an object and blowing the dust from it before putting it back into place. Why had she never told me this before?

"I'm calling Rodgers."

"I doubt he even remembers me."

"I doubt that's true."

I had seen Rodgers exactly once after college. Headed home at an hour so late I can only marvel at it now, I stepped into a subway car and saw him knit together with a woman in one of the seats. He looked up at me but neither of us said a word. I didn't have the confidence to speak to him, but I thought too much of myself to believe a simple *Hey!* would do. If there was anything to our what-might-have-been, if it wasn't entirely in my mind, then he must have felt the same thing. As they rose to get off the train two stops later, he looked back at me. Confirmation. The doors closed.

"I'm calling him." Before I could pretend to protest, Lee was talking to him, making a plan.

"What did he say?"

"He said he'd love to see us. He's up here. We're going over."

"What?"

"What *what*?"

"What is this?"

"It's hanging out with an old friend."

"Remember when we thought he was *so old* because he was twenty-four?"

"I know! He was only twenty-four? God. It's like once you hit twenty-five, you stop using Keats as a measure for accomplishment. At twenty-seven you stop using all those dead twenty-seven-year-olds. And then, I don't know, you try to find some late bloomers to admire."

"Grandma Moses."

"Grandma Moses. Father Time."

"Father Time is eternal. That's different."

When had Keats ever been a model for Lee? I remembered seeing the Norton Anthology on the floor of her room, its onionskin pages unmarked. But what had I known? Nothing of Noah Stone's sad flaccidity. And what had I really known about Rodgers? And what did I know now about Lee and Andy and the state of my marriage? About what was happening inside me? All I knew was that for the first time since pregnancy hormones had flooded my body, I suddenly wasn't so, so tired.

THIS WAS SHAPING up to be the kind of night I no longer had, when my life lay ahead of me like an ocean and I could swim out beyond any mistake. At least, that's what my early twenties had felt like.

After college, both Lee and I moved to New York. Lee was working as an administrative assistant at a nonprofit for reproductive
rights, a short-staffed and underfunded organization, which made
her position fairly thankless, the kind you might take to pay your
dues before applying to law school or pursuing a future in public
policy. If you lacked either pragmatism or idealism, then it was
merely a drab, difficult, not very remunerative job. Lee never struck
me as especially pragmatic or idealistic (she'd never mentioned law
school or public policy) so her motivation remained unclear to me,
but I suspected it was a way to distance herself from her mother's
fabulousness. I had enrolled in a comparative literature Ph.D. program I would eventually abandon, and I was writing short stories
nobody wanted to publish. Lee read everything I showed her and I
loved that she loved my description of a small window with chintz
curtains in the basement of a suburban house. I loved the notes she
wrote in the margins. "This is hit hard on the chin music." "Failure
of sex." "Oh my fucking God!" Her belief in me was legitimizing.
Why would she take the time to read my work if it wasn't good, if
it wasn't worth it? Why would she spend so much time with me if
I wasn't worth it?

And we did spend a lot of time together. We may as well have
been dating each other. We went to a party once in a packed Brooklyn apartment where a young woman told us how she and her fiancé
planned to donate the money they would have spent on wedding
favors to a foundation promoting the legalization of gay marriage.
She was determined, compassionate, doing her part for lesbians everywhere. She wished us the very best.

Lee took me to other parties, occasionally thrown by people I
had read about. I saw the insides of homes I never would have even
known existed beyond the pages of a magazine: Soho lofts bought for

nothing in the seventies, Tribeca lofts bought for a little more in the eighties, whole brownstones in the Village, a penthouse on the Upper East Side. But there was something Cinderella-at-the-ball about those experiences. Something unreal, time-stamped. At the stroke of midnight this ends. There was another city for us that seemed as if it would go on forever. On a Saturday I would say, "They're playing *Gloria* at Anthology" and we would go, and fall in love with Gena Rowlands, her mauve-painted nails, her cigarettes, her pocketbooks, her gun. Then Lee would say "Let's go to the Bronx, Washington Heights, wherever Cassavetes filmed that." So on Sunday we would go, and just walk and walk and walk. There were always more movies, more neighborhoods. There was always time.

Lee would tell me about nights when we weren't hanging out when she would go to a party or a bar and leave with someone she would likely never see again. Maybe I was supposed to view this as self-destructive behavior, but it impressed me. I took it to be a measure of her power, over men and over me. The one-nightness of these encounters I attributed to Lee's attachment to me. At the same time, it said: *Look how easily I could leave you.*

Soon enough, she did leave me, though not for a guy. Linda, increasingly bi-coastal, threw a soiree that Lee reluctantly attended. Her lack of enthusiasm was taken for aloof confidence and she was handed a two-year contract from a French fashion house to be the face of its perfume. Off she went on extended stays in Paris and to a different plane of existence, embracing the birthright she had been trying to deny. When she came back to New York, she still made time for me, but I felt as if she had outgrown and needed to break up with me. Neither of us knew how to talk about it that way, though.

It was a relief —*I can leave you too*—when Ben Driggs Stern came along. At three A.M. in his apartment I couldn't recall what exactly we'd talked about over drinks, but I remembered it being witty. He took my top off. I pulled at his belt. He said, "I like you, Viv," and set me fluttering. Somewhere in the intervening hours he also said he'd like to read something I'd written. Was that before or after he told me he was an editor at a literary quarterly people had actually heard of?

Three months later we were still seeing each other and a story of mine, "Rye, Toasted," had appeared in the latest issue. "Rye, Toasted" was about a young man whose wife leaves him, refusing to see or speak to him. Sad and adrift on a snowy day, he goes to visit his mother-in-law in the hopes of getting through to her daughter. The young man and the mother-in-law are cut from the same cloth and have a strong affinity for each other. She makes him a sandwich and they end up sleeping together. She remembers her first love, the one before her husband. The snow is heavier than expected—the husband returns early from work, just before the roads close. The young man is stuck there for the awkward duration of the night, during which the husband, an amateur chef, expounds on the erotic nature of baking bread. And that was essentially it. A story that didn't know whether it was a slice-of-life character study of two lonely souls with a few well-turned phrases and a cheap, obvious nod to James Joyce or if it was a carbohydrate-fueled sex farce. I wondered, of course, if Ben had published my story only because I was dating him. Did it matter? I secretly imagined this was the auspicious beginning of a career, not to mention a romance. While it didn't return Lee and me to equal footing (we'd never been on equal footing), it narrowed the distance between our new levels.

"No, he's great," said Lee, after meeting Ben. "He's not as pretentious as he first seems. Have you met his mother yet?" His mother happened to be none other than Patti Driggs, Linda West's old nemesis. "I don't see Linda coming to the wedding is all I'm saying," said Lee.

The story of mine that Ben had published was the one that Lee least admired, the one she thought had "too many of those moments that are *literary* funny but aren't, you know, *actually* funny." Ben had told me "Rye, Toasted" had the "Olympian distance" I should strive for. That my writing wouldn't suffer from "a colder eye." Following his advice, I viewed him through such a lens. I began to have inklings that when he'd said, "I like you, Viv," it wasn't the heady beginning of something grand and passionate but rather the full extent of his feelings for me.

Despite our growing dispassion Ben invited me to spend Thanksgiving at his mother's.

"She's not as intimidating as she seems," he said. "I showed her your story."

"You what? You did?"

"She liked it. She said it reminded her of her stuff, starting out. Coming from an egomaniac of her caliber, that's a big compliment."

I wanted to be asked to meet Patti Driggs more than I actually wanted to meet her and I was glad to have an out: it had become something of a tradition that Lee and I would go to my parents' house for the holiday. I had assumed she would break the custom this year, with any number of exciting, possibly Parisian plans to choose from, but her only other offer involved spending it with her mother and Roy, Linda's on-again off-again boyfriend, at Roy's ranch.

"Is Ben coming?" she asked. I equivocated, saying something about him probably needing to stay in the city for work.

Ben Driggs Stern dumped me just before Christmas, and by that point, after what happened with that Thanksgiving, Lee and I weren't speaking. The real breakup.

Now here we were, sitting at an old picnic table on the back porch of Rodgers' house.

"*Andy* Andy?" asked Rodgers.

"Andy Andy," I said.

"Wow. Good for you guys. Cheers." He raised his beer and his twinkling eyes. I was having a hard time not meeting those eyes across the table.

"And what about you?"

"I'm single. I'm single and lovin' it. I just love the fuck out of being single. Does that make me, like, a Charlotte or whoever?"

"I think it makes you a Samantha," I said.

"It makes your references about ten years out of date," said Lee.

"Yeah, that's happening to me more and more. I've decided to give in to it. I'm tired of trying to stay current. It's too much work for too little payoff. I'm losing my edge, it's fine."

"You're losing your edge?" asked Lee.

"This critic said he couldn't figure out whether my last show was 'a very twenty-first-century struggle against the emptiness of being a man or simply underwhelming.' And this woman I'm kind of seeing told me my work can get pseudo-plebian."

"I thought you were loving the fuck out of being single," said Lee. "This woman sounds like your girlfriend."

"I don't really consider people who use words like 'pseudo-plebian' to be girlfriend material."

"She probably doesn't consider people whose work can be pseudo-plebian to be boyfriend material."

"Yeah, it's doomed. Sometimes I'm fine with that. Other times I miss, you know, things like hope." He smiled extravagantly and I was glad to see he hadn't fixed his teeth even though he could afford to now. I had once gone to see an exhibition at the Whitney mostly because it included an installation of his: beautiful tunnels of colored light he had encased in large Styrofoam structures fabricated, seamlessly, from dollar store coolers. The box of curatorial text on the wall spoke of Marxism, religion, a debt to and critique of Minimalism, and though I could make myself see all of that in the piece, what moved me was the very materiality of it, that he had brought it out of his head and into existence. It was titled *Fourth of July*. It reminded me of that party on the roof, the fireworks in the night sky, his hand up my skirt.

Rodgers seemed to be proof that vision plus talent plus drive was still a viable route to success, pseudo-plebian or not. But you had to have the right amounts of all three bubbling away in order for them to react; too little of one and not enough of another and you merely fizzled. Or, I suppose, you got a job writing dialogue for a past-its-prime soap opera.

When the subject came up, I didn't particularly want to tell Rodgers what I did for a living, what I had done with my life. I was supposed to have done better. Around the time I decided to drop out of grad school, my mother came to visit me in New York.

"But you've worked so hard," she said.

"But I don't want to be an academic."

"What do you think you're going to do, then?"

"I'm not sure. Do I have to always have everything figured out?"

The look on her face said *Yes. You're not Lee. You can't live like her. That friendship has spoiled you. It's made you want things you'll never have.*

"No," she said. "You don't. I just don't want to see you throw this away and then regret it."

She was relieved though not very impressed when I started writing for THATH. I had defaulted on some bright promise but the shame of that was residual.

Really, it wasn't shame I felt at all. In college I once tagged along with Lee to see a showcase of student films. The most engaging one was composed of long, still takes of naked thighs, skyscrapers, an industrial park, a family at a picnic table, and what looked like a piece of chicken, all set to "My Heart Will Go On." People laughed and I laughed too, because I knew it was supposed to be some kind of commentary on sexuality or sentimentality or consumerism or agribusiness or copyright infringement or all of the above. I could try to make the intellectual case for the song's use, but secretly I just enjoyed hearing it. I used to try to make the intellectual case for the relevance of soaps. I never admitted that I just enjoyed hearing the song. Yes, THATH strained for highs of the biblical and Shakespearean variety and sank to lunatic lows. But you could argue that soaps were feminist in their focus on the day-to-day lives of women. You could argue that soaps were one of the few mainstream cultural productions in America that dealt with class. With a canvas of thirty characters, THATH had three families at its core: the upper-crust Sterlings, the middle- to upper-middle-class Howards, and the blue-collar Doughertys. You could make all the arguments you wanted and it wouldn't matter. The appeal of soaps was emotional. You could spend years with these characters, typically played by the same actors. They could even die and come back. All those shared memories, all that youth, all that time.

I was lucky to have my job and the truth is, I liked it. I needed it. I didn't want to lose it. I loved Mill River and its swapped babies, its crazy old ladies working on strengthening their cores, its hookers and Judaism. I loved walking down the hall and passing soap legend Darcy Betts, who'd been with the show since its inception, originating the role of Elena Sterling Rappoport. No stranger to cosmetic work, she had refused Botox in order to preserve her unparalleled ability to meaningfully arch an eyebrow. A right brow tick for scorn, two full brow ticks for skepticism, three for delight, a subtle yet unmistakable right half tick for desire. The single full arch followed by a left suspended tick, which she often gave me, I interpreted as solidarity. She would call me "Vivian, darling!" and I would ask her how she was doing and she would say "I'm keeping it light, keeping it lively!"—her mantra, inspired by her favorite brand of fat-free cottage cheese.

I didn't want to talk to Rodgers about my job because I didn't want to have to explain or champion my odd pride in it. But he asked, so I answered. He couldn't believe it. His mother watched the show religiously. Who was that guy, that guy who'd been on it for years, the guy with the cheekbones? Rick Howard? Yes, Rick Howard!

Under Frank's reign, Dr. Rick Howard, world-renowned neurosurgeon, became addicted to Tumestrex, a Viagra-like drug he'd developed, fathered a child out of wedlock, and then removed all childbearing memories from his mistress's brain. He eventually redeemed himself by standing up to a cabal of real estate developers angling to demolish Mill River University Hospital.

"Someone made a YouTube montage of his cheekbones' greatest moments," I said. Now that I thought about it, that montage had been set to Jesse's song "Whatever You Want," which had experienced a resurgent popularity after it was used in a car commercial.

We had to watch it just then, of course, and up came an assortment of Jesse Parrish–related clips. Lee had seen most of them. Jesse as a witty rock star on the *Dick Cavett Show;* once-rare footage of Jesse, incoherent, and Linda, totally loopy, interviewed on British TV; early publicity shots and later stills as a slideshow backdrop to his songs. A picture of Jesse and four-year-old Lee: Jesse leading her to the edge of a pool at the home of a now long-forgotten record

THE SUN IN YOUR EYES

executive. Her small fingers pressed in his large hand. She looks into the water in the serious way children do while Jesse has his head turned to catch something coming from a figure beyond the frame, a portrait, simultaneously, of parental care and negligence. Lee remembered she had been chewing spearmint gum the same light green as her swimsuit. Was it strange that she was allowed to chew gum at that age? By a pool, when she didn't yet know how to swim? She didn't remember where the gum had come from. She didn't remember the before or the after to that moment.

"Do you mind that that's up here? That anyone can see it?" Rodgers asked.

"It was never private. It just wasn't quite as public, or so easy to reproduce. But it's nothing compared to what people put out there."

"Sure," said Rodgers. "So these tapes. Are you prepared for . . . like . . . what if you really do find them and what's on them is just . . . *bad*?"

"That could happen. But I think it's unlikely the way people talk about them. People who were there. Like Charlie Flintwick."

"He's got something of a stake in maintaining that legend, though," I heard myself saying. Lee didn't seem all that offended or stung. Which made me want to sting her more.

"I mean, I wonder if it's like how they say you shouldn't meet your heroes. Because it's always going to be disappointing. Not because they turn out to be assholes but because what you want is that hero fantasy and nobody can be that. So you meet them and you lose what you had in your head."

"I guess what you have to lose depends on how much you value living in your head," said Lee.

Rodgers looked at me with those disbelieving eyes and I looked down, but only before resolutely looking back up at him. When Lee said she should get back to the motel, to see what she could learn about Bill Carnahan, I didn't stop her. I only took Rodgers up on his offer to drive me back later. Until Lee left, Andy's and my old theory about flirting seemed applicable here. I still had the presence of mind to think about it even as Rodgers and I were staring at each other out there on the porch. Nothing to stop our staring, still no call or text from Andy. A kiss goodbye that morning, which felt so far away—a kiss made only slightly less routine by his irritation with me—was the last contact I'd had with him.

"Do you remember seeing each other on the subway that time?" I asked.

"I do."

"I should have said something."

"I should have stayed on that train."

My presence of mind left me then. It didn't come back in the kitchen when Rodgers had his hand on the small of my back, when he brought his face close to mine. Then that theory became a wrong-headed conclusion reached by people who have never been tested.

EVERYTHING IN RODGERS'S home was cared for, everything had a place. Rugs, records, plants, books. He saw the fineness in things. "I like your dress," he had said, standing behind me in his kitchen, his reflection in the window, looking at me. He slipped his arms around me and I was nineteen once more, my dim understanding of the world at odds with what I wanted. I was also thirty-three and married and pregnant and beginning to be aware that my body would never be the same, that you only get so many chances, that years begin to disappear. That you'll pack a flattering dress for a trip when you really shouldn't need one.

I hadn't been drinking but I felt drunk. I mentioned Lee's old suspicion to Rodgers as we leaned into each other in his hallway. "Oh, not on your face," he said. "And anyway, I'd much rather fuck you." A broad, crooked smile. *Holy shit,* I thought. And then I stopped thinking as he pulled me to him and turned me against the wall.

I SLEPT DEEPLY and soundly and woke to an image: a string of white Christmas lights along a dark, narrow bar, a place that had no theme other than alcoholism. Lisette, Andy's girlfriend, had brought us there. About a year after Lee and I moved to New York, and a couple of years before what I would come to think of as "the Thanksgiving incident," the gentrification of Williamsburg was well under way but hadn't reached its apex. Affluent, privileged kids lived there, but in warehouses, not luxury lofts. There were desolate corners and windowless establishments that looked, from the outside, busted and rough. Inside, this particular place was like a VFW post, a barroom and an adjoining room of card tables, a linoleum floor. From the jukebox came the synthesized hovering and racquetball percussion of Joy Division's "Atmosphere."

"I love this song," said Lisette's friend Nate, talking to me. "That voice, it gives me such a hard-on."

"Sure," I said. Nate stepped closer to me, saying nothing for a few long seconds, but apparently forming a question as he looked into my eyes.

"Are you Greek?"

"No. Why?"

"You have Greek eyes."

I lowered my newly Greek eyes and then glanced at Andy. He was watching me with an expressionless intensity that only highlighted the embarrassing nature of my back-and-forth with Nate. I wanted Andy to turn away so I could continue my embarrassing exchange. When he didn't, I wondered what he wanted from me. Some kind of chance opened up for no more than an instant before it swallowed itself and disappeared. It was so brief I didn't know what it even was, but I was disappointed by its disappearance. Lisette came back with drinks and positioned herself in Andy's lap and I wanted to say to him, "You have the luxury of not having to say stupid things to people in public, you have the luxury of looking at me like that without having to think too much about what it might mean because here comes your girlfriend and now she's sitting on you."

"I hear Greece is amazing," I said.

"Oh, man, Greece is fucking awesome."

Nate professed his love for feta cheese while moving his hand to my waist, just under the edge of my shirt. He needed a smoke—did I want to come with him outside? Yes, I did. It would be the fourth cigarette of my life. I went to grab my coat and Andy stopped me. Glowering.

"Really?"

"What?"

"This guy?"

"Well, we can't all be as smart as you, Andy."

"That's not what I mean."

"Why do you even care?"

"I don't—I just—on the level of—whatever. I don't know."

"Nate is fucking awesome," Lisette interjected. "If Viv wants to go make out with him, I don't see why it's your problem."

"Yeah, Andy, why is it *your* problem?" said Lee. She'd been watching the whole scene like a bird of prey, circling on high, waiting to dive down for the kill. The way she swooped in reminded me of that night when she'd led Andy up off that mattress and away from me. It was something secretive between Lee and Andy and yet I figured into it, inextricably.

"Fuck it," he said. Then to Lisette: "Let's get out of here."

"Seriously?" asked Lisette.

"Yeah. And I fucking hate that word. *Seriously.* Like nobody can fucking tell when anybody is being fucking serious anymore?"

"So angry! My goodness." Lisette cupped his face with her hands. "But it's not even midnight yet. We have to make it to midnight." It was New Year's Eve, the turn of the millennium. If Lisette could have shrunk Andy into a figurine and put him in her pocket, I think she would have. He, just then, might have let her.

"Okay. Sorry. I'm sorry. Just forget I said anything."

I would have gone home with Nate that night regardless, but I doubt I would have felt so purposeful about it if Andy hadn't cared.

That spring Andy moved away, for a job in the Bay Area, but then came back several years later. He said it was, in part, because his boss, Jeffrey Sorbo, kept saying to him, "We're so similar," and Andy kept thinking, *If that's true, I'm fucked.* Andy had started working as a programmer for Sorbo right before the technological innovator had started faux-humbly brushing off the labels of "visionary" and "savior" the press began routinely applying to him. Before the adulation from convocation speeches and conference talks had him considering a move into government, just to, you know, shake things up in Washington. Sorbo would have taken Andy with him (Where? Wherever they wanted to go!) if Andy had only believed in his ascendancy. Andy *did* believe in his ascendancy, which is what troubled him. Sorbo would go far, and then go farther, but to what end? What was he really motivating anyone to do when he fired up undergraduates about inventing yet another way for people to distract themselves, trigger a dopamine release, and twitchily buy things in the name of newfangled social interaction? Sorbo wasn't even cynical about it. If he had been, Andy might have been able to cynically go along for the ride but Sorbo demanded a belief in his worldview that Andy couldn't conjure. Maybe it had something to do with integrity? When had integrity come to be synonymous with self-defeat? Andy told me all of this one winter evening, as we were sitting in my studio apartment, essentially the old parlor of a cut-up brownstone. As he spoke, all I could think of was him, fifteen pounds heavier, in that shirt with the satin seahorse on it.

Snow steadily accumulated into the night as Andy and I talked. It grew late and the storm gave him a good excuse to stay at my place, but I expected we would go to sleep and wake up in the morning and nothing else would happen. Only I didn't really expect that. Because of the way he was looking at me, the way I looked at myself for more than a moment in the bathroom mirror. How many times had I hugged Andy? How many times had he put his arm around me? Now, with him next to me by the window, watching the snow float down below the streetlight, all I could think about was how close could we possibly stand without touching?

I went into the bathroom again and got into a T-shirt and sweats (not Sunday-paper-and-a-latte loungewear, but thick, gray, elasticized-ankle *Rocky* pants. *Gonna fly now!*) and Andy took off his sweater but kept on the rest of his clothes. We both got into my double bed. I lay uncomfortably still, daring myself to do something—*you could make it look accidental*—and then backing down. *Why do you have to make it look accidental? Why can't you just be honest and unafraid?* Ten minutes passed on the nightstand clock. Fifteen. Nineteen.

"I'm not sleeping," he said.

"Me neither."

On our sides, facing each other, he slowly moved his hand beneath the waistband of the sweats and my underwear, touching my ass, brushing my upper thigh and then making circles along my lower back. I didn't know where to put my hand so I brought it to his face and I wondered why we weren't kissing yet and it made me think of a movie with a prostitute whose services included everything but kissing, too intimate, too personal, and why did I have to be thinking about that right now? *Stop it. Stop finding ways to distract yourself. Kiss him. Take your fucking sweatpants off.*

He pulled me on top of him. There were smiles, some maneuvering, but no discussion.

That came later. Questions like: Had you ever thought about that? But when had you thought about it? When we first met? In that way that whenever you meet someone new you think about it? He had thought about it then, in that way. Later, he thought about it in a different way. He thought about it out in California. He thought a lot about it on the way over to my place that night. We didn't talk about what was next. Because we didn't want to pressure each other? Because we both already knew.

In the insulated, snowy whiteness of the morning, I crouched down to look beneath the bed for Andy's wallet, which was no longer in the back pocket of his pants.

"It's not under here. Sorry."

"Don't be. I get to see you on all fours."

Who was this? It was Andy. And me: a big, gleeful grin for the dust bunnies.

If Andy had been any other guy, I would have called Lee soon after he left. Eventually I told her what had happened, but only in the broadest strokes. And surrounded it with a false air of disbelief and casualness.

"I'M PREGNANT," I said to the ceiling and Rodgers. Now one more person who wasn't Andy knew.

"Good morning to you, too." Rodgers propped himself up. With the sheet wrapped around his legs he looked like a merman.

"No, really. I am."

I could see Rodgers actively thinking before he finally came out with: "I'm excited for you."

"You don't think it's weird that I slept with you knowing I'm pregnant? Or that I slept with you *at all*?"

"It's kind of fucked up. But a lot of good things are."

"Thank you for saying that. It is fucked up. Not just this"—taking in the bed, the whole of our night with my hands—"but it's fucked up that you seem to be more excited for me than I am for myself."

"I kind of envy you."

"Like you wish you had a uterus?"

"When you have a kid doesn't it relieve you, in a way, of all that self-absorption and striving to do something with your life because there, you've done it?"

"I don't know. You've already done something with your life, though, so I don't know why you're even talking like that."

"And you haven't?"

Without a child, I was another no-longer-young person whose youth fueled her ambition until it stalled out over a lack of drive or talent or money. As a mother, wouldn't I have a clearer purpose? My THATH wages wouldn't be cause for existential questioning or a reminder of some abandoned dream; they would be, say, a college fund. So that one day my child would have the opportunity to be overeducated and underemployed. "You've achieved what you wanted. And you wanted big things."

"It's not as satisfying as you think."

"But it must be satisfying just to be able to say that."

"I guess it is. But a kid! Literally, that may be the most creative thing you can do. You're creating a fucking *person.*"

True, but it also sounded like a sop. My fear was that it was one of the most distracting, preoccupying things I could do. The biggest excuse for not doing anything else. And what kind of person lays that on their child? What if a baby didn't relieve you of self-absorption and didn't relieve you of your dreams? What if your self-absorption remained and your dreams remained just that—dreams—and you were left angry, frustrated, and resentful? For the rest of your life.

"Maybe you'll have new dreams," said Rodgers.

"I never realized you were such an optimist."

"Me neither."

He got up to make us coffee. Already I wondered what I would say to Rodgers if I ever saw him again, the assumption being that I wouldn't. Not any time soon. Would I include him in the mass-email birth announcement Andy and I would no doubt send around to friends and family? (That is, if Andy and I continued to be "Andy and I" and everything turned out okay with the pregnancy.) The bulk email slip-in for Rodgers. Was that wholly inappropriate or actually the perfect vehicle of communication in this instance? I had about thirty-six weeks to figure that out. To hope that questions like this might be put to rest by the arrival of an overwhelmingly strong and calm mother-knowledge that would make my inner voice sound less like mine and more like that of a midwife full of folk wisdom.

As Rodgers drove me back to the motel later that morning, I thought, *This is why people think they can carry on affairs.* His truck wasn't crashing, swerving off the road, running out of gas. The pitch of awkwardness wasn't even all that high. I accepted that this is what happens between people, and people are large enough to absorb it without shattering. Not until we pulled into the lot and I saw Lee standing on the cement parking strip in front our room did it occur to me that I had been wrong. The unit, the twosome of the previous night wasn't Rodgers and me. It was—my stomach sank—Lee and Rodgers. That little dance the night before that left Lee subtly insulted, that gave her a reason to go. Maybe they hadn't sat down and choreographed it beforehand, but still, they were co-conspirators. But for what? My satisfaction? My degradation? A spasm of need reverberated through me and I hastily attached it to Andy.

"Hey," said Lee. "Thanks for bringing her back to me."

Rodgers nodded. Then he walked around to the passenger side. The paranoia bloomed and, if anything, Lee and Rodgers now seemed like parents. Not mine, but strange, shadow parents. I was a child in the grips of learning that what she knows about the world is small, and dictated by other people, and that she sees only what they choose to let her see.

Still, when Rodgers held me to him, despite everything, my body seemed both to sink into and draw a taut energy from his. I didn't move until he did, tilting his head and smiling his crooked, almost embarrassed smile. "See y'round?"

"See you around."

I went over to Lee and we stood there, Lee with her hand to her forehead like a visor, me squinting in the sun, arms folded, as Rodgers drove away.

"I need a shower," I said without looking at her, without saying anything else.

I still smelled like sex. I must have stood in the tub for half an hour, the water running off the pink tile and my back. Soaping up seemed ceremonial. *If you are now or have ever been a whore, do you have to go through a special cleansing ritual?* For a brief, low moment, I wondered if the previous night could count as some kind of archetypal, Joseph Campbell initiation. But initiation into what? The world of adultery? Then I wondered if it was possible to create a scratch n' sniff sticker of an after-sex scent, if that were a thing that people did—have sex, make a commemorative sticker—would I want one, as a kind of sense-memory aid to remind me of Rodgers? I could bury it in a drawer of socks. It would be there when I was old and Andy had died and our child had moved away. I would take it out then and think about a night long ago. I wouldn't have a sticker for Andy. I wouldn't need one. I would have so much of him. I would have a whole lifetime of him. Wouldn't I?

While I was in the bathroom, Lee was busy making phone calls. First to Linda, in Los Angeles, who camouflaged any genuine reaction to the news that her daughter had talked to Flintwick with an effusive interest in the man. *Oh, how is old Charlie? He didn't do anything too unspeakable did he? But I don't understand—how did you run into him? Oh, I see, but what were you doing up around there? Oh, honey, I wish you'd leave this alone. I just don't think you're going to find what you're really looking for.*

The second call Lee made had been to Bill Carnahan. If you weren't on his preapproved list of callers, you had to talk your way past a team of receptionists and a good cop/bad cop pair of executive assistants before you were granted the opportunity to leave a message for the "massively busy" man himself. But Carnahan called Lee back within five minutes, while driving his Ferrari down I-95, headed to a property he owned on a bluff in Rhode Island. He would be there all weekend and hey, he had an idea. Wouldn't you know those photographs he'd purchased from Charlie Flintwick were hanging in a widow's walk he had converted into a carpeted strip of a room that he used for thinking and pacing. It was here that he waited "for his ships to come in." It would be his pleasure to let Jesse Parrish's daughter have a look at those prized possessions. Carnahan loved company, as did his wife.

"What do you think?" Lee asked me.

"I don't know what I think."

She was more or less ready to go, running on some kind of efficient drive that seemed so foreign to me just then. I was standing there in a thin, scratchy white towel that didn't quite cover me, and I was at a loss. Even drying off seemed too complicated to do.

Lee went into the bathroom and came out with two more towels. She wrapped my wet hair up and then began to pat down my shoulders and my arms. I just watched her work on me. She was like a nurse. A blind, bandaged soldier would have fallen in love with her, with her touch, her manner, not knowing at all what she looked like.

"Okay. Stop," I said. Turning away, finding my clothes.

"I'll drive you back home," she said. "And then go see Carnahan on my own."

"No," I said. I should have gone home, but I couldn't. Not now, not yet. I couldn't even call Andy. He'd texted me when I was in the shower.

Sorry I missed you last night. You OK?

I texted him back. The modern telegram, where you leave so much out, including your silence.

OK. Miss you. Love.

Then I got into the car with Lee.

NEITHER OF US spoke. Lee drove, and I said I needed to check in with work. So I emailed Frank, unnecessarily, and then searched "insane custody cases," trying to figure out how to approach our Romola Dougherty story. Two years ago, on the night that a tornado tore through Mill River, Romola had given birth to a stillborn girl, and an orderly, obsessed with the Doughertys' sharp-tongued daughter, switched the baby with another delivered at approximately the same time, presenting it to Romola as her own. Romola hadn't made it to the hospital; she labored in the middle of a power outage at Pine Lawn, the town's psychiatric facility. The baby's biological mother, Peyton Sterling, had been committed to Pine Lawn during her seventh month of pregnancy, when she developed a rare psychomotor disorder that left her immobile and incommunicative. Now, Peyton had come out of that fog, remembered giving birth, and wanted her lost child back while Romola greived and raged. Romola and Peyton had been best friends; they had been troubled and cynical and fun together. They had been pregnant together, comparing notes and confiding hopes, until Peyton slipped out of this world. Romola had blossomed into a wonderful mother. Peyton's mental condition was perfectly fine now but doctors said she could lapse into a vegetative state at any time. Who would you root for? What would become of their friendship?

I tried, but I couldn't get lost in the characters. Out the window, the green rolling hills of western Massachusetts weren't working for me either.

"What did I just do?" I said. "What am I going to say to Andy?"

"Do you have to say anything?" said Lee, as if picking up some place we'd left off. "You guys don't have one of those arrangements where you're allowed a certain number of, like, indiscretions?"

"We didn't build infidelity into our relationship."

"Right. Andy would never stray."

Lee's pronouncements on my husband's nature made me feel proprietary toward him, even toward his capacity to be unfaithful. Her presumptuousness bothered me, as if deep down she knew Andy better than I did.

"Remember that night you met Rodgers? The night that Andy and I—"

I cut her off. "Yes."

"Well. Andy wasn't that into it. I mean, he was *into* it but he wasn't—this is going to sound awful—he wasn't as grateful—as I expected him to be?"

I didn't want to hear this. But, perversely, I did.

"Yeah, well, Andy's not an idiot," I said. "He knew he was being used." Could you extricate utility from friendship? It would be like trying to remove the egg from a soufflé.

"That's what I mean. He let me use him and then he let me know he was letting me use him. In a kind way. All I'm saying is Andy is a kind person. He doesn't hurt people on purpose."

"But I do?"

"No, that's not what I meant."

I thought she might be about to say that *she* was the one who hurt people on purpose, but she didn't say that.

"I know you. And I think I still know Andy. And I think you two are going to be fine."

Reflexively, I wanted to ask her if she was so sure about that. But at heart, I wanted her to be right, wanted us to be fine. Part of me also wanted to believe she still knew me as no one else, not even Andy, did. When Andy and I were planning our wedding, Lee flew in from California early in the week. I imagined that she would steady me but also provide an escape during the tense days leading up to the event. She would save me from the surprisingly unrelenting demands of my mother. I had the thought that if Lee wasn't there, the wedding wouldn't be as worthwhile. That if she was there and impressed by it, it would mean more. The wedding, when I considered it in this light, didn't have all that much to do with Andy. Kirsten, her tea lights, and her vintage dress, came to mind and instead of striking me as shallow and superficial, her approach to matrimony impressed itself upon me as a model. I confessed this to Lee.

"You're not fetishizing an aesthetic in order to distance yourself from real human feeling."

"You make Kirsten sound like a fascist."

"A pretty, put-together fascist. Whatever else is going on, don't the trains always run on time for that girl?"

"Whereas you and I get stuck in stalled cars."

"You get stuck. I get fucking derailed." She released the curling iron and my hair fell into what Kirsten, guest-blogging on a lifestyle site, would call loose, romantic waves. "Oh, perfect," said Lee, regarding her handiwork. "We'll do it exactly like this tomorrow." It was only when she arrived at my apartment the next morning, styling tools in hand, that I realized the knot in my stomach had been worry she wouldn't show. Maybe that was why Lee still figured in my life: to be a lightning rod and to be the lightning itself.

AFTER SPENDING A night in a Narragansett bed and breakfast, we met Bill Carnahan at the marina where he docked his yacht. Carnahan and his wife welcomed us aboard a forty-foot motor boat, what he referred to as their "smaller cruiser," the one that he captained himself and that required no crew, which meant it would just be the four of us out there. Before too long, we were anchored and floating somewhere in Block Island Sound.

As it turned out, my knowledge of yacht culture, which had to that point relied mostly on music videos from the 1980s and James

Bond movies, wasn't entirely off the mark: the exclusive tone, the trashy heart. The day was so brilliant, the surfaces so shiny, that the sun bounced off the railing of the deck and sliced through our champagne flutes when we toasted to "new acquaintances and old habits." Carnahan had the look of an actor in a high-production-value commercial for cholesterol management, erections, or retirement funds—exactly what handsome graying men in JFK-at-sea clothes are meant to sell. He leaned back on a white leather cushion, his hands locked behind his head, legs crossed to reveal a tanned inch of bare ankle between his chinos and Topsiders. "What did I tell you? Worth your while?"

Carnahan's wife, Kara, stirred in her chaise.

"I love this," she said, rolling on her side to face us. She was going for languid, but a hardness about her—blond, freckled, late-forties lip and eye work, diamond jewelry, slim white jeans and a loose white top that in the breeze conformed to her remarkably alert breasts—made her action stagey. As did the trace of a rough Northeastern accent she tried to rid herself of. "You get out here and you almost forget where you came from." Kara Carnahan, in all likelihood, came from an unpleasant place you could never completely forget. "I remember, Bill, the first time you asked me to the beach house. I was expecting the Hamptons. But practically every other yard had a car in it on blocks." Her disbelief was palpable.

"No, it's America out there." Bill nodded landward.

"What does that mean?" Lee asked. She was sitting next to him and inched closer.

"It means they like their trans fats." He reached his hands toward her face and lifted her red sunglasses onto the top of her head so that he could look straight into her eyes. She didn't blink in the gleaming whiteness, but returned his gaze with beckoning skepticism.

"Now don't frown. I know what you are. You're a sophisticated, progressive, cosmopolitan type who is *so* sophisticated, progressive, and cosmopolitan you've come out the other end. You think there's dignity out there, right? You think there's something noble and romantic and dare I say *authentic* about small-town bullshit salt-of-the-earth struggles. That it's all one big Bruce Springsteen song? Well, it ain't, babe. It's a murder ballad. It's a fucking freak show. It's the fucking American nightmare."

"If it's so intolerable, what are you doing there?"

"I didn't say it was intolerable. I said it was a fucking freak show. I happen to like freak shows. By the way, you have the loveliest eyes. Blue like those Dutch dishes. Delft blue."

"I'd say it's more of a Wedgwood, babe," said Kara, exchanging with her husband a look that belied another attempt at languor. Carnahan shook his head and looked to the skies, all *God help me but I love this woman!*

Carnahan then continued his assessment silently, looking Lee up and down. Which is what Flintwick had done. Which is what most people, myself included, did. Only when we did this, it involved a kind of surrender, a giving in to our own desire and curiosity about this woman. Carnahan's stare was colder, less impressed. It registered Lee's beauty as a snake might identify its next snack. Lee must have encountered this reaction before—she didn't flinch—but it struck me that I hadn't. I had relied on her allure, had successfully used it for my own benefit so often in the past that I didn't know if I was more frightened now to consider what that made me or to watch Lee fall short.

With a tight smile, as if something wasn't going according to plan (as if there *was* a plan), Kara suggested a light lunch and how would Bill like to come help her prepare it in the galley?

"Lunch! I like it. Let's do it." He clapped his hands and followed his wife, but not without glancing back at Lee, a glance that promised his return and left little doubt as to where his thoughts would be in the meantime, before slipping below. Carnahan had assured us that this was merely a nautical prelude to a viewing of the Haseltine photographs, but the longer we stayed out there, the more concerned I grew that we might never make it back.

"He likes freak shows," I said.

"I know," said Lee. "But we've come this far. And it's not like we can go anywhere now."

"Yeah, exactly."

"They're probably down there preparing a cheese plate or something."

I rose to my feet too quickly and nausea took hold. Seasickness? Morning sickness? The former provided a convenient cover for the latter, though the Carnahans may have had their suspicions when I declined a mimosa, opting instead for orange juice. (Bill said "fresh-squeezed," and you wanted to find a decontamination station.) Lee rubbed my back slowly but it didn't help.

The Carnahans returned from the galley, Kara with a tray of sandwiches and Bill carrying an extra baguette like a sword. Neither of them had fetched implements with which to tie us up, but they still looked as though that might be their intention. At the sight of the food I remembered I was hungry all the time now. It didn't matter that I was nauseous or that the Carnahans watched us eat as though they were fattening us up for slaughter. I downed everything on my plate and went for seconds.

"We should talk about your father," said Bill.

"I'm curious to know why you find him compelling," said Lee, "why you wanted those pictures."

"I consider myself to be a collector. In my younger days, I used to collect records. I liked Jesse's stuff, sure, but I was never much of a concert-goer. Never picked up a guitar. Now I collect people, in a way. Hedge fund, shmedge fund. I collect. My art advisor said David Haseltines were a must, no collection would be complete without them. But what I love about the photographs is that they transcend my personal bullshit. Not only do they not want anything from me, they don't give a shit about me. They don't even care that I'm looking at them. I don't know if that's because of Parrish or because of Haseltine. Either way, I think I'm drawn to them because they have absolutely nothing to do with me."

Lee kept her composure, even as doubt, derision, and, finally, interest, crossed her face. Kara, meanwhile, was rhythmically clicking the tines of her fork against her teeth and I nearly lost it. I reached for more bread.

"You go for it," said Bill, "I like that." He moved in toward me and brushed a crumb from the corner of my mouth. Then he placed his hands squarely on my shoulders and kissed my forehead, like some kind of dark rite. I wanted to wipe the kiss from my brow before it seeped into my bloodstream, permeated my uterine wall, and contaminated the tiny heart now developing inside of me.

"Are you all right, Viv? You seem a little sunstruck. Why don't you go below for a bit and relax. Put your feet up. We've got a whole theater down there. What's your poison? Home improvement shows? Prestige dramas? Absurdist faux-documentary sitcoms? Prime seventies-era Hollywood? Snuff-film webisodes of blood diamond mining? We've got it all."

"I'll keep her company," said Kara brightly. "I've been dying to talk to you about THATH. Huge fan."

"Thanks, but I'm fine. Really."

Lee, understanding something I apparently didn't, gave me a dissuading look, a French-person pout. As though she were resigned to being left alone with Carnahan. Her fatalism sent a wave of panic through me, and I squelched it with obedience.

Kara led me down into the cabin where she disturbed the hush by vigorously fluffing a couple of pillows along a burgundy velour banquette.

"Sit, sit!"

I sat.

"You can relax! It's okay."

"Okay."

"You have beautiful skin." It sounded taxidermic. Still, I thanked her and told her my father was a dermatologist, which she responded to by telling me her father had been a prison guard. Even in my discomfort, or maybe as a way to my dispel my discomfort, I thought how much Frank would love every word out of this woman's mouth. How would he have written this? When the show's budget had been bigger, Frank extricated a character from a bad maritime situation with the arrival of a cruise ship. He also considered a pod of Good Samaritan dolphins.

"So, I want to know. What's going on with my girl Romola?"

"I'm not sure. I'm supposed to be working on that now."

"I want Romy to be happy, and I know that goes against the grain or whatever, but she's been through so much! She deserves some peace. Let her keep her baby."

"What about Peyton?"

"It's a dilemma. But I like Peyton best when she's mean. I'll take Peyton the bitch over Peyton the good mother any day."

"Can't she be both?"

"Ha. You sound like a professor. Is this what you'd call a teachable moment?"

"I didn't mean to be pedantic. I wonder sometimes if Peyton can have it both ways. Without slipping back into a vegetative state. But, you know, I'm feeling better already. We could probably go back up."

She poured me a glass of water and kept talking. "It's tough. I don't think that women really can have it all today. Something's gotta give. The village is gone."

"The village?"

"The village that used to raise your kids for you and go bowling with you and be all up in your business. I grew up in that village, and it had its advantages. But it didn't have yachts."

The longer our conversation continued, the more ludicrous it became, and I wondered if I hadn't underestimated Kara at the very moment when I should have been on highest alert. If that wasn't her intention all along. We had been down there for over half an hour. God knows what was going on above deck. I told Kara that whatever it was that had come over me had completely passed, thanks, and I really wanted to see those pictures of Jesse, it would be a shame not to, since we'd come all the way here. Wasn't it time to go join Bill and Lee and head back?

"BY ALL MEANS. We'll go up there. Give me a sec, okay? Gotta powder my nose." I didn't know if this meant she needed to use the toilet or something else. All I knew is I was getting tired of trying to read between the lines when I didn't know where the lines were. Alone, I took out my phone, thinking I might try Frank, as though I had lost the right to call on Andy. That's when I saw this:

Hi love. How's the trip? Not too much going on here. Someone at work gave me a copy of that old David Foster Wallace essay on TV. Started reading it at the gym this morning and got distracted by the treadmill's video screen. Hall and Oates trapped in a giant drum kit.
Does this make me part of the problem? Or is the problem so outdated that I'm not part of anything anymore?
Hope everything is ok. Call when you can.

"Shall we?" Kara returned, and I stowed my phone. Her eyes shone with anticipation, prepared to be delighted by what we might find on deck. Which turned out to be Bill, lying in Kara's chaise, a skipper's cap angled on his head. Lee stood by the railing, staring out at the water. Hard to tell if her hair, which sort of always had a rolled-out-of-bed look to it, had been mussed by Bill or by the wind. The bleached-out sun cast longer shadows before it slid behind clouds, the searing white and blue of the late morning giving way to a leaden afternoon.

"Hello, womenfolk," Bill said.

"We interrupting?" asked Kara.

"Lee and I were just enjoying the silence of each other's company."

"I'm thinking it's time to head in," said Kara. "See those photographs you all are so hot about."

"Yes," said Lee, tuning in. "I do really want to see them. And we've already taken up a lot of your day."

"You could say we've taken up yours," said Bill. "You only have so much life energy. I'm so pleased you consented to expend it on me." He wasn't looking at Lee or at his wife. He'd set his sights on me, as if it was my turn.

That's when I thought: I'm out. I'm done. I want to go home. I pictured Andy at the gym, trying to be healthier, for his sake, for mine, and for the sake of our child.

The Carnahans left us to go steer the boat.

"You know," I said to Lee, "the whole self-destructive daddy-issues thing stops being glamorous and just gets sad after a certain point."

"What are you talking about?"

"I'm talking about whatever you let Carnahan do to you while I was down there with his freak wife."

"Nothing happened."

"So what was all that about the life energy you expended all over him?"

"Nothing happened. I swear. I bet you would have preferred if it had? Would that make you feel better? I'm sorry if I didn't debase myself in the manner to which you've become accustomed."

"You think I like seeing you put yourself in that position?"

"Yes, I think it works for you."

"That's ridiculous. And this is ridiculous, what we're doing."

"I told you nothing happened. Nothing, really. So I'm not turning back, not now. But if you want to go, just say so."

"It's just that you're dragging me into something that's really no good."

"I'm dragging you?"

"Yes. I have a life and I'm fucking it up here with you."

"You're not actually trying to blame me, are you? You chose to sleep with Rodgers. You chose to blow off work. I didn't force you to do anything."

No, it wasn't force. She had thrown me a rope that I had grabbed onto, and to pull apart its twisted strands demanded more resolve than I could muster. Woven in there still was the old ingrained inclination to protect her, which had always been a way of protecting myself. I didn't know who I was angry with anymore. Both of us, probably. Fine, I would go with her to the Carnahans' house, I told her, but that was it. *Fine,* she said. Fine.

AROUND THE TURN of the millennium the MBTA overhauled the train station where my father would always pick me up in college. When Lee started coming home with me for Thanksgivings, we would arrive at the small, one-story brick depot and find two empty seats among the discolored fiberglass chairs while I called home on a pay phone. The most up-to-date equipment in that room was a vending machine sponsored by a psychedelic fruit drink brand that existed briefly in the early nineties. A few years later, with the realization of high-speed rail service, the old building was torn down and a proper station was built for Boston's swelling commuter population. Spacious and spiffy, its technological polish suggested efficiency and comfort. It was sleek and we were impressed by the degree to which we were impressed. So it was all the more jarring to see my father when he showed up at the new station in a shearling coat I'd never seen him wear in person, only in old photos. He looked like a time traveler. An unsettlingly young Jonathan Feld had slipped through a hole in the fabric of the universe and materialized here. As though he weren't my father at all, had yet to be. I didn't know how to talk to him.

"Your mother was cleaning out the cedar closet. I can't believe it still fits! Though I'm feeling a little, uh, *sheepish* about wearing it."

"You look like Stellan Skarsgard in *Breaking the Waves,*" said Lee. She was our Sacagawea, the interpreter who spoke everyone's language and knew the terrain or could fake it.

"Is that good?" he asked.

THE SUN IN YOUR EYES

"Oh, it's good. That rugged Danish oil rigger look."

"I'll take it. Rugged Danish. Been feeling more like cheese Danish lately. I'm astounded I can still button this thing."

I didn't mention that Skarsgard's character was maybe Norwegian, I just thanked God for the cheese Danish joke, which made my dad recognizable to me again. On the car ride he referred to us as "you girls"—*Did you girls have a good trip? How is New York treating you girls?* That helped, too.

Lee asked him how "the skin trade" was going.

"It's not what it used to be. Which is both a blessing and a curse." My father took the tone of a disappointed rabbi. Noninvasive techniques and advances in lasers had revolutionized his field, creating a demand for often unnecessary yet lucrative cosmetic procedures. To a man of integrity, which he hoped himself to be, it posed an ethical question. He hadn't gone into medicine to administer glycolic peels and pump cow collagen into the lips of pampered patients. And yet, and yet. Those peels and injections, those beams of pulsed light, had paid for my college education.

He drove us in his Toyota down the leafy suburban streets of my childhood. I envied myself having grown up here, and I envied my parents and their life here. Maybe I had finally broken with this place—it was no longer home—and so I could see it as an outsider. The oak trees shading the yard, the slate path leading to the front door of a white colonial with black trim. Lamplight already glowing through the windows on a darkening afternoon.

"Hello, hello!" My mother called from the kitchen, where she was in the process of baking a pumpkin pie. My mother had generally practiced homemaking in moderation. She regarded cooking, cleaning, and decorating as necessary and sometimes satisfying but didn't consider them exalted art forms. Except, I had noticed, in the presence of Lee. When Lee was around, my mother became a pur-veyor of domestic enchantments: a dinner of simple, delicious roast chicken or an aromatic tajine, dense chocolate cakes served with in-dividual pots of freshly whipped cream; clean, loftily folded linens; a gleaming bathroom. Hospitality mingled with pity and pride in these efforts: *Welcome, Lee! Make yourself at home in a real home such as you never had growing up, you poor thing.* As though Lee had been raised by wolves. Which I suppose is how my mother thought of Linda West. A woman led by her appetites, threatening to those who kept their desires in check, and those even more innocent lambs who didn't even know what real desire was.

The year before, Lee had given my mother a silk scarf from the Linda West Collection (the pricier, upmarket line) and even as my mother exclaimed how gorgeous it was, she seemed wary that some-thing had to be sacrificed in order to produce such a pretty thing. "Your mother has exquisite taste," she said to Lee. "And such drive to get her vision out into the world. I'm not quite sure how she does it." A Faustian bargain must have been struck somewhere along the way, perhaps involving sweatshop labor or the sort of sexual favors euphe-mistically referred to as liaisons? There had to be a downside to this scarf, because if there wasn't, what did that say about the sacrifices *my* mother had made? That they had been in vain? My parents had been invited to a party later that holiday weekend, and I happened to spy my mother getting ready. She tied the scarf around her neck and put on lipstick. Then she frowned into the mirror, took a tissue to wipe the color off her mouth, and untied the scarf and put it away in a drawer.

I never got the sense that my mother's pity and pride made Lee squirm. She seemed to appreciate being taken care of in that mater-nal way. If anyone was put out, it was me, seized by a jealous urge to expose the pumpkin pie act as a total sham.

"It smells so good in here!" said Lee.

"The aroma of a store-bought and reheated pie," I said.

"Excuse me?" said my mother. "I made this from scratch."

I felt like an asshole, though not an unjustified asshole.

My father hung his magical shearling coat in the hall and then came up behind my mother and massaged her shoulders.

"I am glad you're here," my mother said, primarily to Lee but also to me. "We've got a full house this year. Wait until you meet Genevieve." My brother had brought his new girlfriend home from college. They'd gone off for the afternoon but would be back soon. We should know, my mother explained, that Genevieve would be staying in Aaron's room, with Aaron, this being a condition that Genevieve had insisted upon before agreeing to spend Thanksgiving with Aaron. "You should have heard him on the phone—*Mom, Genevieve believes that sexuality is nothing to be ashamed of and that we need to own ourselves as sexual beings.* He could barely get the words out. I think he was reading off a piece of paper she'd handed him. But just so you know, girls, sexuality is nothing to be ashamed of."

"Viv is blushing," said Lee.

"It's just warm in here."

"If you can't stand the heat," said my father. I got out of the kitchen. I thought Lee would follow me but from the stairs I heard the three of them talking about Genevieve. My parents treated Lee like an expert. They asked her for assurance that Genevieve was a phase my brother was going through. Having been a phase herself, more than once, Lee could say yes, it was. Easy laughter, things were positively merry, but if Lee hadn't been there, acting as a counterweight to Genevieve, I wondered if my parents would have been so comfortable with the sleeping arrangements.

What surprised me about Genevieve when she and Aaron returned was her appearance. Cute. Petite, with good posture. Nice enough but not very warm. She probably had excellent time-management skills. Above all, she wasn't impressed with Lee, who I had begun to think of as my family's secret weapon. But Genevieve was impervious to her.

That night, I sat in the den watching Charlie Rose with Genevieve and Aaron when it occurred to me that Lee wasn't there with us.

"Where did you get off to?" I asked when she came in.

"I wanted to ask your dad about this weird area on my back."

She pulled at the neckline of her shirt to reveal an irritated patch of skin just above her shoulder blade.

"Okay." I tried to match her neutral tone. "What did he say?"

"Nothing to worry about. He prescribed a cream."

I tried not to think too hard about it. I worked a crossword puzzle while Lee pulled a recent copy of our college alumni magazine from a pile on an end table and began to leaf through it. My parents kept issues around out of the same sentimental pride with which they'd affixed school stickers to the back windshield of their car. I'd never given the alumni association my own address. If you don't want to know how you measure up, it's best not to keep a yardstick in the house. But Lee seemed interested in the anthropological curiosity of it. She flipped directly to the class notes.

"It's like everyone has invented a new irrigation system in a developing country or written and directed a movie about twenty-somethings."

"Or both."

"Wait, this one is from Chipmunk. Remember Chipmunk?"

"Of course."

"She's a lawyer now, living in San Francisco with her husband, and she's pregnant with her first child. Jesus. I wonder what Moose is doing?"

"Moose is in med school, planning to be a psychiatrist. I read that last time I was here."

"A psychiatrist? How?"

"Do you mind?" my brother asked. "We're trying to watch this."

"Why?" I asked.

"Why what?" he said.

"It's just squawky people who like to hear themselves talk," I said.

"Ironic," said Aaron. Genevieve looked smug.

"Maybe we misjudged Chipmunk and Moose," I said. "They're quite accomplished."

"Well, so are you," said Lee.

"Hardly."

"Things are happening for you. You should have written in here about your story."

"*You* should have written in."

"About being a *face*? About wearing clothes and getting my picture taken?"

"Yeah!"

"Next time somebody asks me what I fucking do, I'm just going to say 'I'm a doctor.'"

It was the first time I'd heard her express dissatisfaction or discomfort with the direction her life had taken. But then, I hadn't been around to listen much lately.

"What kind of doctor?"

"A radiologist. At Mount Sinai."

"But what if you meet a radiologist who works at Mount Sinai?"

"That would be kind of perfect in a universe-folding-in-on-itself way."

I offered up a sad laugh. I believed she didn't have to *do* anything in order to *be* someone. "You're Lee Parrish," I wanted to say. But being Lee Parrish was part of the problem. She would always be Jesse and Linda's daughter, and people would always take an interest in her because of that. She never had to earn it.

"Why *don't* you become a doctor?" Genevieve turned to Lee. "If you really want to, what's keeping you?"

"My defeatist attitude," said Lee. "And blood. I'm not good with blood."

"But you *could* be a radiologist," said Aaron. "They don't really deal with blood." He spoke, not to second Genevieve's annoyance, but as though he had discovered the loophole that would allow Lee to follow her dreams.

My brother had had a thing for Lee since he was fifteen. He'd tried to impress her with bits from various standup comedy routines. The next year, he'd grown sullen and brooding and didn't say much of anything. I would catch him looking at her in the way I wished a boy would have looked at me when I was sixteen. He worshiped her, and Lee played it to the hilt. She even kissed his forehead once and told him he was going to be a "real heartbreaker in a year or two." Aaron must have resented her on some level, found the whole situation humiliating, and now he had Genevieve to throw in her face. The appeal of a girl like Genevieve, as I understood it, was that she did all the work and Aaron just had to show up and be told what books to read, what rallies to attend, and how exactly she could be brought to orgasm.

"Thanks, Aaron," said Lee.

"No problem. But you're not going to be a radiologist."

"I'm not?"

"No," he said. "You're Lee fucking Parrish."

They smiled at each other. Charlie Rose was wrapping things up with a journalist from the *Washington Post*. Carol Channing was the next guest.

"It's about time," I said. Genevieve glared at the screen.

IN THE MIDDLE of the night, when I couldn't sleep, I slipped out of bed and headed for the living room, stopping on the stairs when I heard voices.

"Look at your sister and her friend," Genevieve was saying. "Some people are just more directed than others."

"More directed?"

"People who have beliefs. Who know what they want out of life and go after it. People who care about the state of the world! I'm sorry, but they don't seem that passionate about anything."

I wanted to interject: "It's a holiday. Do we have to be *passionate* on a holiday?" And why wasn't my brother defending us?

"You're brave," he told her. "It's hot."

"Oh yeah?"

They began to honor their sexuality and I crept back to my room.

THANKSGIVING MORNING SHOWED an autumnal gray sky through cold windowpanes. Weather for blankets and lit fireplaces, green grass fading in the yard below, and a quiet street beyond. Someone was already up brewing coffee.

I found my father leaning against the countertop contemplating a mug with the logo of an old pharmaceutical company on it, as though it would offer up answers if he looked at it deeply enough. The jocular Nordic oil rigger of the day before had disappeared.

There was no mantle for him to take up at that moment. He asked me how I'd slept as an opening for him to tell me about his night of tossing and turning. Aside from the usual anxieties that keep a man of his age awake, something was weighing on him. I had always thought of my father as straightforward, but I realized he'd never delivered bad news to me before.

"Do you know what I thought about this morning that I hadn't thought of in years?" he asked.

I shook my head.

"Taking you to the Army Navy surplus store in Kenmore Square. Remember that? You were maybe fifteen. You wanted those fatigue pants."

"I was fourteen. I loved those pants."

"I remember thinking, if that's what you want to wear, that's what you want to wear. Fine by me. Because I knew that was probably going to be the last time you would ever ask me to do anything like that."

"They were German. From the West German army, I think. I didn't want to tell you because I was afraid you wouldn't let me get them."

"Why?"

"I don't know. The Holocaust?"

"Well."

"I can't believe I asked you to take me shopping for those."

"I remember that store smelled like camphor and rubber. The music they played was interesting. Some kind of reggae. I was completely wrapped up in watching you. You were nervous, a little timid, not sure you should be there, but still confident, and you found what you wanted without asking for any help. And as I was watching you do this, I had no idea who you were, but I felt incredibly proud."

I had no idea who you *were,* I thought.

"It was the Slits," I said.

"The what?"

"The music in the store." I remembered everything about that trip, but I hadn't thought my dad did, too. "What made you think of that?"

He looked, again, to his coffee cup, his hands.

"Something happened with Lee. Last night. She came by my study and asked if I would take a look at an inflamed spot on her back. It seemed pretty harmless. I'm a doctor. There *is* an irritation there, nothing serious, a topical corticosteroid would take care of it, but she—"

"What? Did she throw herself at you?"

"I wouldn't say *throw,* but, yes."

What I already knew but didn't want to believe.

Nothing he said would have made that better, so I decided to make it worse.

"Don't flatter yourself, Dad. You could've been anyone, I'm sure. You just happened to be the nearest man with a pulse."

"Maybe that's true. But I'm not just anyone. I don't think Lee is in a very good place. It seems to me like a fairly obvious cry for help. Which is why I'm telling you this."

"So that I can help her stop hitting on other people's fathers?"

"*Vivian.*"

As much as I tried, I couldn't make my father the object of my anger.

"What am I supposed to do with this? Did you tell Mom?"

"I did. We agreed I should tell you. We all care about Lee. But obviously, you're her friend. We want to leave it up to you to handle however you think best."

I had no idea what was best.

He walked toward the tiered metal basket of onions that had been hanging from the ceiling for as long as I could remember. I thought he might try to illustrate something with one of them, an object lesson in how many layers there are to a person. But he just reached in. "I told your mother I would get started early on the stuffing."

"That's it?"

"No. I suppose we have an exceedingly awkward dinner to look forward to."

My father's gift for understatement may have been matched only by his good manners. He wasn't Midwestern, though people often assumed he was. He started on the stuffing while I stood there, mostly stunned by the fact that I wasn't all that stunned.

Before I had much time to figure out where to go or what to do next, I met my brother coming down the stairs, looking disheveled and relaxed, and decided to ruin his day. He asked me if I was okay and I did that thing of not answering, of making it seem like something was so wrong I had lost the power of speech. Aaron wasn't a nervous person, he didn't see trouble everywhere, but when he did see it, it concerned him. He had been a cuddly boy, and though he tried to toughen up (headphones, a hooded sweatshirt, a stony, unmoved look on his face), he hadn't lost his need to comfort and be comforted. I took him out to the front porch, and he folded his bare arms against the cold and stood over me a little. When had he grown so tall?

I played the reluctant confessor. But I hadn't expected my brother to be so calm.

"Why are you bringing me into this?" he asked.

"I'm not *bringing* you in. You're already in it."

"No. I'm not. This is part of some fucked-up thing between you and Lee. And I didn't need to know."

"You really don't care?"

"What do you want me to say?"

"I don't know, something honest? Because what I don't understand is why she went for Dad when she could have easily had you."

"Fuck you, Viv."

He brushed past me and went inside.

Our lawn, its flagstone path, its low row of shrubbery by the empty sidewalk, had a hard quality to it this time of year. This suburb was an old one, old trees, old houses, streets named for old Protestant families. I had read enough to know what happened in places like this, and I wanted to be sophisticated and accepting of the messiness of life. I wanted to be unassuming but I assumed, I assumed. Had Lee planned it? Had she worn a pretty bra? Had my father, the rugged oil rigger, for an instant, enjoyed it? What had *it* been? A kiss? Had his hand touched her shoulder, slid to the small of her back? Why had he seen it so necessary to tell me? Why not let it rest as one of the moments that shape one's secret life? *Lee needs help, I get it,* but wasn't there also some pride on his part, that he could still attract that kind of attention and that he was principled enough to turn it down? Maybe he saw it as his fatherly duty to let me know. Did Lee, familiar with my father's honorable code of behavior, initiate this whole thing precisely because she *knew* that he would tell me?

I waited for Lee to say something to me about what happened for most of the day—how could she not have said anything the night before!—and she waited me out, with such unbearable patience that we made it all the way to the big meal without bringing it up.

By then it was too late for her to leave. Choosing our places at the dining table had the kind of tortured, overdetermined suspense of THATH scenes: Elena Sterling, faced with a tangle of different colored wires, having to pick which ones to clip to prevent a bomb from exploding. Lee wound up between my parents' friends the Manns and Genevieve, who was at the foot of the table. Aaron next to her, me between Aaron and my mother, my father at the head. I kept looking at my mother, but she revealed nothing. She seemed a little mystified that the rest of us let Genevieve dominate the evening's talk. Genevieve asked us if we'd ever heard of Noam Chomsky, told us about her town-gown efforts to introduce local underprivileged children to *manga,* and, while pushing some sweet potato around her plate, enlightened us about the toll exacted by mainstream media on the female body image. Had Genevieve seen any of Lee's ads? Maybe. But would she even cop to reading those magazines?

"It's true, it can be pretty vile," said Lee gently, dipping a toe in Genevieve's stream.

Aaron said something under his breath. All I caught was "you" and "vile." Genevieve didn't hear it. She'd heard Lee, though. And she'd certainly heard Aaron the night before: *You're Lee fucking Parrish.* Their smiles.

"Why do you go along with it?" she asked.

"Good question," said Lee. Like if she had an answer for that, she'd be ready to take on poverty next and then war.

Genevieve garbled Audre Lorde's words about using the master's tools to dismantle his house. And Lee started to say she understood when Aaron snapped.

"Nobody gives a shit, Lee. Just shut up." And she did, mutely looking to me, for help maybe, or forgiveness. I stared down at my plate.

"Aaron!" cried my mother.

"It's fine," said Lee.

"No, it's not."

"Natalie," said my father. "Let it go. Let's try to enjoy the rest of this meal."

Aaron apologized, primarily to the Manns, while my mother gave my father a squinty-eyed grin that contained (just barely) embarrassment, irritation, and incredulity. Natalie and Jonathan. I had the sense of having walked in on someone else's life in what I had thought was my home. My mother found that sheepskin coat in the closet, and it signified a whole world I knew nothing about, a whole secret history. It seemed to me that I was learning something about marriage, though I couldn't have said what.

We finished the meal. As soon as the Manns left, I took up the pie plates and shuttled them into the kitchen with my mother. In years past, the cleanup had always been a group effort, but this time everyone found a reason to scatter. My mother's silence made me think she would have preferred me gone, too, but then, tearing foil for leftovers, she asked me to tell her about Ben Driggs Stern. There wasn't all that much to tell, I said. She frowned.

"I got started too late and gave it up too early," she said.

"It?"

"Oh, you know. Sex. As a vital thing." She sighed. No provocation in her voice, nor was she proud of herself for being frank. It was almost as if she were talking to herself. "I missed my chance, in a way. Men don't look at me like that anymore and I don't look at them, not like I used to."

My mother, looking at men. Men looking at her. Who was this woman? Not the woman who hadn't changed her bob haircut since the birth of her son. She did regularly apply store-bought dark auburn dye to cover her gray, but it seemed more about maintaining the status quo than about her looks. It wasn't that she didn't care. This was the woman, after all, who had determined that I was ready at fifteen for a trip to a salon in the city instead of Kathy's Fountain of Beauty in the shopping strip. So what was it? Better not to be seen in the first place than to be looked at and found wanting? Had that happened with my father? Had he looked at her and been disappointed or, worse and more likely, stopped looking? They had been blinkered horses, canting along together, pulling the load that was our family.

"What men?"

"No one. In the past, I . . . I had . . . thoughts . . . and maybe once or twice those thoughts were met with an opportunity. I never acted on it. Looking back, I don't know if that was courageous or cowardly of me."

"What were these opportunities? I mean, who were they?"

"Nobody you know. I wasn't going to run away with another teacher or a neighbor or anything. It was such a long time ago. I would never leave your father. Not now. I don't have it in me. That's all I'm trying to say. I think at some point even your memories change. They become what you need them to be. Marriage is such a strange thing. Who you end up with. This person who, if you're lucky, makes up so much of your life. In certain ways it seems fated and in other ways so completely arbitrary . . . Remind me not to give this speech at your wedding, will you?"

My wedding. It surprised me how pleased I was to hear my mother, amid her sad talk, allude to my wedding as something inevitable. It had been an abstraction, but maybe I wanted one more than I knew or wanted the kind of relationship in which a wedding was even a possibility. I certainly didn't have that with Ben Driggs Stern.

"When your father told me what happened with Lee . . . I think about these things. About myself. About you. About Lee. I do think she could use a friend right now. But maybe that friend isn't you."

Genevieve came into the kitchen then and was halfway to the sink before she saw us sitting in the breakfast nook, staring at her like a zoo gorilla. She belonged to a different species. Even in refilling a glass of water by the sink she acted with a shining confidence here in her boyfriend's mother's house. No one had ever turned her down or made her feel undeserving. It would be only a matter of time before she would be hurt and humbled, perhaps repeatedly, before the world stopped being a place of promise. Obnoxious as I found her to be, I wished for a moment that she could stay the way she was, unharmed and unknowing. It vanished when she summoned a smile for us, the kind of wan, blinking smile you see on someone actively suffering a fool.

"Sweetie," said my mother, "there's a pitcher in the fridge that's cold."

"Oh, thanks, but my body metabolizes room temp better."

"Of course. Whatever you like."

"Thank you, Natalie."

Ms. Feld. Call her Ms. Feld. Your shit stinks too, Genevieve. And could you maybe offer to wash a fucking pan or something?

"Aaron is so young," said my mother, when Genevieve left.

"He's always seemed old to me. I usually end up feeling immature around him."

"I think I know what you mean. But he's still *such* a boy in certain ways. I'm not too worried about Genevieve, I'm more worried about whoever comes after her. Ben Driggs Stern. Do you always use his full name like that?"

"Yes. Unfortunately."

"Poor kid."

"Me? Or Ben Driggs Stern?"

She laughed and for an instant, she became Natalie to me again, not my mom, and I wanted her to have run off with whoever it was who had presented her with an opportunity all those years ago.

The security light by the kitchen door clicked on, and my mother stood to see who was knocking on the glass pane. Lee. She came in from the cold, huddled in her parka, her eyelashes wet, her eyes bloodshot.

"Could I talk to you?" she asked my mother and then gave me a look I'd once seen on a wounded doe that had wandered from the local deer sanctuary into town. Animal Control eventually shot the bleeding creature in a parking lot behind a multiplex. My mother ushered Lee in and took her coat.

I went up to my old room so I couldn't even try to listen. There were now a few plastic storage containers stacked by the desk and at the foot of the bed. But above the dresser was still the Bikini Kill poster I had taped to the wall, a postcard of Garfield eating lasagna, and a picture of Helena Bonham Carter I put up during my *A Room with a View* period. All of it was from a time before Lee, which didn't quite compute. My life always already had her in it. Years later, I would experience the same disbelief, the same ontological whiplash with my son. The always already.

The knock at my door came from Lee, who held her packed bag at her side. She had insisted on calling a cab to get her to the bus station, even though my mother had offered to drive. She was so sorry. She felt so alone and she missed me, but I had Ben now, and she understood that changed things. She didn't know what else to say. I wanted to tell her that I didn't have Ben, not in any way that meant I no longer needed her. But the last thing I wanted just then was to need her.

My mother later told me she had sat Lee down, fixed them each a cup of tea, and tried to get across that if she was upset, it wasn't so much on her own behalf, but on behalf of her children. On behalf of Lee, too. Natalie, ever the anti-Linda. If it had been reversed, what would Linda have said to me? But it could never have been reversed.

I wouldn't go so far as to call it a bright spot, but I have to admit to a certain satisfaction that nobody, including Aaron, ever told Genevieve what happened, though she saw the taxi pull up, saw Lee get in. We closed ranks because we still had loyalties and we still knew where they lay.

Lee later apologized to me again, and I told her I forgave her. I really thought, at the time, that I had. That the moment with my father was, after all, a cry for help. But I never truly forgave her for damaging our friendship or for hurting me. I never let myself believe that's what she'd done.

A WELL-GROOMED MAN in a chambray shirt, dark jeans, and work boots greeted us at the door of the Carnahans' house, which sat on a tiny peninsula jutting out into the sea.

"He's got servants," I whispered to Lee.

"Yes," she replied, annoyed with my astonishment. "They're not servants. They're personal assistants." I forgot they'd had various helpers when Lee was growing up.

Carnahan appeared. "Let's go have a look at dear old Dad, y'all," he said.

We followed the Carnahans through airy rooms, all glass and

white walls, to a rickety back staircase they hadn't yet gotten around to renovating and maybe never would.

"It reminds me of a mental institution," Kara said. "But in a good way. Know what I mean?"

I nodded. Possibly Kara was alluding to the deep Freudian scratches in the wooden banister and dark paneling along the wall. It wouldn't have surprised me to reach the top and find an old nursery covered in yellow wallpaper. Instead, below a skylight was a hallway freshly painted in a soft soothing gray, leading into a rectangular observatory. Wide windows opened onto the ocean and the sky, and a thin shade made of some UV filtering fiber cast the room in a shadowy light.

A series of black-and-white portraits lined the wall. Most of the well-known photos of Jesse, the ones that had graced his albums and been reproduced many times over, had been taken by Linda, candids she snapped with her old Brownie. Their intimate home-movie feel welcomed you into a rarefied world: Jesse in the Chateau Marmont; out by his Corvette in the desert; leaning on a fence at a scrub-covered ranch in Topanga. David Haseltine's images had intimacy too, but not one that extended to the viewer. In their ongoing interiority was a vivid psychology that bled through the surface of the image, but nobody else could be a part of it.

In one image, against a backdrop of flocked, floral wallpaper, Jesse stared directly ahead, daring Haseltine to catch the combination of boyish sweetness and lock-up-your-daughters sexuality. This simultaneous vulnerability and confidence must have made it hard to say no to him. But the photograph also crystallized that look, formalized it, made it into a mask, behind which you could almost glimpse Jesse laughing, quietly and a little viciously, at all of it.

Next was a shot of Marion looking at Jesse as Jesse cast his gaze down toward a dusty beam of light coming through the window of another room in Flintwick's lake house. They looked so contemporary—Jesse in his cardigan and T-shirt and Marion in her white button-down and light blue trouser-like jeans. On a side table next to Marion I noticed a glass bottle of water and a china cup placed on a saucer. The small touch of finery surprised me, evoking a loose luxuriance. Was that saucer Marion's doing? Or was it Jesse's? His etiquette, his Southern ways. The stillness of the picture was appealing, though a little blank, until I saw the picture to the other side of it, the moment just after, as Jesse looked straight at the camera. It hummed with the tension of him not looking back at Marion. Marion was looking ahead at Haseltine's lens too. Their expressions: *Is this what you wanted?* As though both Jesse and Marion knew in advance what Haseltine's frame was going to reveal here: a couple that wouldn't last.

Transfixed by the photos, I almost forgot to be angry with Lee.

"Wait," said Lee, pointing to an object on the dresser Marion was leaning against. A chain with a pendant, a narrow silver bar about an inch long. The way the light caught it, I could make out the Hebrew letter *shin* engraved along the top. "That's Big Mort's."

"He gave it to Jesse?" I asked.

"No, no, no. Big Mort gave it to my mom when she left New York for L.A."

"Maybe Jesse had it for a while?"

"I don't think so. Linda wears it all the time. I think she must have been there. These were taken the day he died?"

Carnahan stepped forward and made a show of exhaling. "Yes," he said. "Tangled web?" Kara gazed out at the undulating waves, going for a troubled Bergmanian gloom but reminding me of the blonde in ABBA. Neither of them seemed to understand that we had just awakened something dormant, something we had mistaken for the ground before it started to move beneath us.

THE CLOSELY SET cottages, patchy grass, and power lines of what Carnahan had referred to as "America" came into view at the end of his circuitous private drive. In the car the giddy shiver of a narrow escape came over me. But Lee didn't want to feel that thrill with me or talk about what had just happened. "I'll take you to the train station now," she said with cold focus.

"Lee."

"What? You don't want to be involved. I get it."

"But I am involved. So, what are you going to do? Where are you going to go?"

"I'm going to look for Marion Washington, for real."

She'd tried to find her months before, she explained, without success but also without much urgency. According to the Internet, Marion didn't exist after 1978. She had never spoken publicly about those last days with Jesse. She didn't remember any of it, is how the story went. Vilified and with a chunk of her life lost, she disappeared from the public eye.

But maybe she did remember. Not what happened to the tapes but something else, such as what Linda was doing at Flintwick's that day. We didn't have enough leverage to make Linda talk, and clearly leverage was what was needed. There I was—using words like "leverage" and "we."

I wouldn't be getting on that train.

"Lee, let me help."

"I'll probably have to hire a private investigator or something."

"Maybe. But maybe not." We were twenty-five miles away from

our alma mater and its extensive network of archives and databases. Twenty-five miles away, it dawned on me, from Patti Driggs.

"Why would she want to talk to me? She hates Linda. Besides, what would she even know?"

"Isn't it possible she might have a clue as to Marion's whereabouts?"

"Won't that be weird for you?"

"Because I dated her son for a few months eight years ago? I never even met her."

Lee decided it was worth a shot.

"Thank you," she said.

"Of course," I said. As if there was no question. As if I didn't then take out my phone and reread the message Andy had sent me, start to reply, and delete every inadequate attempt. I'd been doing that with him, in one way or another, for months. Years, even. I couldn't do it anymore.

"Lee, I need you to pull over. I have to call Andy."

OUR WEDDING VOWS had mentioned responsibility. How it was inseparable from loss. It had a heaviness to it and this was its finest quality. If you didn't feel its weight, you didn't have enough to lose. But Andy and I hadn't exactly written that part of our vows. We'd cribbed it from Frank, lines he'd written for the show that were unexpectedly beautiful. ("You distract them with campy hijinks and people think the poignancy comes out of nowhere," Frank had said. "But it never comes out of nowhere.") Was it a cop-out, I'd asked Andy? No, he didn't think so. He didn't think it was cheating. It was, he added, a nice way to honor Frank, even. To be honest, I don't remember the wording of our vows, only that they made me feel giving and loved and expectant, that we were about to make our lives that much larger. That we would each take care of the other. I should have committed those words to memory. I should have known them still by heart.

There was a lot I didn't remember about our wedding. It came back to me in flashes and out-of-sequence moments. Andy and me, alone in a room just after the ceremony, Andy biting into an apple, a post-match victory snack, like orange slices at a junior-high soccer game. My father's guiding hand on my back, his other hand in mine as we danced. The Hasidic frenzy of the hora, an injection of shtetl into our modern marriage. My brother's elegance in raising his glass for a toast. Kirsten presenting a bare, highly toned upper arm to Frank, and Frank, in his deadest of deadpans, saying: "Cardiofunk?" Jack Caprico giving me a congratulatory kiss on the cheek by way of introduction. How it lingered because of the full, bristly beard he'd grown for his run as Trigorin in a production of *The Seagull*. Lingered, too, because it was stupefying. All I could think was: Jack Caprico touched me. Later I would see, out of the corner of my eye, Jack Caprico talking to a tall, clean-shaven man in a lowly lit alcove, Jack Caprico doing most of the work and Andy, the tall, clean-shaven man, graciously listening but not working for anything and it would make me so proud. I would also see Andy talking to Lee, the two of them out in the courtyard, and it occurred to me that the last time I had seen them together like that, paying that kind of attention to each other, was in college. The feeling it gave rise to was akin to jealousy, if jealousy was a comfort.

My parents were talking with Nancy and Tim Elliott, Andy's mother and father. Admitting to each other how excited but nervous they had each been. My mother confessed to breathing easier now that she could see how beautifully it was coming off. She'd had her doubts earlier, as their town car crossed the East River on the way to the venue.

"F. Scott Fitzgerald wrote that the view of Manhattan from the Queensboro Bridge is always the city seen for the first time, in all its wild promise. But I'm afraid what you see when you head in the other direction is, well, not quite so promising."

Nancy nodded and smiled considerately, either at a loss as to how to follow up or because she was too kind to acknowledge my mother's stiff pretensions. Small talk had never been my mother's strong suit, and she often left it to my father. You could say that she was too introverted for it, that she found it uncomfortable and wasn't a very good fake with people she didn't know particularly well. You could also say this made her socially demanding, that she failed to understand how accommodating and how generous conversational inconsequentiality could be. That sometimes, especially if you had a sparkling drink in your hand, you could talk about traffic or even a feat of urban engineering without referencing its literary pedigree.

She had steadily, strangely pecked away at our wedding plans ever since Andy and I had started making them. "What does one wear to a wedding in a foundry in Queens?" she had asked. I hadn't wanted to dignify her remark with a response, to explain that the foundry was an impeccably renovated nineteenth-century industrial space now used for parties. That we weren't trying to be aggressively unconventional or challenging in our choice, that many people had hosted lovely events here before. But what *does* one wear to a wedding in an old Long Island City foundry if most of one's clothes converge along a Cambridge-Wellfleet-Tanglewood axis? That bohemian school-marm look of dressy shawls and velvet in the winter, linen sacks in the summer, shoes with sensible soles. A way of dressing much influenced by the designs of Linda West, come to think of it.

Linda catered to that customer, but only to a point, refusing to full-on frump it up. And Linda arrived there by a different path, signposts including the floating bias cuts of Madeleine Vionnet and the gauzy cover-ups for afternoons by a crystalline pool in L.A. No Virginia Woolf, no weekend matinees of *The Caucasian Chalk Circle* at the American Repertory Theatre. My mother might have bought a Linda West dress and worn it to a wedding, but she wouldn't have been caught dead in one at a wedding that Linda would attend.

The coppery shantung jacket she wore over a celadon sheath turned out to be a good choice, picking up the warm bronze of the brick walls, giving her a glow. Something Elena Sterling Rappoport might have in her wardrobe for a charity luncheon. But Linda was effortless and blasé in a slouchy cream silk top, wide-leg black trousers, and a black satin blazer. It made me think: *Right, this is what one wears to a wedding in a foundry.*

I had placed my mother in a humiliating position—the kind of quiet humiliation that might require a minute or two of deep breaths in a bathroom stall. The kind that had led to her concern about what one does and doesn't do. I'd wanted her to be humiliated, just a little, because her bloom of anxiety reminded me of the perfecting impulse that overtook her whenever Lee had come to stay with us. That extra effort she made, the tajines and grapefruit-scented hand soap packaged to look as if it came from an apothecary, that only Lee occasioned. Linda came up to all of us and said, "What's that you were saying about wild promise? Sounds like the name of the cheap perfume I used to douse myself in when I was a kid." I caught a glimmer of embarrassment in my mother's eye.

Linda took my mother's hand and clasped it while performing a vaudevillian pantomime of disbelief: *How did we get here? It seems like only yesterday I used to be a girl. Who knows where the time goes? Sunrise, sunset. Ah, life!*

"Natalie," she sighed.

"It's lovely to see you, Linda."

"Congratulations!" Another head shake. "*Right!?*" Linda gestured to me like an auto-show attendant presenting a much-anticipated new car model. She leaned in to kiss me and in an almost-whisper said, "Gorgeous. Just gorgeous."

"Thank you. It's Lee's doing."

"Yes, well, Lee's very good with a makeup brush, but you can't *apply* radiance like this."

She had a way of telling you what you wanted to believe about yourself.

"Hello, Linda," said my father, jumping out of whatever he'd been saying to Tim in order to jump in here. "You're looking very dapper."

Linda smiled. How silly he was—a well-meaning but confused man who never quite understood how to talk to women and certainly didn't know anything about how they dressed.

But I think he knew exactly what he was saying. Linda's outfit accentuated her femininity, but he made it seem as if she were a drag cabaret emcee or circus ringmaster. He had sensed my mother's distress and come to her defense. They were comrades in arms. Strange that this should have surprised me. But it did. Like a secret passage—like what I had always taken for bookshelves was really a door to a room in our house where they would go. I could see them in there, after that Parents' Weekend dinner, my mother reproaching my father for his Talmudic questions-begetting-questions act. My father saying he could do only so much to cover for her insecurities. They must have agreed on a strategy for the next time they would see Linda, the weekend Lee and I graduated from college. When the dinner plans fell through, when Linda had to fly out earlier than expected, I could tell they were relieved, though maybe a little disappointed, missing the opportunity to put some plan of theirs into action.

They would hash out certain terms in this room and then head back into the world, where all I saw was their adherence to those terms, not how they'd reached them. The adherence this evening: my mother attempting to mingle, my father lightly hugging Lee when he saw her, the first time since that Thanksgiving weekend, keeping a good two or three inches between their bodies but not a protesting-too-much distance. His coolness toward Linda. At the same time, he'd noticed what she was wearing, looked her over, taken her in.

"And you, Mr. Feld, do very nice things for that suit," said Linda.

My mother was all patience. Linda was basically a glorified tailor, wasn't she, and therefore qualified to make statements about the fit of garments.

"I love seeing all of us in our finery," Linda added.

"You must be so used to it, though. Getting dressed up, going to galas and that kind of thing," said my mother.

"Oh yeah, it's all very run of the mill. I take absolutely no pleasure in it whatsoever."

Neither of my parents had sharpened their wits quite enough to meet Linda's sarcasm. My mother simply chuckled lightly, shifted the tone and said, "You must be Roy?" to the man who had been politely standing behind Linda. Edged out of the inner circle, like Nancy and Tim, who now looked a bit lost. They had expected to be the recipients of all the weird, rivalrous energy that my parents were directing toward Linda and in the absence of that, they didn't quite know what to do with themselves.

I had met Roy a couple of times. Linda had started seeing him when Lee was still a child. Roy wasn't the first boyfriend Linda had after Jesse, but Lee never got to know the others. One night when she was eight, she heard what sounded like muffled hyperventilation and, concerned, got out of bed. Out by the pool she found one of these men going down on her mother. She didn't yet know what that meant, didn't know those words for it, but she stood there long enough to grasp the mechanics of it, though not long enough for Linda or the man to see her. Lee encountered another man in the kitchen one morning who made her breakfast. "What, you don't *know?* You gotta mix some butter in the syrup and *then* you dip that bacon in there! *That's* how it's done." Then he looked at her and said, "Shit, you're like a little Jesse, man. It's like Jesse's watching. I can't do this." Lee said, "Do what?" He said, "Keep fucking your mom." Lee never saw him again. Roy was the only one who seemed at all capable of being a father figure. Lee never caught Roy and Linda in the act, and she decided this was due to Roy's discretion and regard for her welfare because it couldn't possibly be due to Linda's.

Lee had told me that Roy was always costumed—suede jacket with arm fringe in back-in-the-day photos, mutton chops and Western wear around the time Linda met him; ponytail and desert boots for a while there in the nineties—never merely dressed. This evening he seemed to be going for International Architect just back from Berlin. Dark suit, dark shirt, no tie, angular glasses, close-cropped receding hair.

My parents exchanged introductions with Roy, neglecting to include Nancy and Tim, who stood there looking on, as though they had forgotten they didn't have to stand there and be excluded.

"So, Roy, if memory serves, you're a television producer?" my father asked.

"That's right. I'm essentially retired now, though."

"Would I have seen one of your shows?"

"Possibly," said Roy. "Did you own a TV in the eighties and like poorly paced ensemble comedies?"

"Oh Roy, come on," said Linda. "He practically transformed the medium."

Roy hailed a server carrying a tray of seared tuna on sesame thins.

I didn't know all that much about Linda and Roy's relationship, but I imagine it's emasculating to be the man who knows he can never be loved like Jesse and be willing to stick around nonetheless.

I just remember catching Andy's eye then and thinking: *We won't treat each other like that. I would never treat you like that. I won't be Linda and you won't be Roy.*

I MADE LEE pull into the next rest stop and I found privacy and cell reception at the edge of a wooded area, behind a tractor-trailer.

"I'm so sorry," I said.

"For what?" said Andy.

Upon hearing his voice, I convulsed and then involuntarily started rocking back and forth. I must have looked like those men I'd seen praying at synagogue on High Holidays when I was a child. I didn't know where to begin. I could no longer distinguish between the symptoms and the causes of what was wrong. I hadn't, until just then, conceived of what I'd done with Rodgers as a betrayal, not really. I'd been thinking it had very little to do with Andy, but *that* was where the betrayal lay.

"For everything." I sat down on the ground to control my strange swaying. "For leaving things weird between us. For not calling sooner."

"Where are you?"

"We're heading to Providence."

"You're not coming home?"

I thought I had the shaking under control, but really it just got diverted into a kind of whimpering moan. A pained sound, an animal one. I couldn't help myself. My body was taking over.

"Viv?"

"Yeah?"

"Are you okay?"

"No. I mean, yes, I'm fine. I don't mean to make you worry. And I really want to come home. I really do, but there's something to this now. I can't leave Lee now."

"You've found something?"

"Yeah. I'm not sure what, exactly, but I think it's important, and I need to help her see it through. It's like I thought this trip was about one thing and now it's about something else. I don't mean to be cryptic, but do you know what I mean?"

"You mean it's not just about you being bored with me and your life?"

I hadn't realized how hard I'd been pressing the phone into my ear until I let it go just then, almost dropping it. I never thought I'd had the desire to jump out of a plane, to freefall, to want that release that exists only because you risk not coming back. But that's what I'd done and when Andy asked that question, it was like a parachute opening. I could catch my breath, look around, locate myself, and think: *Holy fucking shit.*

"It wasn't boredom. It's not boredom. I can't explain it very well. I wish I could, but I feel like I'm only just figuring it out in any way that makes any sense."

"Well, whatever it is, it makes me feel like shit, Viv."

"I'm so, so sorry."

"You keep saying that."

"Because I am."

"Yeah, I get that. I just. I don't know. I have to say I liked it better when Lee was out of our lives."

"Was she ever really, though?"

"She was out of mine, yes."

"Really?"

"Really."

"So there's no part of you that wishes it were you here with her, that she'd asked you to come with her instead? No part of you that thinks your life wouldn't be better if you were with her instead of me?"

The questions I had never asked, but that had been there all along, now tumbled out. Why did Lee choose me over Andy? Because it had seemed that she had, and sometimes, ever since, I found myself trying to suppress the thought that I was a substitute. That Lee had substituted me for Andy. And not just that, but that Andy had substituted me for Lee.

I wished I could see his face.

"I got over her a long time ago."

"Did you?"

"Yes. I did. And I kind of feel like I've been waiting for you to catch up. I thought this trip might help."

Andy, out there, ahead of me, waiting for me to catch up to him. Despite all of our plans, all of our commitments, I don't think I had ever thought of him quite that way. As the future. If only I had.

"I want to come home. I do. And I'm going to, as soon as I can. But I don't think I *can* until I help Lee now, because it's bigger, it seems like it could be bigger than just finding the old tapes. She's going to need someone to be there with her for whatever this turns into, I think. And right now, that person is me. What I mean is, this isn't about me or you. It's about her."

I expected an angry *It's always about her.* At least that's how I would have written it in a THATH scene.

"All right," he said.

"Okay."

"But when you get back, do we need to, like, start taking a cooking class together or get some drugs or whatever people do to spice things up?"

"No, we don't need to take a class. Or get drugs."

"Because we could. We could take a drug class."

"We don't need to take a drug class."

"You sure?"

"I love you."

"Viv?"

"What?"

"It sounded like you were going to tell me something else and then you stopped."

"No. I'll be back so soon. I promise."

I didn't say, "Please wait for me" or "There is more and I will find a way to tell you about it." *About something that happens all the time but that I didn't think would happen to me. And something else that also happens all the time so you almost forget how astounding a prospect it is, just even on a biological level. I think you and I can do this together. Ambivalence about it feels ungrateful, like asking for too much. I'm asking for too much. But that's what I'm asking for.*

I wiped my tears away and waited for my face to dry before getting back in the car with Lee.

From *The Talking Cure: Selected Interviews, 1967–1992* by Patti Driggs

*A*round 1990, I thought I might revisit the Jesse Parrish profile I wrote. It had been twelve years since his death and more than eighteen years since I had published what now strikes me as a prickly and perhaps ungenerous, though not inaccurate, portrait. That piece ended with these words about Jesse and his wife, Linda West:

> I can't tell if I'm bringing too much irony to bear on him or not enough. They are both performing something when it comes to their identities. Her Jewishness? His Southernness? By which I mean they are able to turn it on and off. I want to see this as fluid and liberating rather than a con. But I don't know how. Theirs is a language I can't quite speak, whose grammar I haven't mastered. Then again, I have never owned a caftan or purple velvet pants, never known the disappointment of their being at the cleaners.

For the new piece I had in mind, I wanted to hear more from the women who had been in Jesse's life. There were a number of them. They came across as accessories, in both senses of the word. Supporting players. And yet they each, in their own way, were greater than. I wanted to explore that. I went so far as to track down the reclusive Marion Washington, Jesse's girlfriend, who survived the car crash that killed him. She wouldn't speak with me, and ultimately I never followed through with this story. I did, however, conduct some preliminary interviews, including this conversation with Elise Robin, a friend and admirer of Jesse and Linda, and author of the widely read memoir Free Lunch: The Life and Times of a Rock and Roll Muse.

Patti Driggs: When did you first meet Jesse?

Elise Robin: I should remember. I should have the exact moment crystalized in my mind. But it's more like he was just there, always. And then he wasn't.

PD: Is this still hard for you?

ER: It is. I think it's always going to be hard. He was just such so special. Even our relationship, I don't know how to describe it, it didn't fit into any common category. It was platonic—he's like the one guy I *didn't* screw—and I guess you could say he was like a brother, but it was romantic. Everything about him was so romantic.

PD: What set him apart for you, why wasn't he like all the other guys?

ER: What set Jesse apart was his sweetness. He was just a real sweetheart, like a gentleman, like Cary fucking Grant. Like if Cary Grant were thirty years younger and magic and showed up at your door with powdered donuts and a big bag full of grass and took you to the last place on earth, or California, that had waitresses on roller skates. And he would talk to you like he had to know what you were thinking, no matter how far out it was.

PD: What were you thinking?

ER: I don't remember offhand, but I could go look in my overwrought diaries for you. It was scintillating, I'm sure. No, but really, Jesse was interested in me, as a person. Not like, what could he get out of me or what could I do for him. He always looked out for me. I remember we were at this party once—I'm not gonna name names here. I don't like trouble the way I used to. But this pretty famous musician was there, you can probably figure out who I'm talking about, and he comes up to me and he's doing his thing with his British accent and Jesse, kind of joking, was like, "Hey, slimeball." And this guy was like, "At your service." He *was* a slimy guy. He oozed. Jesse says, "Elise here sure is a knockout." And Slimy goes, "Will she lay me out flat?" Jesse says, "I expect she'll lay you however she likes. Or not at all. She leads with her heart." And the tone of it was like he was saying to this guy, "Know who you're dealing with,

don't mess with her." It wasn't territorial, it was protective.

PD: In a way that you appreciated? It sounds pretty objectifying.

ER: Oh, Patti, c'mon.

PD: I think it's a fair question.

ER: Well, look, I loved the scene I was in, but yeah, it could be pretty shitty, pretty frustrating as a woman. I didn't have the perspective I have on it now. But you know, I never burned my bra because I never wore one in the first place. For whatever that's worth. But with Jesse, at that party, I had this image of him kneeling down in front of me with a sword and swearing his loyalty to me, and I'm in one of those medieval dresses? Like he was my defender, but I was in charge.

PD: Did you ever see another side to him, that wasn't so sweet?

ER: Sure. I mean, he wasn't a cardboard cutout. He was an actual person. He could be a jerk. He could be a colossal asshole, too, don't get me wrong.

PD: How so?

ER: Well, like when he wanted Linda to get an abortion because he thought having a kid was going to fuck up his career. I mean, he didn't call it his "career." That's only how people talk now. I could see how he might feel that way, but he didn't even go to Linda first to talk about it. He went to his manager. Like his manager was gonna tell Linda not to have the baby? Well, it got back to Linda, of course. I think she was more angry about the manager thing than about anything else. I'm not suggesting she didn't want the baby, either. But I feel like she kind of dug in her heels after that?

PD: Were you close with Linda?

ER: Oh yes, I loved Linda. I loved her the way I loved young nuns in movies. That kind of sisterly adoration. She used to give me her clothes. We would be lounging on these sumptuous floor pillows—everything was so sumptuous—and all of a sudden she would get up and go to her closet and come back with the most exquisite scarf or some dynamite hat, a flowy white gown she had and she would tell me I had to have it.

PD: The two of you would play dress up.

ER: Patti, what do you want me to say? We would play dress up while the rest of the world was going to shit around us?

PD: I'm just trying to get a picture here.

ER: Well, it's not like this is all we did. But, yeah, this is how I remember her, us, then.

PD: You were a sort of charity project for her?

ER: No! She wasn't dumping her stuff on me. They were like treasures she was bestowing.

PD: I see.

ER: The thing is, everything was a treasure because it was hers. She was so real but also just beyond. She and Jesse both. They floored me. And I know I was starry-eyed and maybe I still am. But people say that like it's a bad thing, like the alternative is better? Give me the stars and their infinite sparkle! The stars and their star child.

PD: What was Jesse like, as a father?

ER: He was a wonderful father, despite everything. Once Lee was born, I mean, there was no question. He was in love.

PD: No question.

ER: Look, you can be ambivalent and still be in love. Story of my life, practically. But I went over there, pretty soon after they got back from the hospital and Jesse was holding Lee, kind of swaying with her. Really sweet, but also he looked a little like he'd just smuggled her in from someplace. Like he'd gotten away with something he couldn't quite believe. And he was letting me in on it. He couldn't take his eyes off her. And he said to me, "She's my girl. Dancing the moment she came out."

infrasonic

frequencies

∽

Lee, 2010

Sometimes I think, if I had a child," Lee said to Viv, "it would be a quarter him. It would bring him back in a way."

Lee put on *The Garden of Allah* because she wanted to hear her father's voice as she drove. Arresting as those Haseltine photos were, there was something removed and unknowable about them. She had seen pictures like that of herself, in a magazine or two—that was the art of it. No wonder a sociopath like Carnahan admired that quality. But there was nothing inaccessible in her father's voice. This album was the one she'd listened to the least. She hadn't wanted to hear her father losing it. But lately she'd come to understand why people—Andy—loved it so much. Andy had told her once that Jesse abandoned it before it was done and that Brian Reiger, the producer, had salvaged it, building and layering instruments and effects that balanced out Jesse at his most caustic and bitter. The production made it bearable. Still, it was painful.

"Yeah. I haven't really thought about it like that," said Viv, distracted, as if she'd been caught daydreaming in class. "My child will be a quarter Jonathan and a quarter Natalie. But also a quarter Tim and a quarter Nancy. Do you think that means a quarter of the time he or she will be emotionally distant and a quarter of the time ever so subtly making me feel like I'm not good enough for Andy?"

"I wouldn't underestimate heredity. Is Andy . . . when you talked to him . . . is everything okay?"

"I don't know. I think he understands. About trying to find Marion. The rest—I couldn't say on the phone."

Viv was going to have a baby. The great divide. The great multiplication, then the great divide. Viv didn't follow up. She didn't ask if Lee really did want to have a child. She didn't invite Lee into her world. As though this was one place she could go without her, where Lee didn't belong, or at least a place that Viv had gotten to first. Which wasn't entirely true, though Lee thought better of enlightening her now. It would only be spiteful and what good would it do. How betrayed would Viv feel, to learn that she and Andy had shared that? But, then, they hadn't shared it because Andy never knew anything either, that she'd been pregnant. How different would life be if he had? Completely? Not much at all?

They say it won't last, that you're too fast, but they don't know, how you come and go. It was "Hey, Linda." A song, presumably, for her mother. How did she do it? Lee wondered. Linda and her robust, industrious verve had mystified Lee for so long. She had tried to understand it, escape it, succumb to it, match it. But she had never thought to doubt it. It had occurred to her only lately, murkily at Flintwick's and then more clearly coming into focus in the old widow's walk where Carnahan kept those pictures of her father, that Linda's relationship to her own past may not have been so tidy as it seemed. That her mother's full-bodied, full-tilt charge ahead might be a defensive stance. An obfuscation of her history—obfuscation, yes, Lee had taken a class or two in college. A diversion. Eyes over here! Nothing to see that way. Move it along.

Ahead on the highway, she saw a billboard for a furniture store, the same one she'd seen years before, driving up and down this artery as an undergrad. The mustached trio of owner-brothers, their sectionals and dinettes, hadn't changed. Soon enough, they were on local roads, the periphery of the campus, on the tree-lined street outside the university-owned Queen Anne where the dean of alumni relations and Linda's former publicist lived. They parked, turning off the car stereo just before "Yours" (the song written for her, the one unambiguously lovely song on this troubled record) would have come on.

"The dean might not remember me," said Lee. Solely for effect, what you say, even when you know people always remember you. "But it's worth a shot. She'll probably recall Linda's generous donation in any case."

A red door, a curving, decorative brass knocker, and then: "Lee Parrish! How *are* you? What are you *doing* here?" The dean, beckoning them into her parquet foyer, wearing a black dress and leopard-print heels, her dark hair smooth with a bouncy salon finish. Ready for a dinner-dance in Boston where she would deliver a version of the speech that almost always ended with her exhorting her audience to "Contribute!" Her catchphrase.

They had come at just the right time, the dean explained. A few days later and it would be graduation: "Absolute delirium!" They likely wouldn't have caught her nor would she have had the chance to listen to Lee's story about how they just happened to be in town (*old friends, road trip, girl time!*) and how Viv, a fellow alum and feverish workaholic, could really use access to the library while they were here. The dean thought nothing of making a phone call to grant them temporary entry cards. Even putting them up in a guest suite.

"Ladies, I've gotta run," she said, putting on a jacket from Linda's spring collection. "By the way, this pulls everything together. Your mother remains a genius."

"That she does," said Lee.

This place. It all came back to Lee quickly, though now it was like wandering through a life-size diorama. The brick buildings with slate shingled roofs, each lifted out of a period drama, the archways that opened onto the main green, gas lampposts, leafy trees dappling the spring sunlight. They passed a carriage house refashioned for academic offices and a classroom, where she recalled discussing (or rather, sitting silently and listening while other people discussed) Baudrillard. It had never occurred to her that *this* feeling is what *that* was about and she wondered whether she was always going to catch on fifteen years after the fact.

Their room for the night was in one of the newer dormitories, furnished with a sofa and club chairs upholstered in a dated gray, turquoise, and magenta fabric. It reminded Lee of a photo shoot in which she was told to hike up her pencil skirt, put one high-heeled foot on a similar chair, lean into the actor who sat there in a suit, and pull him toward her by his tie. The high-low tableau of beautiful people in expensive clothes on a set art-directed to look like an office park where you didn't come to work so much as have anonymous sex. Which was perhaps a form of work itself. She had given them a range of expressions: hungry, playful, mirthless, I-know-better-than-you, Do-I-know-better-than-you?, Pride-in-a-job-well-done, and Nice-tie. The end result looked a lot like I-am-very-hungry-and-I-would-like-to-eat-your-tie.

They dropped their bags and set out across campus for the humanities library. The white building with the 1960s punch-card façade hadn't changed much—the bike racks and the brickwork sidewalks, the wide steps where she had first encountered Viv. But midcentury design had acquired a patina in the intervening years. Instead of seeming, as it once had, slightly dingy and outdated, it now seemed like a place with history. Which brought her own history back to her. It seemed to Lee as if she had watched the scene in a movie: two girls sitting out here one afternoon, one of them getting up and running away. Power-walking away. The way you can watch yourself in a dream. It was only a dreamlike logic that allowed her to make sense of the fact that she was standing here right now.

Across the street stood the tall, wrought iron gate that was opened twice a year, once for a snaking formation of nervous freshmen to pass through on their way to the main green for convocation and once for only slightly less self-conscious seniors to walk out of during commencement. In a few days, it would be time for that second ceremony. She had a vague memory of lining up to move through the gate as a freshman, meeting a group of friendly students who invited her to join them for a meal-plan dinner later. She did, and it was pleasant and they had a few laughs, but then they never saw much of one another after that. She didn't see some of them again until four years later, when Andy graduated and she and Viv still had a few semesters to go. They acknowledged each other on the green with minor smiles, as if to say, "That was you, right? Well. Good luck with the rest of your life!" Viv asked her in a politely lowered voice who those people were and she replied, "I never really knew."

How arbitrary it could all be. If she had gone to a different school. If she had never met Viv. If she had never met Andy. New York, after she had been away from it, often conjured Viv for her: the sun in the summer and the way it could cast a quietness over the streets, the subway lines that took you above ground, over the river or out to the beach. This place now started to seem less of a simulation of itself and began to conjure Andy.

Sometimes when Lee thought about Andy, she thought of the way Linda and Jesse described meeting each other: an instant attraction in a kitchen at a party. With Andy it wasn't exactly attraction but something similar. He was so easy to talk to. He reminded her a little of Alex Garcia, who would skip sixth period in high school to go lie with her on the floor of her bedroom and look up at the ceiling, the stereo on, saying whatever came into their heads. That Alex turned out to be gay didn't really surprise her. Isn't that, in a way, what had probably drawn her to him? She wondered about Andy. He didn't express an immediate, sexual interest in girls, but he didn't express much of an interest in guys, and she initially figured it wasn't that he was gay but that he was so into music, to an extreme, maybe to the exclusion of sex, with anyone.

A week or so into college, she heard *Motel Television* coming from his room, like a flare in the distance: *over here.* She thought about turning back down the hall. If she knocked and went in right then, she would have to tell him. It would be weird not to. But who knew how that would change things? She had recently begun to think about her father, about being her father's daughter, the way she thought about her looks. For much of her childhood, she hadn't *thought* all that much about either, she had just accepted that her life contained certain facts: her late father was Jesse Parrish and she was pretty. Linda sent her to a progressive private school where a majority of her classmates were the sons and daughters of famous people. She never felt particularly exceptional in that respect. While she knew that the way she looked gave her certain advantages, she had taken it for granted. She hadn't tried to manage or manipulate her beauty until she became aware that it had an effect on other people. It compelled them and sometimes alienated them and sometimes confused them. It could do all of that to her, as well. Like with Roy, when she was fifteen, when her legs were still a little too long for the rest of her body but her breasts were balancing it all out. Roy was what then? Linda's good friend, industry event date, and occasional lover? He was around a lot, in any case. And Lee, from the age of ten, when Linda first started seeing him, had liked him. He joked with her in a way that Linda never did, called her Robert E. or the General. General Store. General Vicinity. General Ization. And he lived on a ranch where he had chickens, horses, a llama or two, and even, briefly, a donkey he named Steven Bochco, after his one-time professional rival. She couldn't recall Linda ever being very involved with her school projects, but Roy knew what cuneiform script was and seemed genuinely interested in her report on ancient Sumer. He also once helped her construct, out of cardboard and cushioning balloons, a container that would protect an egg and keep it from cracking when dropped from a second-story window. All this changed the summer after she started high school. He still used those nicknames, but they had become clunky. Now they were reminders, souvenirs of an easier time, a time before she felt him looking at her and then quickly looking away when her eyes met his. Roy never made a pass at her, thankfully, but his restraint (never in doubt, yet never wholly without effort) left her self-conscious. She lost him, in a way, and she lost some remaining part of her innocence. There were, of course, other men who came into Linda's life without Roy's restraint. But by then she knew to expect it.

"Hey, can I come in?" she said.

"Yeah!" Andy said. "Get in here."

"I know this song."

"It's the perfect song," said Andy. "The whole record is fucking great. You like Jesse Parrish?"

She took her residence hall ID card out of her bag and, almost contritely, showed it to Andy, anticipating his embarrassment.

"Wow. You're *that* Lee."

"I'm that Lee."

"I should have known. I mean, it makes sense. I know who you are. I mean, I don't mean it like that, like I *know who you are* or I know all about you or anything. But. Like. Right."

He didn't tell her, just then, that he had read the biography Linda authorized and allowed herself to be interviewed for, as well as the other one, which she hadn't and which was less flattering though nevertheless obviously written by a Jesse Parrish enthusiast. Later, over time, he admitted that he'd watched various concert films and sent away to an address in Michigan for a compilation of fuzzy clips on VHS. He'd seen a picture of Lee as a toddler, curled up in her father's guitar case. Another one of her on Jesse's shoulders. But he'd seen images of Lee only as a child and he imagined she would be beautiful like Linda (and like Jesse) but not as troubling as her mother. He'd wondered whatever happened to that girl, who would be his age. And he'd even permitted himself to fantasize that if they ever had the chance to meet, they might get along. She might be the kind of person who would recognize something in him and might provide him the kind of understanding her father's music did. Far-fetched, all of this. Preposterous. But it's where his mind had gone on occasion, playing it out to a point where he might meet Linda West. Not that he was dying to meet her. He never quite grasped her appeal. Linda West had been all about sex, which he knew he was supposed to think was a good thing, those photographs of her in a sheer blouse with no bra, her nipples hard, but it also embarrassed him. He wasn't embarrassed, though, when he said this to Lee. Or maybe a little, but mostly, by that point, he was open, even brave with her, and she was the one who struggled to be as forthright and unashamed with him.

"Right," Lee said. They stopped talking for a minute. She looked at her hands, at her father's ring, at an elm tree outside the window. Then she asked him how his classes were going so far. He went into great detail about the scheduling conflict he was trying to work out during add/drop. It involved a film theory class he wanted to try and the fact that he'd taken AP calculus in high school so he should be able to enroll in the advanced math course that was more optimally timed. She thought that might have been the first time she ever heard someone use the word "optimally" in conversation. She wished him luck and, speaking of timing, said she had better be off to her late-afternoon survey on architecture and urbanism.

She wrote "Parthenon" and "Vitruvius" and "morphology" and "cobbler" in her notebook and when the lecture was over, she walked to the record store near campus and bought a copy of *Motel Television*. She had heard all of her father's music before. At eleven, she had listened to "Yours" over and over as though it contained a message for her from beyond the grave. Still, she'd never experienced the connection that Andy did. How a song, like nothing else, can possess you.

Linda had all of Jesse's output at home, of course, not just all of the albums and singles on vinyl but also eight-tracks, cassettes, and all the recently reissued CDs. But Lee hadn't brought any of it with her to college. That evening, while her roommate (a very nice girl she had very little in common with) was out at dinner, she put it on. As she listened to it, she imagined Andy listening to it, and she heard a heartbeat there that she hadn't picked up on before. She listened to it straight through and when her roommate returned, she apologized for being rude and then put on headphones, lay back on her narrow bed, and listened to it again. If this is what people were going to project onto her, was that so bad? She had read an interview once with a young actress, the daughter of a more famous actress. No disrespect to her mother, who was her greatest champion (and whom she spoke of as one might a lighthouse or the Statue of Liberty—shining and exemplary but sexless and not in competition with her), said the young actress (whose career would later tank), but you want people to like and respect you for *you,* and she often found that hard to come by. Lee was beginning to understand this. She'd been somewhat sheltered from this growing up in the world that she had. Most of the kids she knew were more or less like her in this regard. Lee wanted people to like her—or *not* like her—for who she was, only she wasn't really sure who or what that was.

Days later, she approached Andy in a corner of the quad, and they both pretended they hadn't been avoiding each other.

"Do you know what you need?" she asked him.

"Uh, no. What?"

"You need to come with me tonight."

She took him to a party that an older girl she knew from high school had invited her to. A house off-campus throbbing with people. Entering it was like making your way inside a dark, warm muscle as it contracted and released. The pulsating absorbed her so she became part of it. Which is what she wanted, to move with it and not to think. She wasn't so sure about Andy. She could sense him not wanting to get separated from her. She didn't really think he was going to dance. She knew he was going to stand there and she would dance and he would watch her. Which he did. And then she would pull him in and he would be hesitant, reluctant, but she would make him stay and dance with her until he lost himself. Which he never quite did. She couldn't tell if he looked bored because he thought that's how you were supposed to look in a place like this, or if he actually *was* bored.

"Do you want to go?" she shouted.

"What?" he shouted back.

She took his hand and pushed their way through until they had expelled themselves back onto the street.

"Sorry," he said. "It's not really my scene."

"Oh, you have a scene?"

"Yeah. I've got a scene."

"What's your scene?"

"I'd say it's centered around long, uncomfortable pauses. And a very close relationship with my right hand."

"Did you take something?" Almost laughing, almost proud of him.

"Yes, but I don't know what the fuck it was. Can you get me back to my bed please?"

"Yeah. Of course."

He couldn't find his room key. So she took him back to her bed, where he fell asleep before either of them had made enough noise to wake her roommate. She thought better of getting in there next to him, letting him wake up with her in his arms and misleading him more—misleading herself. She took a pillow and lay down on the floor.

They woke Sunday morning to the first fall-like day of the year. A bright blue sky and a few gentle cumulous clouds. A day made for wrought iron gates and piles of leaves and wool sweaters and apple cider, the kind of New England fantasy Lee had growing up in Los Angeles. A day that demanded, at the very least, a walk. The coolness of the air seemed to do Andy good, though they walked slowly, aimlessly, more in recuperation than invigoration. They stopped for hot chocolate (on the idealized beverage equivalency scale, in the same class as apple cider, which proved to be elusive in reality), taking it with them as they continued across campus and up along streets of old houses with small historic plaques and sizable yards. Then they cut east, downhill, toward the stadium.

"I used to play football," said Andy.

"You did?"

"Yeah, varsity."

"Really? So, do you have, like, a varsity jacket?"

"I do."

Lee laughed.

"Is that funny?"

"No, it's not funny. I don't know why I laughed. I just had no idea. You're like a scholar athlete."

"Well, I'm not much of an athlete anymore. It was just something I did growing up. It wasn't a big deal in my town. I broke my arm junior year and I was out all season and that was it."

"But you were kind of a jock."

"Yeah. It was very character-building."

"Do you miss it?"

"Sometimes. Sometimes I miss being on a team. I wouldn't exactly say I'm a joiner, and I always kind of want to think of myself as a lone wolf, but I'm not. Can I tell you something?"

"Of course."

"This is weird. That we're here, walking around, and a month ago I was just, like, in my room."

"Is that a Beach Boys reference?" One of maybe five Beach Boys songs, including "Kokomo," she knew just by osmosis, just from living in the world. But she figured Andy would appreciate it.

"I guess it is. Everything is a reference now. But do you know what I mean?"

She did. It meant she would have to stop with the superficialities and they would have to talk about her parents.

"I know these things about you and about your life," he said. "So I feel like I know where you're coming from, but maybe I have no idea."

"I have no idea either, sometimes. So."

Andy was staring at his feet as he walked, as if to hide some frustration with her. As if he had risked something and she hadn't.

"I'm not being glib. What I'm trying to say is you love my father. He clearly means a lot to you. You obviously know who my mother is. But what I'm trying to say is that *I* really don't know who they are. I've listened to *Motel Television* I don't know how many times in my life and, honestly, I never really heard it until about a week ago. So maybe you do know where I'm coming from, even if I don't."

"What did you hear when you heard it?"

"Oh, the things people talk about. Haunting. Heartbreaking." She knew she wasn't close to arriving at what it was she actually heard. "What do you hear?"

"It depends. It changes. But what I love about that record, in particular, is that there's such a prettiness to his singing but you can feel this edge to it, like he's trying to keep it from curdling into something else, something kind of vindictive. And the music, half the time, is already there, over that edge, if it's not loping toward it. I think I just really admire the effort, how pretty he wants it to be, and then I just love the failure, when he gives over to everything underneath. The production on that album was genius. It adds this sheen to everything and that probably made it go down easier. It's so easy to listen to. Like, the last song, "Waves," it's basically a lullaby, right? It might as well be spooning you, the take that's on the album. But have you ever listened to the demo version? They put it in the box set but before that it was an extra track on the bootleg of his 1972 tour. It's the same melody but the arrangement—there is no arrangement really. It's just Jesse and it's really intimate and, I don't know, like, *wounding*. It's kind of a precursor to the stuff on *The Garden of Allah*. When things got really troubled."

Andy being spooned. Like he had any experience with that. He still had never mentioned a girl. But she hadn't yet mentioned any of the boys she'd known either. None of whom she'd ever spooned.

"I should stop talking," he said.

"No."

But he did. So did she. The long, uncomfortable pause that was "his scene." Only it wasn't that uncomfortable. Their silence contained a reverberation, as though they were still communicating on a low, infrasonic frequency. They picked up on each other's vibrations. His: *I want to keep walking with you.* Hers: *Yes.*

WHEN LEE AND Andy sat across from each other in a café, books splayed, she would think, *I shouldn't touch my lips like that or let my hair fall into my face* and then she would touch her lips and let her hair fall in a way that most likely made him want to touch her lips and brush her hair back. She didn't know why she did that with Andy. More to the point, why she did that and then found herself encouraging him toward other girls.

"Like what about Sarah or Porter down the hall?" she asked.

"Moose and Chipmunk?" he said. "No."

She figured it was her role to discourage his negativity, but she just couldn't. Moose and Chipmunk. His negativity was perfect. She asked herself, *Why not Andy?* There was a night, out walking with him, when he took her hand. He wasn't even tentative. He just took it, and she let him. As long as she did, they were suspended, safe, moving along in a hypnotic state. It brought them to wherever they were going and then she must have let go. Neither of them ever mentioned it afterward. Soon she started sleeping with Jeremy from her playwriting workshop, effectively establishing a pattern later borne out in her relationship with slimy-yet-seductive Bruce.

She thought the whole thing with Bruce and Mind Faith might have finally dulled Andy's feelings for her, but he was still there for her when she came back to school. He practically took her in. Though she didn't know what she would have done if he hadn't been there, she was also annoyed at that fact. It made her want to lash out at him and then feel guilty about it; take up with Noah Stone in a sexless relationship. A penitent one. Like a nun.

Noah tried. He said he wanted to but he almost never could. She would lie there while he went down on her and think: *This is nice and it's enough.* But then there was a month or so when he had a lot of dental work done and barely touched her and finally she felt the not-very-nunlike frustration of it. That night at his place, the night of that party, when all he wanted to do was hold her and fall asleep, she couldn't take it any longer.

"Did you not have fluoride in your water? What's the deal with your teeth?"

"It's my gums, actually. And it's not that."

She didn't feel entitled to an explanation from him and felt even worse that he trusted her enough to offer one: his antidepressants. She hadn't thought Noah had enough emotional range to be depressed. Even as he told her this, she still didn't see him as an entirely real person. He held her after he shared this with her and she ran her fingers along his face until he fell asleep. Then she got out of the fortlike bed he'd constructed from lumberyard scraps. She didn't know for sure but she thought maybe Andy was secretly still a virgin and maybe she would be doing him a favor. That's how she'd justified it when she pulled him up off that mattress, taking him away from Viv and over to the sofa in the room they called the study. But he probably wasn't a virgin because it seemed like he knew what he was doing, the way he touched her as though he was guiding her and not the other way around. When she came, she wasn't thinking about anyone else and then she looked down and saw he still had on that T-shirt with the seahorse and she thought: *Oh. No.*

IF SHE HAD once been irritated with Andy for some reason she could never quite understand, taking her free-floating anger out on him, soon it seemed as if all that was left between them was a sadness she had created. She could never bring herself to tell him what it was, that she had been pregnant, could never bring herself to tell any of them. Even when Noah had picked her up after her appointment at the clinic, he apparently believed she just had this "ovary thing" to take care of. Viv had no idea, though she'd seen her go off with Andy the night of that party. Viv's eye through the crook of her elbow.

Viv probably assumed Lee had had several abortions by now. Viv was someone you thought was unassuming, until you got to know her and you realized she assumed so many things. Had Lee told her at the time, Viv would have offered support and understanding. Still, something, something less than judgment, less than disapproval or disappointment—knowledge—would have been there ever after, would have become part of who Lee was to her friend. Viv would have seen it as one more way in which Lee had more experience, was somehow deep in a way Viv envied. Maybe this is how Lee wanted to think of it herself. For a while she had clung to her abortion as a private identifier, something that belonged to her.

That job out of college, when she went to work at the reproductive rights center—she tried to convince herself that that was where she fit. But she didn't, any more than she had fit in Bruce's chapter of Mind Faith. Not any more than she would fit in the world of luxury brand ambassadorship.

She would come home sometimes and hear, in the hall by the front door, the sound of Viv and Andy watching a movie, talking or laughing. It surprised her that her instinct wasn't to insert herself between them, to claim one of them as her own. Instead, she would head back down the stairs and find another place to be. It got easier later that year, when Andy started seeing the awful Lisette. (Who probably wasn't even that awful, in retrospect.) With Lisette came a certain alleviation, and then Andy graduated, and then it was just Lee and Viv.

Though she kept things from Viv, she never felt she had to hide from her friend. To pretend she wasn't, on a good day, moody, and on a bad day, sometimes panicky. What Viv was able to do was take Lee out of herself. She provided a focus. Viv's surprising self-absorption came as a relief to Lee—because the absorption extended beyond Viv's self. Lee once described their college relationship to Barbara, her therapist, in terms of paper towel commercials. Lee was the blue liquid that tore through weaker sheets and Viv was the strong, fibrous brand that could soak up big spills. Barbara laughed and asked if ads for bladder control garments weren't perhaps even more on point, cementing Lee's respect for her.

INSIDE THE LIBRARY, Lee and Viv sat down at a computer station to see what, if anything, they might find on Marion before they visited Patti Driggs during her office hours the next morning. Viv assumed the air of a focused secretary. Her keystrokes were like heels down a corridor. Lee loved how seriously Viv was taking this, using words like "cross-reference" as she called up various public records, searching for any scrap of information on the whereabouts of Marion Washington. A number of Marion Washingtons popped up but, upon further digging, each of them turned out to be wrong.

"Remember microfiche?" said Viv.

"No, not really."

"You never used it?"

"Nope."

"Did you ever even write a paper? I don't think I ever remember you writing a paper."

"I wrote papers. I even took exams."

"What did you major in? I can't remember that either."

"American Civilization."

"What is that, really?"

"An oxymoron. Just kidding. God bless the USA."

"I'm sorry. Of course you wrote papers."

"Well, I was never the most diligent student. I didn't have the best models. Linda never went to college. She just took some business classes. Jesse dropped out of undergrad after a semester."

Viv nodded, half-listening while she focused on the screen in front of them and opened up several digital archives of old newspapers and periodicals.

"You should have finished your Ph.D."

At this, Viv stopped typing.

"Why do you say that?"

"You're, like, in your element here."

"The library is my element?"

"I just mean, you've always been kind of scholastic. You're really into researching stuff."

"Well, sure, and if that's all a Ph.D. was, then maybe I would have gotten one. But it also involves a lot of bullshit political maneuvering that I didn't want to engage in. And I think I've been much happier writing for THATH. But thank you for making me feel like Edward Casaubon."

Lee didn't know who that was. But she knew saying as much would only further the opposition here: Lee as breezy hedonist, Viv as studious pedant.

"I wasn't aware it was still a sore spot, Viv. Sorry."

"I wasn't aware it was either. It's being back at a place like this, I guess."

"It makes me glad that we're not here anymore, that we're not twenty-one or whatever. That it's a long time ago already. But I also can't understand where it all went."

"I know."

Lee couldn't quite bring herself to tell Viv that the other day, in the car, driving to see Flintwick, when she told Viv that the low point of the past few years was standing in the supermarket aisle, stirred to tears by an MOR evergreen—that that was the kind of sad and pathetic story you share precisely because it doesn't reveal much beyond an awareness of your ordinary inability to resist the near-universal sentimentality of pop music. Who isn't sad and pathetic in that way? She'd told Viv a little bit about her depression, about what she might have inherited from her father, the sketchy relationship the Parrishes historically had with mental health. But she had described this as a concern, not a comfort, when really it was both. She had noticed, living in Los Angeles and driving more, that she sometimes found herself in a fog at the wheel. She was operating at a deficit. Her inclination wasn't to pull over and collect herself, but to just drive on through and let whatever might happen happen. She'd wondered if her father had ever experienced something similar, something that may have been taken, romantically, for recklessness. Maybe recklessness was just a passionless disregard for yourself and others. In New York, where she didn't have a car, this fuzziness had sometimes led to poor decision-making with men. It resulted in a couple of qualified performance reviews at her nonprofit office job. But once she left for modeling in Paris, where she understood about sixty-five percent of what people said to her, her slightly erratic, distracted behavior was rewarded, if not encouraged. There are contexts where liabilities become assets. Her father had known this. Flintwick had called it pathological, his need to be a star, but what else was Jesse supposed to do with his excess of charisma?

French people loved Lee. She always showed up for work and she could be counted on, but she wasn't all there, suggesting she was absorbed in something fascinating beyond what was in front of her. She gave in to her absentmindedness instead of trying to focus and make sense of what was happening around her. She was told this came through in her photographs.

Toward the end of a shoot once, a producer stepped forward and said, in English: "Okay, that's all, fucks!" And Lee, brought back to attention, had said, *"What?"*

"Porky Pig! Looney Tunes?"

"Oh. Oh! That's all, *folks.* I thought you said something else."

"I did!"

Lee erupted as though something much funnier had just occurred, and the photographer took a few more pictures before pronouncing her "so wonderful." From then on, "That's all, fucks" became an expression she often said to herself.

There was a point, however, at which she couldn't easily be pulled out of her not-there-ness. A point at which it could become less than charming. She never reached this point in Paris, but she'd been there before, in college, and she was there again.

Had it been the same way for her father? Was *The Garden of Allah* what that sounded like? Or did it sound like whatever was on the tapes that had gone missing? Finding the tapes might provide an answer but what did she really think that answer would do for her? What was really sad and pathetic, so much so that she couldn't even bring herself to tell her therapist, was this search for something she knew she wasn't going to find. Because it was all in the past. And everything everyone has ever said about that: *You can't go home again. Don't look back. Getty over it.* Searching for these tapes, as if they would reveal something to her about herself. What could they possibly reveal other than her own delusion? Once, against her better judgment, she had attended a Jesse Parrish tribute concert to benefit a cause she no longer remembered. She did remember encountering backstage two old rock crones in leather jackets. Garish hair. Pendants resting atop puckering cleavage. Heavy rings on their fingers. There was something who-gives-a-fuck fabulous about them, which they must have known. But you would never, ever want to be them, which they also must have known. Like the shrine she and Viv had visited in upstate New York. Anything can become a caricature of itself.

Using her father as a reason to pull Viv back into her life, or push herself into Viv's, was sad and pathetic. She had gotten as far as admitting to Barbara, in that contemplatively lit office high up in a residential tower on the Upper East Side, water towers in the distance, that she missed the way Viv had idealized her. It used to make her feel possessed of some lasting, captivating power. Viv must have seen *something* in her. *The way Viv attached herself to me, as though she might really start going places now that she had me as a friend, as though her life might begin and it was almost like I kept waiting for her to realize she bet on the wrong horse.* Barbara said: I think it's interesting that Viv, as you've described her, never seemed all that envious of you, of all that you had or had been given. And Lee thought, *No, Viv didn't really seem envious, more like pleased to have been let in on it. The more I gave her, the more I got—I fed off her adherence to me.* Barbara said: You tend to talk about your relationship as if you're somehow the bad one, as if you're bad for Viv. Lee: You don't think that's the case? Barbara: I'd like to hear why *you* think that's the case.

Lee didn't tell Viv about any of this.

Viv found various accounts of Marion's relationship with Jesse and the accident but nothing about what had happened to her since. One article by a conspiracy theorist proposed that while there was a crash, there was never any accident, that Marion and Linda had plotted to kill Jesse and carried the whole thing out together, *Diabolique*-style. The writer presented it as a given that the wife and the mistress wanted to do away with Jesse mostly because they were women and women did things like this. It made Lee sick and uneasy—not the accusation itself, but the tone of psychotic familiarity. Along with the caveat: "Full disclosure: I've never met Linda or Marion. I don't know what they're like, personally." As though he very well could meet them, and it wasn't an issue of access but of timing or disinterest on his part. As if he were too busy doing so many other important things. As if Linda, Jesse, and Marion weren't his betters.

They wrapped it up and went for fried egg sandwiches and spinach pie smothered in red sauce at the coffee shop they used to go to all the time, after Andy graduated and she and Viv latched on to each other. Still the old striped awning, maybe a fresher coat of green paint on the woodwork around the front windows. How often had they sat here, at the laminate-topped tables? They must have usually been part of a group because this is where everyone in their set ended up, but in Lee's mind, they didn't have a set. It was just the two of them, sitting at the counter. The owner's daughter would let them turn the radio to the state school station, which in Lee's memory was forever playing *Taking Drugs to Make Music to Take Drugs To*. Moments from so many late nights spliced themselves together.

Viv: "My grandmother thinks my voice is sexy."

Or: "I felt weird bringing popcorn into a documentary about Herbert Marcuse. Nobody else was eating anything."

Or: "It was a good thing I stayed in. I got to see that episode of *Melrose Place* where Kimberly checks Peter into the hospital to give him a lobotomy."

Or: "He told me he was glad I was editing his article because I'm kind, patient, and gentle."

"Those are good things to be," Lee had said. She couldn't remember who the "he" in question was. Someone who worked on the same school publication as Viv? Someone who was sort of a dick but who Viv sort of had a crush on?

"Yeah, but there was something so condescending about *him* saying it or else it was the way he said it. It made me want to say, *Shut the fuck up, you pompous fuck. Like I'm only here to balance you out with my docility.* I didn't say it, though. I just kind of raised my eyebrows then smiled. All kind, patient, and gentle."

And: "Why can't I talk to him? Why do I turn into a big, boring piece of rubber? He's smart and he's nice and he looks so smoochable."

"Everyone here is smart and more or less nice and more or less smoochable. It's something else, something you can't measure in those terms."

Lee couldn't articulate what else *it* was. She knew only that it felt a lot like this: sitting with someone and wanting to keep sitting with them, to keep hearing what they said.

She half expected to see people they knew here now, which was irrational. The people they did see looked so very, very young. The owner had passed away, the owner's daughter was out, her son said, as he handed them menus. She and Viv really had to stop this reunion tour of greasy spoons. Though the food was fine, same as ever, the whole experience was like using the little toilet at an elementary school: familiar, workable, but mostly uncomfortable. Lee had thought that while they were here in Providence, they might visit their old house, the footbridge over the highway, the park by the water where they used to sit and look out. But on further consideration, it seemed wiser to spare themselves all of that.

They paid their check and walked outside. From up the street came laughter and voices out of the dark. A guy shouting "Booooom!" and a girl going "Aaaahhh, fuck you, Kevin. You scared the fuck out of me, dude." Lee tried to remember, from her own experience, why teenagers liked to be loud on street corners. Nothing occurred to her. But as she and Viv went back to their room, she was glad for the noise, for all the space the loudness occupied. She didn't feel like talking anymore tonight.

"YES, COME IN." Tiny Patti Driggs sat at a big desk in a room that might once have belonged to a couple of maids when the arts building, with its marble entrance hall and grand staircase, had been a stately home. Lee could almost see them, two girls looking out of the leaded window, beyond the terraced garden, down at the small city below. Thinking of bigger cities they could run off to. Patti had lived in those cities and now she was here. She took her eyes off what she had been reading, removed her glasses, and blinked up at them. "Do I know you?"

Before Lee spoke, Patti stood, instantly energized, a spider scuttling across its web. All in black, she appeared ready to take the stage with a mime troupe. Her bob was serious. She smelled clean and citrusy. Her wine-colored lipstick feathering into the little lines around her mouth was the only hint of weakness about her. Linda could have recommended a good product to keep the color in place, and Lee could just glimpse such an exchange happening: the détente between two old enemies whose former allegiances no longer meant anything because their sides no longer existed, but whose shared singular history made them, in effect, comrades.

"I *do* know you."

"I'm Lee. Lee Parrish."

"Yes, you are. I've seen your picture. Pictures."

Lee wasn't sure what to make of this. But then, Patti Driggs had written a book about photography. Copies of it lined a shelf on a wall full of other books. Photographic prints, one of which had the meticulous formal qualities Lee recognized as David Haseltine's, covered the other wall.

Patti waited for Lee to say something.

"If this isn't a good time—"

"Have a seat. It's a fine time. I think. Though that may depend on why you're here."

Lee and Viv took the pair of dark wood spindle chairs facing Patti.

"I didn't mean to surprise you," Lee started, "but I wasn't sure if you'd be willing to see me, and I was hoping to ask you about something . . . Excuse me, this is my friend, Vivian. Feld."

"Vivian Feld. Why do I know *that* name?"

"Small world? I knew your son," ventured Viv. "Briefly."

"Yes, well, women tend to know Ben briefly."

Viv stifled a laugh. Patti wasn't laughing. Because she wasn't terribly outspoken or performative, Viv could give the impression of being quiet or shy. But she wasn't. She was more socially skilled than she gave herself credit for. She could keep people talking. She seemed to be collecting material she continually collated into an ever-evolving manual for how to live. "It was a long time ago," Viv continued. "But he's married now, isn't he? I saw the announcement in the *Times*."

"That announcement is going to outlive the marriage. They used to call that sort of thing fishwrap. Now everything lives on forever, doesn't it?"

It sometimes seemed to Lee that they were all engaged in a kind of generational cold war. It was clear who would win (had already won) but what a hollow victory. Is that what their parents had wanted? For their children to live in their shadow? It would seem that Patti had only vanquished herself. Once appealingly tart, she had completely soured.

"Listen to me." Patti softened a bit. "It's not even ten-thirty and I'm in full hypercritical bloom. Let's blame it on end-of-semester stress. Tell me, what can I do for you?"

"It's a long story. But I would really like to find Marion Washington. I haven't had much luck tracking her down. We happened to be close to campus and I thought, I don't know, maybe you might know something, having been a part of that world."

"That world, yes. What do you want with Marion?"

"I'd just like to talk to her about my father and their time together, whatever she remembers of it."

Patti inhaled through her nose, her mouth a thin, imperfect line. In her eyes that quick inner spider nimbly went to work.

"I never quite got Marion. But then I never quite got Jesse either, much as I wanted to. Much as people thought I did. Linda, though, I understood. Every now and then, I think, if I'd been just a little more imaginative at the time, a little less convinced of my own perspective, *she's* the one I should have written about. The more interesting subject. Though I'm sure, in retrospect, she's more than happy I gave her short shrift. I didn't paint the most flattering portrait of your parents. I did a very good job of using them, though. Maybe you hold that against me. Maybe this is what it feels like when one's chickens come home to roost. Though maybe I'm projecting, and that bad blood seems like ancient history to you."

"My mother still thinks of you as her nemesis."

"Nemesis! That's a little strong. I didn't realize I was anyone's nemesis. I should be honored anyone cares that much." Lee couldn't help but think that Patti knew exactly how much Linda cared.

"But I've always been partial to that Faulkner line," Patti continued. "'The past is never dead. It's not even past.' I'll admit my first thought, on seeing you standing in front of me, after the instant it took me to realize who you were, is that you'd come seeking revenge on Linda's behalf. Or even your own."

Revenge? Lee had read Patti's much-lauded essay about Jesse, with its brief, condescending inclusion of Linda, but she hadn't thought it was all that riveting or all that revealing or all that *anything,* really. Not enough to warrant vengeance. Like Linda, she didn't quite get why everyone thought Patti was so great.

"I'm the first to grant that it was damning, that piece I did on

Jesse. But that was a defense mechanism, me trying to hide my in-fatuation with him. If you read it again, you might find it to be one of the most fawning profiles ever committed to the page. I have my regrets. But it's a time capsule now. Linda has lived a lot of life since then. As have I. Marion, too, I'm sure.

"I had the same impulse as you, some years ago, to find Marion. Mine may have been more journalistic, more essayistic, though may-be that's just what I told myself. There had to be some more valid reason to legitimize my lingering interest in Jesse. It couldn't just be an obsessive schoolgirl crush on a dead man. I also thought a profile on Marion might truly be fascinating. Marion and Linda and the other women in Jesse's life. I'd just finished writing my second novel, and I was tired of being in my own head. Ready to get back to something more reportorial. It was about a dozen years after the crash. The world was already a different place, and Marion wasn't in it much from what I could tell. But I did some digging, connected some dots, and I found her. She wasn't going by Marion Washing-ton anymore. She had changed her name to Marion Morris and was living in Big Sur. She became a psychologist. I called her up at her practice in Carmel, and she was cordial enough but she didn't want to talk to me. Can I ask you what it is you'd like to know? What do you hope to get out of talking to Marion?"

Lee's guard went up. "What did *you* hope to get out of talking to her?" Lee challenged. Patti seemed mildly amused to have the tables turned on her.

"I wanted a story. I also wanted a little bit more of Jesse."

"That's what I want, too. A little more of my father."

Patti softened for a moment, in her eyes, her posture. The gaze she'd directed at Lee became more searching, less critical. As if she'd initially been looking at Lee to find exactly what she expected and now she wasn't sure what that was.

"I hope you have more luck with Marion than I did."

"Thank you for the information."

"You're welcome." Patti, to judge from her writing, had never been much for sentimentality. To feel strongly about things in a negative, critical way was all right in Patti's world, but to express the positive was to make yourself susceptible. Patti checked herself. "Speaking of fishwrap, I read an article recently about Linda and her company, her wildly successful move into e-tailing, or whatever you call it. She's done very, very well for herself. I always knew she would. I should consider myself lucky she still harbors such strong feelings about me. It doesn't seem right to ask you to say hello to her for me, though." Patti eyed her one more time then turned to Viv.

"What about you, Vivian? Shall I give Ben your regards?"

"WELL, *THAT* WAS something," said Viv. "I almost want to call up Ben Driggs Stern now and ask him how I can help. Do you know, when we were dating, he showed her a short story I'd written and she told him it reminded her of her own work, when she was starting out. I thought she was dismissing it as derivative, but he said, no, that was high praise coming from her. That she was always looking for her own reflection but she didn't often find it."

They were outside on a bench below Patti Driggs's office. Though Lee wanted to run with what Patti had just told them, what she wanted more was to sit there for a moment and let the sun warm her face and her bare arms.

"Why don't you write anymore?"

"I do. I write all the time."

"I don't mean for THATH."

"I don't know. At a certain point you have to grow up and let these things go."

"What's so grown up about letting it go?"

"There's only so much time in a day. There are certain realities in life you have to accept, you know? Maybe you don't know."

"I understand realities, Viv."

"I know you do. I'm sorry. I'm just being defensive about it."

"I wish you didn't have to be. You have something that engages you."

"Maybe if I go with you to find Marion in Big Sur it'll inspire me. Bring out my inner Henry Miller."

An image came to Lee—nano-sized Henry Millers inside of everyone. Like that movie where Dennis Quaid was a miniaturized Air Force lieutenant injected into Martin Short's blood stream and zaniness ensued. Had she spent her whole childhood watching TV and movies on TV? Or did her mind just always go there and, if so, what did that say about her mind?

"Would you really come with me to Big Sur?"

She had wondered how to ask this of Viv. That is, she knew *how* to ask—the same way, more or less, she'd asked anything of Viv, including, from the very beginning, asking her to join a cult. It was like whatever she asked was always directly in line with Viv's id. Even when they first met on those library steps. Her one and only Reach Out! Viv had fled, but not very far. The question now wasn't *how* but *why*? Why ask Viv to come with her? Why had she encouraged Viv to come with her in the first place? And put Viv in that kind of position with Andy. And called Rodgers Colston. And when she saw where it was going with Rodgers, why didn't she do anything to stop it? Barbara had asked why she thought she was the bad one. *Because look at what I do. I don't know how to let someone know I need them and I don't know how to say goodbye.*

Viv would go back to her life with Andy and she would tell him she was pregnant and she wouldn't tell him about Rodgers, or she would, but it wouldn't tear through them; they would give with it, like the reasonable people they were together. The reasonable duo they had formed. Viv may have romanticized a certain destructive urge in others, Lee above all, but when it came to her own life she was too level-headed and honestly too lazy to behave like that herself. Andy was the same way.

WHEN VIV CALLED her after that snowstorm, it had all seemed obvious and inevitable. Lee expected she would go through the motions of feeling happy for her two friends at their wedding. That's what you did at weddings. She didn't expect that she *would* feel happy—not just happy for them but for herself. As if Viv and Andy were actually beaming love. Transmitting it to her. She'd experienced a similar surprising sense of belonging a few days earlier, doing a practice run styling Viv's hair. When she'd first read Kirsten's tutorial on "loose, romantic waves," she'd thought, *What the* fuck*? This was Kirsten's life now? This was Viv's?* But then she couldn't stop paging through all of Kirsten's posts on brow pencils and "splurgy pjs." The girlishness of it, which initially put Lee off, drew her in. It wasn't something that excluded her, but something she and Viv could share.

She found herself gently squeezing Jack's hand when Viv and Andy said their vows. And Jack, who'd been through a bitter divorce and custody battle over his young daughter, squeezed back. Viv's parents had walked their daughter down the aisle and, in what had always struck Lee as a bit of regressive parlance, given her away. But Lee felt that she too had given Viv away that evening. By the time Viv and Andy got married, Lee had been back in L.A. for almost a year and it was so much easier to be far from the place where Viv and Andy had made a home together. She hadn't exactly left because of them but, after that snowstorm, she'd had an inkling that time was about to be up.

Her fizzy happiness boosted by champagne carried her along through the toasts—she kept hers simple, spoke of hearing their laughter through the door, left out the part about turning away from it—through the buffet dinner and on to the dancing. She hadn't known Jack was such a good dancer and then she remembered that years ago he'd been in that Hitler youth/swing dancing movie where his character had fallen in love at the dancehall with a sure-footed Jewish girl. She couldn't remember if big band music saved either of them in the end. But Jack must have learned from the choreographer on set how to move his body in a conscious, muscular way that looked, and felt, effortless, light as watercolor. She was aware that people were looking at them while trying to appear that they weren't looking at them. Which she had experienced before, and it was amplified here because of Jack, who had reached that level of fame where even if everyone didn't know exactly who he was, they knew he was *someone*. Even with his Chekhov beard.

All her life Lee had heard about the great love her parents had. A tumultuous love of such elemental force that it bound them to each other always even when it couldn't keep them together. She had wondered if she would ever have anything that compared. Maybe falling in love was effortless and light, but love itself was something else. Maybe she'd had that something else and hadn't recognized it. With Andy. With Viv, too, in a way. Maybe she wouldn't have what Linda and Jesse had but here, dancing with Jack, she was outside the realm of comparison. So far outside that she didn't dwell on the unsettled expression she happened to catch on Linda's face in between songs—an expression that quickly hid itself behind a standard teary-eyed smile.

Later in the night as the party thinned, she spotted Andy out in the stone courtyard. A hearty aunt in a black sequined dress that looked like jazzy mourning garb had just said goodbye. He was momentarily alone, standing by the dying flames of the fire pit. The cake cutting was over. He looked dazed and pleased.

"Hey," she said.

"Hi," he said.

"This was all so wonderful."

"I'm glad you could make it." She knew it was late in a very long day and that he must have been tired of making conversation, but: *Glad she could make it?* The kind of thing you say to anyone. Wasn't she a *part* of it? She had cleared her calendar a year ago and flown in days early.

"I never knew that, what you said before, about standing by the door. I never thought of you as a standing-by-the-door type."

"Sometimes you see things happening between two people. I don't know that you were falling in love then, but it was that thing where you think it's going to make you jealous to see it, but it actually makes you kind of hopeful. You know?" A revision. A lie, in other words.

"I mostly think of those days as me being hung up on you." There was no melancholy in his voice, no hint of anything other than having so thoroughly moved beyond that time in his life that he now considered it a youthful folly. How ridiculous he'd been, moping over her. How different he was now. She had no hold on him. Which was fine, totally how it should be. So why did it bring her up short?

"Jack seems cool."

"He is. It's early, I guess, but I really like him."

"I hope it works out for you guys." He said it as if he knew it probably wouldn't but wanted to be charitable. As if he felt sorry for her. For whatever it was about her that made things not work out. The iridescent bubble she had floated over here on just popped.

"That's very nice of you, Andy."

"I mean it. I hope it works out. I want that for you."

"Because we're still such good friends."

"The way I see it, you're the one who stopped being my friend. Not that you were even that great of a friend to begin with, but you know, I never minded that. Because in a way, you were never just my friend. And it's not like I expected we'd fuck and that would change everything and all of a sudden we'd be together, but I didn't think you would basically ignore me afterward. I thought that whatever it was, it had meant more than that. But you made it pretty clear that it didn't."

"But it *did.* I was so stupid and messed up then. I made everything so weird between us and I didn't know what to do about it. I'm sorry. I really am sorry." She couldn't tell him in full why it was never the same. Not on his wedding day. Not with Viv in her ivory gown, yards away, chatting with a guest but turning to see them, gratification on her face.

"Well, if it brought Viv and me closer together, it was a good thing," Andy said. He looked in Viv's direction, looked at her the way he had at the bar that one New Year's Eve. Which had really been the first time Lee recognized something going on between them. Not the laughter behind the apartment door, but that gaze. Lee realized she'd been wrong. She had thought she was giving Viv away, but the truth was Viv and Andy were giving *her* away. They'd already done it and she just hadn't known.

But now here she was, with Viv again, not wanting her friend to leave her. She thought of Flintwick, talking about Linda and the "freaky frisson" of the past and present dissolving into each other. Freaky Frisson sounded like a bad stage name.

"Let's see if Patti's information is still accurate," said Viv. "But if it is, yeah, I would go with you to see Marion."

Viv's offer was a relief but it came with some deflation. Maybe Viv couldn't face Andy yet and wanted more time. Maybe she wanted to meet Marion. For the sake of curiosity? For material, like Patti Driggs? A free trip to California, because of course it would be Lee's treat? Maybe she knew that Lee didn't want to do this alone. Maybe Viv thought: *If I do this, I will never owe her anything again.* There was something valedictory in the offer. As if they both knew this would be the last time. Andy would understand this when Viv called to tell him she would need a few more days. He wouldn't be upset because he would know where things stood. It had always been Viv going along with her, surrendering to her, but this didn't feel like surrender. It felt like a favor, and a bit like pity.

OLD PICTURES OF Marion Washington were all over the Internet, but only one image of Marion Morris lived online. Third from the left in a group of attendees at a mental health conference in 2002, she was obscured by a broad-shouldered man in a suit but her face was visible in profile. She would have been about forty-five then, and though she seemed to have lost some of her vivaciousness, she had retained all of the grace from the Haseltine photographs on Carnahan's wall. She was clearly the woman they were looking for. It wasn't difficult to find an address for her office along with a phone number.

"My name is Vivian Feld," Lee said to Marion's voicemail. "I was referred to you by a friend of mine. If you could call me back, I would really appreciate it. Thank you."

"Why do I get the feeling this isn't the first time you've used my name like that?" Viv asked.

"I've never used your name like that." Which was true even if it didn't feel true because it had come so naturally to her.

"So, what, you're going to set up a fake appointment under an assumed name and then head across the country and ambush her?"

"First, let's see if she calls back."

Marion did, the next morning. She wasn't taking on new clients now but she could refer Vivian to an excellent colleague of hers. Marion had the same alto voice that Lee remembered, not from childhood, but from a few seconds of old footage repeatedly used in the various documentaries about Jesse: Marion answering the door to their hotel room while Jesse tunes his guitar in front of a cameraman. Marion is in the background, by the door, and you hear her say, "Excuse me?" and you can't make out what the man at the door says but she replies evenly, "No, not right now." Nothing coy or breathy about her. She closes the door, turns around, folds her arms, maybe thinking, *This is what I want, but how many times do I have to listen to him tune his guitar?*

"You're going to think this is crazy," Lee said. Marion didn't laugh. She must have heard that lame line, in a professional capacity, who knows how often. She didn't hang up when Lee told her who she really was. Marion grew quiet and then Lee thought she heard a faint sniffle.

"Lee?"

"Yes."

"My god. You were just a little girl the last time I saw you. You would be amazed, or maybe you wouldn't be, by the strange calls I've gotten over the years. People pretending to be other people in order to talk to me about Jesse. Nobody has called here yet pretending to be you. Only you, calling and pretending to be someone else. Although maybe you're not even really you."

"I *am* me. I don't know how to prove it to you on the phone. I could send you a picture. I look like my father. My mother, too. We could video chat and you could see."

"Video chat? I don't video chat. But why don't you go ahead and tell me why you're calling. We can take it from there."

"It's about my father. I wanted to talk to you about him. I know you don't remember a lot from that time. But I'd really like to talk to you."

"Where are you calling from? Could you come see me? I think we ought to talk in person."

"DO YOU REMEMBER that guy we sat next to," Lee asked, "the last time we flew to California together?"

"With the leather bag, and the book, and '*You laugh with your whole body*'?"

"Yes. That guy."

"I remember thinking I ruined your chances with him, if you wanted a chance with him, but I couldn't tell if you wanted a chance with him. I'm sorry—did I ruin your chances?"

"No. I don't think I knew what I wanted. We were performing for him. What I remember most was his girlfriend, waiting for him, at baggage claim. She was so, I don't know, she just looked so *substantive*. I don't know how else to put it. I couldn't stop looking at her. She made me feel out of my depth. Like she knew so much more, about how to go through life or something."

"Well, how much could she have known? She was with a guy who hit on you for the greater part of the flight."

"Was he hitting on me? I don't know if that's what it was. Maybe he was just a dick and she would figure that out sooner or later and move on. But maybe she was aware and she knew him in some more complex way that either justified his behavior or in some way accounted for it. I guess what I mean is that she made *him* more complex for me. It made me feel stupid. Thinking that I knew what it all meant."

"Don't you think that maybe you've been that girlfriend? Not that you've always dated douche bags, but that you've been that woman for a girl who was like you? That some girl has seen you in a room and thought how substantive you were?"

"It's pretty to think so."

She was waiting for Viv to correct her, almost as if she had laid a trap. *Isn't it. The line is "Isn't it pretty . . ."* But Viv didn't correct her. Viv just smiled.

DRIVING ALONG HIGHWAY 1, Lee recalled the beige leather seats and the chrome ashtrays of the white Mercedes convertible Linda used to drive, with Roy or Stephen or Monty sitting shotgun (Monty—she had almost forgotten about Monty, with the spurs on his boots because he was a cowboy or because he was an actor, she wasn't sure. *When* was Monty? Pretty early on. Maybe he *was* a cowboy. He never landed any roles). Linda always drove, and Linda's boyfriends always came along for the windblown ride. Sometimes the boyfriend sat in back, and Lee got to sit up front with Linda. As she grew older, she was kind of embarrassed that she was in front and there was a man back there where there should have been a child or a dog.

It was easy to feel you were in a car commercial as you drove along this coast, maybe even the one set to Jesse's "Whatever You Want." The young couple who keeps driving, past the party they had set out for, because what party could compare to the air through an open window, climate, time, and fuel efficiency on your side? But no ad could capture the mythic drama of mountains pushing up into cliffs that sheared off into the Pacific, dark and vast beneath the rolling whitecaps. Looming, indifferent redwoods that dwarfed you and your tiny car. Marion had the right idea. To live by the ocean amid giant, primeval trees. Marion, it would seem, knew how to disappear into a different life.

Bixby Bridge. 1932. Linda used to yell, "1932!" as if it was a very significant year. "What do you think Big Mort and Bubbe were doing in 1932?" They were still children, though Big Mort was already working as a stock boy, on the other side of the country, in apartments in the Bronx and Brooklyn. They went to sleep with their brothers and sisters, four to a bed, and they shined their worn shoes and saved up for a piece of penny candy or a potato chip. Jesse's parents were alive then, too, his father the son of an ambitious grocer, his mother a future debutante. Jesse's great-grandfather had been alive during the Civil War, his childhood home destroyed in Sherman's March. Meanwhile Linda's great-grandparents were in Russia, where their homes were also destroyed. Different story.

Lee remembered being on the beach here with Linda and Monty— yes, it was Monty. "Seals!" Linda cried, pointing to a rocky outcropping in the water, and Monty made barking noises. Seals were a good omen, Linda said. But those were sea lions, Lee pointed out, not seals. Were sea lions also a good omen? she asked. Linda said, "You are so much your father sometimes." Before Linda could say anything else, before Lee could comprehend the look in her eyes, Monty rushed Linda, threw her over his shoulder, and ran with her along the dark sand.

The road began to curve away from the ocean, out of the sun and into the wooded coolness. They were getting closer to the turn-off that would take them to Marion's place. Lee wasn't going to turn back, but if something had gotten in their way, a roadblock, a rockslide, a rabid mountain lion frothing on their hood, she might have been secretly relieved. She hadn't felt this urgent toggling on the way to Flintwick's or to see the Carnahans or Patti Driggs.

With Bill Carnahan she'd dreaded the return to a certain way of interacting with men that made her feel ashamed. She had actually tried to pretend she was undercover, like in one of Roy's old procedurals, when you got to see the hot actress in a dress instead of her usual street cop clothes, putting herself in danger for the sake of some greater civic purpose. But Lee was putting herself in danger only for the sake of putting herself in danger. Carnahan hadn't made much of a physical advance on her, though. When he got her alone, he had merely brushed her cheek with the back of his manicured fingers and likened her skin to the soft inside of a flower petal, asked if she knew what the Japanese expression *mono no aware* meant. In retrospect, it was absurd, but in the moment, she'd felt stripped. As though footage of every past humiliation were being played on a screen behind her and Carnahan was watching it all. She'd tried to think what Viv might do in her place, but Viv wouldn't be in her place. So then Lee thought: *What would my mother, my inviolable, indefatigable mother, do?* Keep him talking by pretending you're slightly interested in what he says. Give him something, but not too much. Be like the photographs of your father. When this worked, Lee felt as though Linda had been with her. She was grateful, and even unnervingly proud.

MARION LIVED IN a redwood cottage built into a hillside at the end of an unpaved road. The sun shone in one direction and shadows crossed the other so that grasses, succulents, purple wildflowers, and a lemon tree grew out front, while in back a creek ran below a leafy canopy. No wind chimes. No stained glass sun catchers in the windows. No New Age tchotchkes. None of that. She came to the door, a slim woman of average height in a white shirt, chinos, and red espadrille flats, a few thin silver bangles at her wrist, her hair cut in a short Afro. The Marion in Lee's memory wore silk dresses, huge sunglasses, platform shoes. Her fluffy hair fell over her shoulders.

"You really do look just like both of them," said Marion as they introduced themselves. "It's astonishing."

"Genetics," said Lee, not knowing what else to say just then, immediately regretting how it made Marion's remark sound obvious and left little room for expansion, which hadn't been her goal at all. It was like something she would say to Linda to shut her down. *God.*

"I can't get over how beautiful it is," said Viv, relieving them all of the silence. "You get to live here." She started them on a course of conversation by which they learned that Marion had moved here more than twenty years ago and lived by herself for the most part. She had never married. Morris was her mother's maiden name and she had adopted it after the accident.

Marion lead them into an open room where the sun streamed in through the windows onto a Mexican rug covering a rustic floor made of thick pine planks. White walls and a white, acrylic-topped dining table offset the woodsiness, as did an arcing chrome lamp in the corner. The furniture could have been recently purchased or could have been decades old and in good shape because it saw so little wear and tear, since it was so often just Marion here, alone. She had art on the walls, a hanging textile, a couple of deeply saturated abstract paintings and a few drawings. A framed postcard—or maybe a headshot—of an older man in a suit, an inscription inked across the top, but Lee couldn't make out what it said or who it was. No pictures of family or friends, though perhaps she kept those in a different room.

Lee recognized someone or something in Marion's manner, how she was both guarded and open, as though one was a corrective to the other. Almost as though they were paint colors that she was mixing every so often. It took Lee a minute to realize it was herself she recognized.

Marion brought out a tea tray and a cutting board with wedges of cheese, a jar of jam, and a loaf of bread. A pain de campagne. Lee knew Linda would call it a PDC. *Oh, this PDC is to die for!* Rather, *this PDC is TDF!*

Marion poured the tea into cups on saucers. She asked about their trip, where they'd been before coming here. They told her about Flintwick ("Charlie had no use for me," Marion said. "He thought I was a distraction and a nuisance. But he always had a strange relationship with women in general") and about the Carnahans ("The trouble with late capitalism," she said). They told her about Patti Driggs, who had led them here. ("Patti would have eviscerated me if I'd talked to her. Even if that wasn't her intention, it would have been the result.") Lee held off mentioning the Haseltine photos, Big Mort's pendant on the dresser.

"So you remember Charlie Flintwick," Lee said, "from back then?"

"Right. There's that small matter of my coma. My memory loss."
A little deprecatory: comas and amnesia—so melodramatic. "Look,
people hated me back then," she said. Public opinion had never been
kind to Marion. In the instances where she was treated as more than
a footnote, she was characterized as self-interested, careless, and par-
asitic. She was only nineteen. At that age, independence is inter-
twined with self-interest, freedom with carelessness. It's tempting to
grab on to people you shouldn't. Viv at nineteen, when Lee met her.

"People still hate me. Still! I do own a computer. You can't help
but read things. But these are people who didn't know me and didn't
know Jesse. That not-knowingness leads to a purer hatred. It's an
innocent hatred, untouched by reality. And maybe more dangerous,
in a way. It's hard to know how to react to that kind of hatred. All
I knew is that after the crash I didn't want to talk to journalists or
anybody, and it was easy when I had nothing to say on the subject.
That coma was the best excuse I ever had."

"I write for a soap," said Viv, "and when we get stuck on a plot
point my boss likes to say, 'I hear a coma a'callin'!"

Marion laughed. Quiet. On the sly side. Marion would never clap
her hands together in theatrical delight, never chortle or guffaw the
way Linda sometimes did. Lee must have known what Marion was
going to say next, must have been expecting it. Why else, really,
would she have come here?

"My memory came back a few weeks after I woke up. I remember
the time I was with your father. I remember taking care of you when
you were just a little slip of a thing. We drove up here with you once
and I had been dreading it. I didn't think I was a kid person. But you
were a great kid. I was essentially a kid myself." Marion's eyes filled
and Lee felt herself tearing up too. This always happened to her, not

when she saw someone crying but when she saw someone fighting it and failing. "I remember going to New York, to Flintwick's, and I remember Jesse in the studio. I have no idea what happened to the tapes, though. They would certainly be worth finding. There was one song, in particular, that I so loved. It was called 'Winter.' I'll still hear a fragment of it in my head from time to time, but I can't get the whole thing. I would love to hear it again."

"You remember everything?" Lee asked.

"Not everything. But a lot of it. Yes."

"Do you remember a photographer named David Haseltine?"

"Of course. He came to Flintwick's. He was a lovely man. Very unassuming, understated. Not one of those sexy-sexy photographers. He was kind. I wasn't used to that. Kindness for its own sake. But I'm sure he had his own motives, too. Maybe that's how he got good pictures. I never saw the shots he took of Jesse and me. For all I know they're with the tapes."

"Carnahan has them."

"Carnahan does? He gets to look at Jesse and me? Oh, that makes me shiver a little. Has he got us hanging on the wall?"

"Yeah. He's got them in a special climate-controlled room. He says they inspire him. Does that make you feel better or worse?"

"I'm not sure."

"I saw something in one of them. This silver chain and pendant that belonged to my mother. Belongs, I should say."

Marion poured more tea for herself and cupped her hands around it a little ceremoniously. She looked down into it and then back up at Lee. As if to signal a beginning.

"Does your mother know you're here?"

"No."

"Have you talked to her about this?"

"She doesn't want to talk to me. But I was hoping maybe you could tell me what she was doing there? Because she must have been there that day."

"She was. She came out from California to get Jesse back. It sounds very high school, doesn't it? Or like your soap, Viv. But I wasn't too far out of high school when I met Jesse, so there you go."

She stopped, collected her thoughts. Viv reached for more bread and jam, like popcorn at a movie. Viv would probably be mortified to know that Lee had always noticed that, if food was placed in front of her, Viv rarely refused. Lee suspected that if she someday did something unpardonable to Viv, more unpardonable than anything she'd done before, she just might be able to win her back with passed appetizers.

"Do you know what it feels like to be a phase?" Marion asked. "My father loved Nat King Cole. 'When I Fall in Love.' 'Unforgetta-ble.' I would never have admitted it growing up, but I thought love should be like those songs. There were moments like that with Jesse. I know he was attached to me. I believe that. But we didn't have that grand sweep, that nobody-else-in-the-world feeling. There was always someone else. Linda. Still, when Jesse died . . . I *still* miss him sometimes. Actively, physically miss him. I wonder how that can be when my own body feels so different. How could my *body* still miss him? That was Jesse, though. I could understand why your mother had come out to get him back. I'm telling you this because you're not a child anymore. You haven't been a child for a long time. And you've come to me."

Lee nodded. Viv put down her food.

"Linda showed up at Flintwick's the same day that David Hasel-tine came. She just turned up unannounced. It was all very civilized at first. People came and went, the guys Jesse was recording with, like Chris Valenti. But that afternoon it was just the three of us. It sounds absurd, but we had lunch together and then we went for a swim. Linda borrowed one of my bathing suits! It wasn't like we all stripped down and went for a dip in the lake. Jesse and his women or something like that. It was more like, here we are and it's a gorgeous day and why shouldn't we make the most of it. I think we all thought that was how adults in the seventies were supposed to behave. We were trying to be very mature about things. Haseltine arrived, but I don't recall him shooting at that point. That was later in the afternoon and then he left. He went back to the city. But I think it upset Linda terribly. The idea was to get pictures of Jesse for the album he was making. But Jesse wanted me in some of the shots. Me and not Linda. It was kind of awful. Charming as Jesse was, he couldn't outcharm the awfulness of what he was doing. Using me to provoke Linda. And I did it, too. I'm sure I wanted to provoke her. I'm sure I didn't know any better."

Marion had placed the heel of her right hand on her knee and as she spoke she kept extending her fingers toward Lee, as if she were touching her without making contact.

"It worked, of course. Linda and Jesse started fighting when Haseltine packed up. I went back down to the lake. I didn't want to hear it, though I could still make out their voices from the water. I don't even know how long I was in there for, only that it got cooler. The sun sank behind the trees and then it was quiet. I wrapped myself in a towel and went back inside and I found Jesse in that room, that bordello of a room that Flintwick had. Linda was gone. He was drinking and he warned me not to walk in there with my bare feet. There was broken glass all over the place.

" 'We're getting a divorce,' he said. And I thought it should have pleased me to hear that, but there was something about him sitting there in that sordid room, getting drunk, that made me very uncomfortable. At the same time, there was this charge from him choosing me over Linda. I went to wash up and get dressed and I kept wondering if he would get up and come be with me and I wanted him to, but I was also scared that he would. I no longer knew what he was capable of or what I was capable of. But he didn't come to me. He was picking up the glass when I came back, and he'd cut his hand. It wasn't deep, but he looked so helpless all of a sudden. So I pulled him up. I literally pulled him up from the floor and led him to the little sink by the bar and cleaned off the blood, bandaged his finger. It was as if I only had to touch him to set everything in motion. One thing led to another. He took me to bed, or I took him, and the next thing you know—"

Viv stood up.

"I'm so sorry—I have to—like all the time now—sorry." Marion pointed her to the bathroom. Marion looked at Lee as if trying to gauge her thoughts. Could she tell that Lee was imagining what the sex must have been like? Was there a meanness to it? An electricity that hadn't been there before? A violence? Lee had been in a situation once that was similar enough, with a husband and wife about ten years older than she was—triangulated in the same way—and she had felt powerful, as if she had never been so in control of someone else's desire, and at the same time, never been so used. She'd been in just about every situation over the years, hadn't she? Except for married, with a kid. Apparently she had a special knack for triangulation, though. Viv, Andy, herself.

"You should stop me," said Marion, "if you don't want to hear this. I don't want to make you uncomfortable, but I'd like to give you the full story."

"No, please. Go on."

"Why don't we make ourselves more at home then." Marion settled into a corner of the saddle-brown leather sofa, taking her feet up and placing a throw pillow in her lap. Lee took the other corner and let Viv have the recliner.

"Sorry for the interruption," said Viv.

"Not at all. So where were we? I wanted to go out. To get out of that house. So we went into town for dinner. Only one place was open at that hour, a bar where they had tables and served some food. I had a chicken sandwich and French fries and I'm sure it was mediocre, but I couldn't eat it fast enough. Jesse was looking at me, like, *Who* are *you?* I guess he'd never seen me eat like that. He was drinking. More than he was eating. I should have taken the keys. I should have driven us home but he was so possessive when it came to his car. He'd let me drive it before but I could tell he didn't like it so I had it in my head that he was *the driver*. I remember walking to the car and he had his arm around me and I had my hand in the back pocket of his jeans and he walked me to the passenger side door, a gentleman, and we were leaning against the window, kissing. I loved the way he felt up against me. It was my weakness. I don't know if he ever knew that. But that was my weakness."

Marion was both there and not there. When she shifted her gaze from an empty space on the wall, she looked almost surprised to find that Lee and Viv were listening to her.

"So we got in the car and Jesse was driving. He liked to drive fast, of course. It didn't matter that the roads were dark and slick and there was a fog. We were the only ones out there on the mountain road that led back to Flintwick's place. Then there was a turn and out of nowhere there were headlights up ahead, off to the side, and someone was just standing there in the middle of the road. Standing there and not moving. Jesse swerved and we went over."

Marion waited for her to understand.

"It wasn't suicide?"

"Not the way you might have thought."

"Who was it, in the road?"

Marion said nothing and Lee's stomach turned. Marion gestured for her to hold on and went to heat more water at the stove. Maybe she was one of those people who found tea to be healing. Lee had tried to be one of those people once. After that god-awful Thanksgiving when Natalie Feld had sat her down, put on a kettle, and it really did have a calming effect. Before she drank it, she'd felt a lot like a wild animal that couldn't help biting the hand that fed her. (Shouldn't the Felds have known to stop extending their hands in her direction already?) But the tea soothed her. As though its heat restored some humanity to her. She'd liked the ritual of it and the idea that she might one day make perfectly steeped tea for someone in need. She went to a lovely little shop where a serene and seemingly wise woman sold her several loose-leaf varieties. The canisters sat untouched in her cupboard until she moved and then they sat in the cupboard of her new place.

Marion stood over Lee, filling up the cup she hadn't realized was empty.

"I never got a good look. I couldn't be sure. But when I was in the hospital, your mother came to see me. They'd moved me to an intensive care unit in Manhattan and she came almost every day and she sat with me and talked. I was unconscious. She thought I couldn't hear. Or maybe she thought I could."

"What did she talk about?"

"I don't remember much of what she said, mostly the cadence of her voice, and a few stray things. Like you remember parts of a dream. She told me about the Catskills. About riding in the back of her father's Cadillac when he drove the family up to Hirschman's for the summer. Speeding along at night, with the windows down, in the passenger seat of a car that belonged to a waiter at the resort. Linda said she loved the total darkness of the country because it was nothing like the street-lit night of the suburbs and in that darkness she could pretend the waiter was mysterious. On their last night together—and I recall this vividly—he told her he'd write to her and she said, 'Can you write like you fuck?' Linda said he looked as if he was trying his best not to appear horrified. She never heard from him again."

"Well, that certainly sounds like her," said Lee.

Marion continued. "She hadn't been back there, to the Catskills, since those Hirschman's summers. Not until the day she came to Flintwick's. By then Hirschman's was shuttered. I remember driving by that place and pointing it out to Jesse because I thought it was something he might be into. That he might want to go explore the ruin. It was all boarded up behind a chain-link fence. The roofs of the buildings were falling in, and there was this gigantic empty pool. But Jesse just shrugged when I suggested we take a look. He quoted someone, a writer who said nothing ever looks emptier than an empty swimming pool, but I could never remember who it was. He never told me about Linda's association with it."

"It was Raymond Chandler," mumbled Viv. "The line about empty pools."

"Is that right?" asked Marion.

"*The Long Goodbye*."

"Oh," said Marion.

So her father and Viv had read the same books. Lee wasn't sure what to make of that. What pushed its way into her consciousness just then was the moment, as she had kissed Jonathan Feld, when his hand had moved to her breast for a long second. And the look on his face when he finally pulled away. Rueful and confused but with an intensity she'd never seen from him before.

"Okay," said Lee. "Hirschman's. Where Linda apparently had the time of her life."

Marion didn't seem to get the reference, though she seemed saddened by Lee's cynicism.

"I'm sorry," said Marion.

"Don't be. *I'm* sorry. I mean, this is why we came here. Please. Keep going."

"That's about it, of what I remember Linda telling me. How she knew the area, how she knew those roads."

"You think it was her in the road," Lee said.

Marion pulled into herself, closing her left hand around her right wrist and folding her arms to her chest.

"I don't know. I have no proof that it was her. All I know is I woke up with a scrambled mind and a gut feeling. Linda came to see me one more time in the hospital after I regained consciousness. I told her I knew she had come to visit me the weeks before, that I had heard her, and she said, 'Heard what?' She said they must have had me on some really good shit." That quiet laugh again. "Maybe they did. Maybe I imagined it all. I asked her what she wanted with me. I was in a lot of pain and I didn't have the strength, the inner resources, to challenge Linda. She was so . . . who she is. And I was so very young. She told me she wanted to give me half. Jesse had a will and he hadn't updated it, so his estate was hers. She was going to keep half of it for you and give the rest to me. I didn't know what she was trying to do. Buy my silence? Assuage her guilt? I told her I didn't want the money and she sighed, as if I was being naïve." Marion's voice caught. "She was wearing that pendant of her father's.

'It's done' she said. Just like that. She never came to see me again. She was right, though. About me needing the money, of course. The hospital bills were astronomical. But it was also as if she knew I would need to start again. As if she couldn't, but I could. And she was giving me that chance."

It seemed Marion had been over and over this in her mind and still hadn't quite figured Linda out. She had turned it into a vexing case study, establishing a professional distance so as not to be personally destroyed.

"I changed my look. I cut my hair, dressed differently. I went to college. Then graduate school. Sometimes my ego would get the better of me and I'd wonder if people recognized me. But people rarely did. I realized Jesse was the context in which people had known me. You couldn't have 'Jesse Parrish's black girlfriend' if you didn't have Jesse Parrish. In time, I became someone else. I probably would have become someone else regardless. I always knew I would lose him somehow."

"Maybe. But not like that," said Lee. There was something lovely about Marion's self-sufficiency and endurance, but also something remarkably sad. Her solitary life in a fairy-tale cottage in the forest. If there wasn't a prince, there ought to have been a woodsman, at least, or some dwarves.

"You never heard from Linda again?"

"No, we don't send each other Christmas cards." A bitterness crept into Marion's voice. "I went into one of her shops in San Francisco once, out of curiosity. I even tried on a tunic. It had a very nice drape. I have to give that to Linda: a sense of proportion in clothes, if not in life."

It seemed to Lee that she ought to be shocked by what she'd just heard, by all the implications of it, and maybe that would come later. Or maybe this is what shock felt like: having the dream where you discover an extra room in your house, only waking up to find that room really is there.

Lee felt herself on the verge of tears, coupled with a stubborn urge to keep it all in. As though she didn't want to give someone the satisfaction. But who? Marion hadn't hidden her feelings. And if Viv wasn't overcome with emotion, she at least looked like someone who was trying to be concerned for the sake of a friend, while also spreading one last schmear of soft cheese on a piece of bread. She moved slowly, as if she knew she shouldn't be thinking about hors d'oeuvres at this moment, but nevertheless going for the hors d'oeuvre. It broke the tension.

"I have more where that came from," said Marion, noticing the time on her watch and turning on a floor lamp. "We could have dinner if you like. Where are you staying?"

"Nowhere yet," Lee said. "We'll probably go to Carmel or Monterey, find a hotel for the night." Linda would stay at a posh inn just down the road from here when she used to come for spa weekends with Roy or Stephen or Monty. A cabin at Deetjen's the couple of times she tried the great outdoors family thing with Lee. She couldn't have known Marion had been so close all this time.

"Why don't you just stay here?"

Lee shook her head. "Oh, no. Thank you, but that's okay."

"It's no trouble. I would like it. I go into the guestroom and I can practically feel it accusing me of neglect. Please. Stay."

Lee didn't need a lot of convincing. She had been going, going, going, all to get to this and now that they were here, she let fatigue overtake her. She wanted someone to take care of her, and Marion would do that. She didn't have to think about what came next, only had to go out to the car and bring in her bag for the night. It was a piece of luggage that Linda swore by for travel. As usual, Linda was right about these things. It held all she had needed this whole time and there had still been room, a deep inner pocket, in which to keep safe the Haseltine photo that Flintwick had given her. She pulled it out of its rigid cardboard case. Days ago (Had it really been just days?) when Flintwick first showed it to her, she had seen a complacent man, one who maybe knew that complacency didn't play well so he should disingenuously try to appear a little more troubled. But now she saw it the other way around—Jesse tightening a valve on his worry after he'd let a little of it leak out. It was of a piece with the entire Haseltine series. It had that quality that captivated Carnahan: involving-but-uninvolved. Like the waves and the rocks and the towering trees around here. You could observe the terrain, you could wander in it, it could move you, it could hurt you, but it had no need for you. No need at all.

Marion's face came alive when Lee showed her the photograph. Bewilderment, scrutiny, avidity. Marion was looking at a code she had once been able to decipher easily by virtue of daily practice. She was rusty now, but give her a minute. She would get it. It would come back to her.

"You know what I haven't thought of in years?" she said. "How Jesse used to call me Maid Marion sometimes, like Robin Hood. I never told Jesse that I'd only ever seen the Mr. Magoo version. I didn't want to spoil the romance."

"I know it's not so simple, but he must have loved you a lot," said Lee.

"He did," said Marion. "In his way."

"You should have this," Lee said.

"Oh. No. No, I couldn't. You keep it. It's yours."

Lee didn't argue when Marion handed it back to her, but she didn't really believe what Marion had said. Yes, she could keep it, but it wasn't hers.

IN THE DARK, in the cool, soft sheets of a queen bed, under the white matelassé cover, neither Lee nor Viv was asleep.

"If it's true, she's a monster," said Lee.

"Lee, if it's true, she was out of her mind. She didn't know what she was doing. Other than trying to kill herself."

"By stepping in front of his car? So either they went or she went? So he's either dead or he gets to live with her death on his hands for the rest of his life?"

"But that's what she's had to live with. His death on her hands. If it's true."

"How do you find her so defensible? You always have. I'm asking for real. I'd love to know how it's possible because just for once I'd like to stop hating her."

"She's not my mother."

"No, she's not."

"We all do things we can't take back."

"Yeah, we all do things. Believe me, I know that. But not manslaughter. I know you're feeling guilty about sleeping with Rodgers, but it's not the same. It's hardly the same thing. I should never have called him. I should never have started that whole thing."

"I do feel guilty. I feel terrible. But it's also like I feel guilty that I don't feel guilty enough. Maybe that's what it is, what makes me sympathetic to Linda. I'm not trying to excuse what she did or explain it away. I can just feel for her, that's all."

"When are you going to tell Andy that you're pregnant?"

"As soon as we get back."

"You should go home, then."

"Now?"

"We got what we came here for. I should go see Linda on my own, anyway."

"And the tapes?" Viv suppressed a yawn.

"Who knows. Maybe Linda has them after all, locked away somewhere."

"You make them sound like Rochester's wife."

Linda was never a big reader, not like Jesse, but she liked the Brontë sisters. When Lee was reading *Wuthering Heights* in high school, Linda said she liked their anger, ate a pecan sandy, and then walked out of the kitchen where Lee sat at the table with her book. Lee didn't immediately understand what she felt at that moment in Linda's wake—admiration for her mother. She hadn't registered any anger on the part of the Brontë sisters before Linda mentioned it. But once she did, she began to burn through the book, whose first few chapters she'd found a slog. Then she read *Jane Eyre* when it wasn't even assigned. She'd loved how dark and gusty it was, and she loved Jane with her stormy feelings and her sense of right and wrong. Jane was a bundle of contradictions, but was she ever hypocritical? Lee let the thought drift as she and Viv lay there silently in Marion's guest bed.

A light salty breeze came through an open window. It was different from the beachy, smoggy air of the Southern California coast, of her childhood. It was more rugged and moodier up here. Linda, as best Lee could remember, always took her (and the boyfriends) north. Never south, to La Jolla or to Mexico, never east, to the desert that Jesse had loved, where his ashes had been scattered. So when

Lee went to the desert for the first time, it wasn't with her mother but with Alex Garcia, who had his license a year before she did. Alex with his long skateboarder shorts and his smooth, tan skin. He thought the trip to Joshua Tree was all about his coming out to her, and she pretended it was, for his sake. Alex Garcia was paunchy now but still had the same clear complexion and dark, razor-straight hair. Living in Oakland. Working for a start-up that sold eyeglasses online. He wore a Buddy Holly pair himself. That she gleaned from the social network she had belonged to for about two seconds. He had written in her yearbook that he didn't know what he would do without her. But he'd figured it out pretty quickly.

"Viv," said Lee. No answer. She turned, propped herself up on her arm, and looked at her friend. How unknowable people were when they slept, how unreadable, especially the ones most familiar to you, who made up so much of your life. Lee could have touched Viv's shoulder and roused her from her private world. But she didn't want to. She contemplated Viv's face, the half-closed hand resting on the pillow, the steady breathing, the slightly open mouth. She thought that Andy, at times, must have looked at Viv from the same vantage. Andy would continue to do so, while this would soon become only a memory for her. Not quite so distant as Alex Garcia, but a memory nonetheless.

IN THE MORNING she woke to an empty bed. *The more things change,* she thought. Viv was already up and dressed, as was Marion, sitting at the dining table drinking coffee that Lee could smell from across the room.

"You lose something," she heard Viv saying, "when you find that one person. Other people fall away. Even if they don't go anywhere. You miss them and you miss who you were with them."

"It is a loss," said Marion. "And you may need to mourn, despite everything you may have gained."

How strange, if flattering, to be mourned when you were still right there in the next room. But was Andy really the one person in Viv's life? If he hadn't entirely been when they left—if Viv's decision to come with her on this trip was rooted in a struggle against that—then that struggle had now been resolved. Time for Viv to go home. She knew what this trip was for Viv, just as she had known what that trip had been for Alex Garcia. So, was that manipulative on her part? Or was everybody, ultimately, just getting what they wanted? Viv got to have one more adventure, the kind she couldn't quite admit she'd outgrown. And Lee got to be the person who could give her that. She got to feel needed. Unlike with Andy, who'd also made her feel necessary once, but whose needs she could never properly meet. But in a way, now she was giving him what he required of her too—what he needed more than another apology or the whole truth. She'd first had the realization that she was on the outside looking in at Andy and Viv's wedding. Letting go of Viv now was letting go of Andy, finally. She wanted to tell him this so that he wouldn't hate her, but there wasn't really a way to tell him. She had to hope that if he thought about it, he would somehow know. The boy who had loved her would have thought about it. If that boy was long gone, then she was only trying to reach a ghost.

"Oh, Lee, I hope we didn't wake you. Viv said you were up for a while last night. I hope you slept all right, considering."

"Yes, thank you."

"Come sit down. I'll make us all some breakfast."

Lee watched Marion move about the kitchen, slicing up the rest of the PDC and soaking the bread in an egg and vanilla batter. Heat-ing a skillet. Preparing a fruit salad. She read the expression on Marion's face as satisfied purposefulness. What if she just stayed here? What if Marion went off to work and Lee cleaned up, picked flowers, gathered wood for the fireplace, and had dinner ready for Marion's return? What if that was her life from now on? She recognized Marion's satisfaction because it reminded her of the fulfillment she was so surprised she felt when working with Linda. Most of Lee's prior notions of business had come from eighties movies. Power suits and big mahogany desks and gold paperweights in the shape of ducks. She had grown up around Linda West, Inc., but she hadn't grown up *in* it. She didn't know Linda the Executive—the strategic thinker, the creative mentor. But when Lee was foundering professionally (and in other ways too), Linda had taken her under her wing and put her to work. She rotated Lee through several departments in the company, a process of accelerated rope learning, and then made her a vice president, overseeing talent acquisition in New York. Yes, Linda said, it helped to have Lee as one of the more public faces of the company, but first and foremost, Lee was an excellent judge of character, an asset in this role.

Linda had foreseen this, had recognized what her daughter most needed at the time and tried to help her attain it. Like a mother would. Lee hadn't known Executive Linda very well, but she was even less familiar with Maternal Linda. For most of her life, it seemed as if Linda made a mess and then either didn't recognize it as a mess or simply excused herself from the disarray. Lee had been left to sort it out. But work was an arena where Linda looked after her. This is what she would miss. She couldn't go back to it now if what Marion had told her turned out to be true.

IN THE REARVIEW mirror Lee could see Marion standing by the door of her cottage, waving them off. Marion would head inside and eventually make her way back to the guest bedroom where she would find the photograph of Jesse that Lee had left for her.

"Are you sure you want to go see Linda alone?" Viv asked when they were back on the coastal highway.

"I think I have to. Besides, if you don't get back, you're going to get fired and I need to know what's going to happen to Romola and Peyton."

"You don't even watch."

"I'm going to start."

"You better do it soon. THATH has a rich history but not much of a future."

"What will you do if it goes off the air?"

"I don't know. I'm like an iceman. Or a maker of mouse pads. I wonder if I could go work for Carnahan. He's got that thing for appropriating obsolescence. He's got his butler waiting on him in vintage factory wear and small batch denim. Maybe I could dress up like a town crier and be their in-house storyteller. Kara Carnahan loves THATH. I could keep it going for her."

"You could be her Scheherazade."

"Oh my God, could you imagine putting the Carnahans to bed every night?"

"Yeah, like, here's a glass of warm milk to go with your bucket of raw meat. Sleep tight!"

At a gas station they stopped for coffee and on the cardboard sleeve of Lee's cup was an ad for a neo-caper movie that Jack had a supporting role in. More than a month ago she'd received a text from her ex: *Thinking about you. Getting hard.* She hadn't replied. Was there an expiration date on these things? The message was still on her phone. What would she even write back at this point? *You still there? Still hard?*

Back in the car, Viv took over the driving. She was so ten-and-two. Lee had always loved that about Viv: how Viv, despite wanting not to be, was so ten-and-two. She didn't even realize she'd been staring until Viv said, "What?"

"Nothing," said Lee. She busied herself with finding a playlist Jack had made for her. It was a great playlist. And she didn't mind being reminded of him. He'd never yelled at her, never spat at her or threw a plate at her. Of all the relationships she'd been in, all of her encounters with men, theirs was one of the least demeaning. She scrolled to a song that made you want to go out and have one last really fucking great night. When you played it loud, and you had to play it loud, it reminded you of your whole entire life and then made you forget about everything for one pure moment.

Viv wondered aloud if one day the world would have changed so much that if they were to, say, dance around their kitchen to this song, it would have to be the equivalent of that "Ain't Too Proud to Beg" scene in *The Big Chill.* Lee wasn't sure. If you turned into whatever the current equivalent would be of a self-satisfied yuppie who just couldn't fight the rhythm, then that's what you turned into and it didn't matter what the music was. You were a joke. But the more she thought about it, the more she thought about her mother and grudgingly felt she had to give Linda credit. How Linda got over rock and roll early, got over those boys. All but one of them. Linda loved the music of her youth as much as anyone, but she never pushed it on you, as if her generation were the only one that had ever really been young and grown older. Maybe the best thing about the music of Lee's youth was that it had already lost its innocence. So the nostalgia you felt when you heard it wasn't for what you believed was a better time, just a different one.

"So, when we get to the airport, is that it?" asked Viv. "I kind of feel like you're sending me away, and it's going to be years before I see you again."

"It's not as dramatic as you're making it sound."

"If I'm being dramatic, it's because you fucking made me that way." Viv shook her head. "Stop laughing. It's not funny."

"I'm going to see Linda and hopefully get some answers, and then I'll go back to New York and you'll see me as much or as little as you want to. As much or as little as Andy wants you to." Lee's mind landed on something. "Remember that girl at that party, like, years ago, who thought we were a couple?"

"Yeah!"

Neither of them knew how to finish the thought.

ELLEN SHELLEY HAD the air of someone continually carrying a clipboard. Her whole body hummed.

"Lee-*eeeee!* What are you *doing* here? I mean, come in!" Ellen, at the door of Linda's house, like a mad scientist steering Lee into a chamber where ordinary humans were subjected to abnormally high levels of energy. Lee almost expected to be given a jumpsuit to change into. "I thought you were in New York? I mean, I thought you were on vacation? I mean, fuck, you know what I mean. I wish you'd called and let us know you were coming. I would have prepared."

"What would you have prepared?"

"Shit, I don't know. A snack? I would have ordered something special. Made a goddamn reservation."

"A snack reservation?"

"I don't fucking know. Something, *okay*?"

Ellen swore gratuitously, the way that actresses profiled in men's magazines do. Lee recalled that Ellen used to go on auditions when Linda first hired her as a personal assistant seven years ago. Linda had had a number of assistants over the years, and while all of them performed more or less the same tasks, they each seemed to serve a different purpose for Linda. One or two were Linda manqués, also-rans of her scene who never burned as brightly and always needed money. Some of them were strivers, absolute Linda loyalists, never a bad word about the boss. A couple of them, by the end of their tenure, couldn't hide their grumpiness, and Lee probably should have sympathized, though she never really did. She had only ever cared about one. Sally Andrada, who had worked for Linda while Lee was in high school. Sally looked and dressed the way Lee thought she ought to look in ten years. Long, not very neat, light brown hair with blond streaks, as if she surfed a lot when she wasn't on the clock. T-shirts, jeans, boots. Sometimes skirts, long or short, but almost always with a pattern, textiles being her thing. Always as if she never tried too hard (though maybe she secretly did), and as if she knew you probably wanted to be her, but she wasn't going to make a big deal about it, or even a small deal (which was usually worse, as these things go, than a big one). No reverse-snobbery: *Look at you people and your money.* But nothing of the sycophant about her. Just a conscientiousness: she wanted to do a good job, she wanted to move beyond where she came from (Sally from the Valley) and she understood how Linda could help her get there. Her talent had brought her under Linda's tutelage, but she still couldn't keep a note of protective sarcasm out of her voice when she referred to herself as a "textile artist."

"Don't ever talk like that! Don't deprecate yourself or your art that way," Linda had admonished her. "Your art is your work." Sally thanked her. Linda then allowed a little time to pass before asking Sally to book her an appointment for a wax.

Lee cared what Sally thought of her. She imagined Sally had a boyfriend who wasn't entirely worth her time, but still. Lee never wanted to do anything that would make Sally complain to this boyfriend. *Can you believe that girl? But what do you expect?* Sally left sometime when Lee was away at college. She could look her up, find out what had happened to her, but she preferred to just hope it was something good.

"Is my mom around?"

"She is, she is! Um, I think she's out back. You want to wait here?"

Ellen hustled her into the living room, sitting her down on the eraser-pink George Sherlock sofa, its cushions like giant hamburger buns. This wasn't the house where Lee had grown up, but that sofa was like a floating home.

"Hey, just so you know, Linda hasn't exactly been herself the last few days. I don't know what it is, but she's been a little, like, withdrawn or something. She canceled a few meetings. There was this benefit dinner she bailed on last night. I don't want you to be alarmed or anything, but. Just FYI."

"Okay, thanks for letting me know."

It didn't matter that Lee hadn't answered Ellen's question about what she was doing here. Talking to Ellen was like being at a cocktail party or trying to have a conversation with someone looking after a toddler. Ellen spirited herself through a set of French doors and while Lee waited, she looked at her hands, at her father's agate ring. As a girl, she had worn it on a thin chain around her neck and then at sixteen she had it resized for her finger. She rarely thought to take it off because it was so much a part of her. It had been a talisman of sorts, a silent marker of a special power granted to her. In the way that children play one parent off the other, the ring was a reminder to her mother: I come from someone else. But she had forgotten that Linda had given her the ring in the first place, after Jesse died.

Ellen reappeared carrying a tray with two glasses, a pitcher of still water, and a small plate of cut-up lemon.

"Linda's coming in a sec. Um and she told me to go home early, so I'm gonna"—Ellen set the tray down on the wide coffee table and rotated her hands in front of her like turbines as she searched for the words she wanted—"head the fuck out!"

"Okay. Have a good rest of the afternoon. Evening."

"Would you. Could you just. I mean, go easy on her, okay? Whatever it is. Like I said, she's having a rough time."

Lee wondered when she'd developed a reputation for being a bitch. She had heard "standoffish" before but she didn't think she'd been particularly known for nastiness. Though she'd never thought Linda needed coddling, either.

"I'll see what I can do."

Linda approached just then, from around a corner. Looking very British Woman in Kenya in a rumpled white linen camp shirt tucked into wide-legged khaki pants and flat sandals. Big Mort's pendant peeking out of a lapel.

"Thank you, Ellen," Linda said. "I'll see you tomorrow." She put her hands in her pockets, her Charlie Chaplin–slash–Marlene Dietrich-in-menswear move, and shuffled into the living room, looking at once apologetic, stern, and worried.

"Hi," she said. "Did you just get in?" She poured two glasses of water, released a lemon slice into each, and dropped into an armchair facing Lee.

"Yes and no. I was with Viv, in Big Sur. I dropped her off at the airport and then came here."

"Big Sur, huh? You've been to see Marion, then."

Of course. Of course Linda would have known.

"Yes."

"And what did she tell you?"

"She told me what she remembers."

Linda's face twitched preemptively into a kind of bullying expression Lee had last seen on Will, a half-English, half-French director of high-concept music videos. They had gone away together for a weekend to a Mediterranean villa, where he asked her to sleep with his good friend Max. A variety of motivations were supplied, chief among them that it would get Will off. He didn't need to watch, just knowing it was happening would do.

"I don't think so," she had said.

"Really?"

"Yes, *really*."

And he had said, "All right, look, if you don't like this, if your delicate psyche can't handle it, then don't do it. But don't make me feel like I'm exploiting you or I ought to be ashamed. Because I'm not."

"My psyche isn't delicate. You'd just like it to be. It gives you a better speech."

Lee knew what to do with the you-and-your-delicate-psyche tack, how to turn it around, but Linda's expression had already morphed into something else, something Lee was less familiar with.

The only other time Linda had looked at her this way was when they took their golden retriever, Fred, to be put down. Lee, twelve, had acted surprised that Linda had decided to go at all, instead of sending Fred off with a staffer. Her mother indulged the act, she let Lee be superior and indignant. Linda cried but didn't fall apart and Lee, bereft and angry, had understood, however dimly, that Linda's show of strength was for her benefit, so that she could fall apart and have a mother who would be there to put her back together. And

Linda did—for the rest of that day. Instead of going home, where everything would remind them of Fred, they went to the Beverly Wilshire hotel (no Chateau Marmont scuzziness at a time like this) where they put on robes and ordered room service and got into bed and watched *All About Eve* (Linda's choice) and *Meatballs* (Lee's). Lee never had another dog. She probably ought to get one now.

"I've been waiting for you since your call," said Linda. "After you saw Charlie Flintwick. Do you believe her? Whatever Marion told you?"

"I don't think she's lying."

"You've always had good judgment. Your judgment is unerring. What gets you in trouble is that you don't trust it. That's probably my fault. I didn't encourage you enough or something. I knew where this would lead, you going on this . . . quest. I knew it was only a matter of time. I've had thirty years to figure out what to tell you but I'm still not sure what to say. Marion isn't lying. I don't know that I would trust her memory entirely, but she isn't lying."

"I want to hear it from you."

"Where would you like me to start?"

"Oh, I don't know. The beginning?"

Linda shook her head, as if she couldn't believe she was about to do this, but also, surprisingly, as if she admired her daughter. Rather like the way Patti Driggs had looked at her. As if she hadn't quite thought Lee had it in her. As if Linda saw some of herself in her child.

i love you
more than
anything
∾
Linda, 1978

At Hirschman's there was a waiter named Robert Rothman. What she had liked about Robert was that he drove fast; they flew down roads in the dark in his Ford Galaxie. He had thick black hair, and he called her *darlin'* in an already retro Elvis Presley kind of way. "Whoa, darlin', where'd you learn *that?*" But he listened to folk music, like everyone else then, and also some soul records that spoke to a sensitive, anti-establishment streak in him. But not too strong a streak because in September, Robert would be off to Bucknell, pre-med. At sixteen, she might not have been able to articulate it, but she knew that Robert was challenging the values of a culture in the way a child challenges its parents—to make sure that at the end of the day they were still there, firmly rooted. The disdain that Linda was already developing for her own middle-class upbringing somehow felt more dangerous than Robert's because it was more detached from any overarching, idealistic principle, more manipulative and self-serving.

Sometimes Linda wondered about her scruples. How she could look down on her father. He would have done anything for her and somehow that wasn't enough. Big Mort, in his extravagance, booked Linda and her older sister, Lori, their own large room at Hirschman's, with two double beds they would sneak out of at night, Lori to see her swim instructor and Linda to the cabins behind the dining hall where Robert and the rest of the waitstaff lived. Big Mort. Never to his face, though. Always Daddy to his face. She let him down again and again, and he loved her unconditionally.

She had been thinking about Robert Rothman and those summers at Hirschman's while she drove from her parents' house up to Flintwick's studio to see Jesse. The thick-ankled women in costume jewelry and the Borscht Belt banquets of her adolescence. It startled her how at home she felt on these roads, like being in a dream, a place your mind conjured so you know the landscape and you know what comes next. All those winding country and mountain routes she'd taken in from the back seat of Big Mort's Cadillac and then the front seat of Robert's car. She felt girded by the advantage of being on home turf. She needed to be self-possessed when she saw Jesse, not desperate or angry or scared or sad. Or she would be all of those things but self-possessed enough not to show it. Certainly not in front of Marion. Marion made Linda feel old, worthless, and unseen. It was the first time in her life she had felt that way, and it shocked her.

Jesse wasn't expecting her, but she knew what he was going to say. Let's settle this. Finalize it, formalize it, whatever his attorney was advising him to do. You'd think Linda would be the one with representation. If not a high-powered, corner-office-in-a-glass-tower lawyer, then some friend of the family, a Big Mort associate. But it was Jesse who saw to these things, whose sense of tidiness, propriety, and manners always lay beneath the careless rock-and-roll surface of his life. (Probably why he had so much trouble with drugs. They were an escape for him, a way to lose control and reorder his mind, whereas for Linda they remained recreational. Linda had dropped acid the way her mother played bridge. And speed had been lovely but then it got to seem like a lot of work. Cocaine, when it came along, was wonderful for parties. Heroin she just never ever touched.) It always surprised Linda that Jesse was neater than she was, that he cared about housework. That's what Patti Driggs didn't get in her hateful profile, painting Linda as the dazed yet doting wife. A foolish woman in a ridiculous scene of 1950s domesticity transplanted to 1970s post–sexual-revolution California. What Patti Driggs didn't get, or didn't care about, was that Linda wasn't a good wife in that sense. Linda's disheveled yet stylish look was an embodiment of the way she approached the world. She didn't wear any old thing, she had a method, a vision, but she also never thought too hard about it.

As she drove, she thought how Jesse was a better lover than Robert Rothman or any of the other men she'd been with. She *loved* him. He was sexier than any of those other men. God, he was sexy. He was so sexy that she still wanted him, even when he would unload the dishwasher (before they hired a housekeeper) in a fed-up, put-upon pedantic way. *It's not that hard, Linda, to stack the plates that match and put them in the cupboard. Could you try it just once?* Patti Driggs had no clue about Jesse. Linda had said, "Fuck the dishes," as she positioned herself on the countertop and pulled him to her. With Robert, nothing very emotional entered into it. It was undiluted fucking. They didn't even have to speak. Their bodies completely took over. She had never lost herself this way with Jesse. She cared about what Jesse thought. Perhaps she was only being sentimental about those rides in the car with Robert in the hopes of feeling better about losing Jesse now.

She wore the white peasant dress with the red embroidery that she'd bought in Mexico (would he remember?) and whiskey-colored boots. She looked airy, not nearly as nervous or doomed as she felt.

This wasn't like her, this suppressed panic at the impending end of things. She was usually already moving on.

Big Mort hadn't said, "I told you so." Neither had Mom. So she had to hand it to them. Jesse might as well have been from another planet. When she announced her plans to marry Jesse, Big Mort said, "So he's a good old boy, huh? A good old goy is more like it!" But he hadn't forbidden the marriage or threatened to disown her. Was it any wonder he loved *Fiddler on the Roof* so much? Temperamentally, was there ever a character more like her father than Tevye? If Linda were the type who chose to settle for the butcher, stay in the village, and cling to tradition, would Big Mort have loved her as much? Lori had married a lawyer, moved two towns away into a four-bedroom split-level, and produced two precocious grandchildren who regularly came over for Friday night dinners. Her father loved Lori, but not as much as he loved Linda.

"Life will go on," Big Mort had said when he first heard about their separation. And hearing that had made Linda feel surprisingly better, albeit briefly. She still had her youth, sort of. She was (only?) thirty. Having Lee hadn't destroyed her body. A few thin, translucent stretch marks on her hips. Breasts still in good shape. Lee. Had she really not thought of her until just then? And in this way? Terrible, terrible mother. She was going to be mature about this. For her daughter's sake. She would let Jesse go, be a grown-up (but remind her, what was so great about being a grown-up?). Whatever they became to each other, she and Jesse would at least have to be two parents on good terms. Perhaps this would be what finally turned them into parents. Linda still hadn't gotten entirely used to identifying herself as a "parent." Sometimes she couldn't believe she was allowed to be a mother. You needed to pass a test in order to drive a car, for God's sake, but not to raise another human being.

Life would go on, as Big Mort said, but not the life she wanted. So here she was, hoping to win Jesse back. To make him realize where he belonged. She could have picked up the phone first, but her impulsiveness and her immoderate heart had propelled her here instead. She hadn't really understood about Marion, though. Hadn't underestimated her so much as totally and mistakenly discounted her. She had assumed Marion was for Jesse what various men had been for her: a way to pass time. She hadn't considered her a rival. Not until Marion came to the door when Linda arrived at Flintwick's, flustering her. Gorgeous Marion. Linda expected to see her in one of those spaghetti-strapped terry-cloth jumpers, no bra. But no. She wore a trim button-down shirt tucked into jeans. Oh and wasn't Marion so mature herself, welcoming Linda inside so calmly and cordially. Not putting on adult airs, but an honest-to-God adult, if such a thing existed anymore. Fuck maturity. Really now, couldn't Jesse have answered the door himself? Couldn't Marion have exiled herself from the house for this?

"Hey, Linda," he had said. Like the song he'd written, "Hey, Linda," only it came out sounding tired. Instead of playful and flirtatious (as it did in the first chorus) or beseeching and desirous (in the second). "Come on in. You look pretty." Why did those words, which he'd said to her so many times before, and which were the truth (she did look pretty, she knew it) now leave her feeling humiliated? They seemed to strip her of her power.

How easy it had been when they first met. She had been living with a boyfriend, another musician, a more famous one, they had thrown a party, and Jesse had cornered her in the kitchen. The next day he came back for her. Within a week she had moved in with him. Romance (if that was the word for it) had until then been easy for her. She hadn't been one for long and messy goodbyes. She had always been the one who left. But she couldn't leave Jesse. She believed they belonged to each other. She didn't know how not to be with him. Their time apart had merely been a pause. Jesse, however, didn't seem to know that he still belonged to her.

Jesse and Marion were planning to go for a swim and there was something about this place, Flintwick's libertine fantasies in the form of a house, that led Linda to think it was the most natural thing to join them. That's what you do with your husband and your husband's groupie at a place like this. Marion even had a swimsuit she could borrow. A blue maillot with red stripes. She changed and in the process, snagged her dress on the pendant that hung around her neck, Big Mort's pendant, which he gave to her when she went to California. A gift that had made it seem less like she was running away and more like she was taking an extended field trip with her parents' permission, but she wore it all the time. She tugged too hard to free her dress and the clasp broke, so she left the necklace in a little pile on a bedroom dresser.

There was a photographer there, too. His very presence, there in that Adirondack chair, made Linda vain, to the point where she wondered how he could keep from turning his lens on her, how he wasn't compelled by her beauty—not as a man but as an artist. Once he got his camera out, he didn't seem at all interested in getting her in the frame. His focus was Jesse, which was fine, but it killed Linda when Jesse asked for Marion in some of the shots and this Haseltine guy didn't see anything wrong with that. He was happy to oblige. She was expected to sit it out unnoticed. Not for her. She made her way over to the studio and that's where Jesse found her, by the mixing board, looking through scraps of paper, lyrics, musical notations, in his handwriting.

"Let's talk, Linda," he said. So up she went with him to the house, where he poured her a glass of expensive red from Flintwick's wine cellar. Jeez, this place. The living room—draped in velvet, elk antlers on the wall—looked like a cross between an opium den and a hunting lodge. She had no doubt Flintwick had decorated it himself. They raised their glasses to their absent host. Marion made it easier on her by heading back down to the lake, betraying no insecurities whatsoever, as though safe in the knowledge that when she returned, it would all be over. The nerve.

Linda and Jesse had married in Mexico. Jesse'd had a small part playing himself in a film being shot there, and they had stayed on for a few weeks afterward. Linda hadn't invited her family because—could you imagine Big Mort and Mom and Lori turning up there? They were mutually exclusive, the Weinsteins and sleepy Mexican beach towns. She tried to be nonchalant and breezy about it ("Barely even a wedding, you didn't miss much, there were no caterers") but she knew that cowardice and avoidance were at the root of her behavior. Jesse knew this too, which was one of the reasons she had married him. He took her seriously enough to be perceptive about her. The absence of her family worried her, especially at the end of the ceremony, which was not at all Jewish and did not include the ritual breaking of the glass. In that moment a pang of fear struck her heart for the world she was choosing to live in and what lay ahead of her. Then Jesse swept her into his arms and whispered "I love you more than anything, Linda," and the sound of the ocean evened everything out.

But then, she got her broken glass after all, the shards on Flintwick's floor like some sad, contorted echo of what she had missed on her wedding day. She hadn't even wanted a wedding day, not like other girls did. But her love for Jesse had domesticated her.

They had started talking, about his record and about Lee. Then she had asked him and then pleaded with him to come home and he said he couldn't. "Home," he said, as if it were a philosophical concept he'd struggled to comprehend and given up on, confused. As if he were playing dumb with a fucking interviewer. He wanted a divorce. So she threw her glass at him (she missed) and then she took two more from a liquor cabinet and hurled them at the stone fireplace. Jesse just stood there, infuriatingly unmoved. He didn't even try to restrain her while she flailed against him, so that it might turn into an embrace. She had to embrace herself, slipping to the floor, pulling her knees to her chest, crying into her fists.

"Linda, I'm sorry," he said.

"Fuck you," she said. "Fucking fuck this." She stood up, disgusted, mostly with herself. She wiped her face, smoothed her hair, put her dress on (she was still in Marion's one-piece), quietly got in her car and started driving. She looked in her rearview mirror to see if he was following her. Nobody was following her. What a fool she was. Patti Driggs was right after all. Patti Driggs was so smart. Patti Driggs was the smartest fucking person who ever fucking lived.

From the road, she could see what looked like a welcoming place to stay the night. A ski lodge in the off-season, golden light emanating from its long glass windows. Like an Alpine chalet. Something out of a Swiss or Austrian holiday she had yet to take. She had envisioned, wrongly, it turned out, lots of blond, knotted wood. Like the movie version of *Women in Love* when the two couples go to Innsbruck. She hadn't read the book (Jesse had) but she loved Alan Bates. She would see anything he was in. Alan Bates. She wondered why their paths hadn't crossed yet. Isn't that what happened when you moved in famous circles? If their paths did cross, if she could make them cross, she wondered what her chances would be with him. Fifty-fifty? Sixty-forty? Eighty-twenty, because of what you heard about him liking men? What was this kind of thinking? It was Big Mort and his gambling buddies turning life into probabilities.

Her room at the *Women in Love* ski lodge, with its thin blue carpet and pink walls, didn't look Austrian or Swiss. Less Alan Bates, more Norman Bates. It made her hesitant to take a shower. Water down the dark drain, Janet Leigh's eye. Bernard Herrmann. Stab, stab, stab. But she had to wash this day off her. Pulling the Mexican dress over her head, she felt her bare neck. She'd left Big Mort's pendant on the dresser at Flintwick's. Shit. Shit, shit, shit. She couldn't go back there. Not now. Jesse would think she'd left it on purpose. Quite frankly, she was surprised she *hadn't* left it there on purpose. She would have to ask Jesse to send it to her. Or she would have to ask her lawyer to ask his lawyer to send it to her.

She sat on the bed in her towel, combing her wet hair. She pulled a pair of jeans and a T-shirt from her travel bag. She realized how hungry she was. In the dining room of the lodge they had candles in little glass hurricane lamps on each table. Dark wooden chairs with spindled backs. White tablecloths. A large chandelier hanging from the center of the sloped ceiling. There was one family in there, on the other side of the room, a mother and father and a boy and girl. Her instinct wasn't to nod to the adults, parent to parent, but to look to the children, as though she were a child herself. And she didn't immediately comprehend why the waiter held her gaze for an extra beat. Had she done something wrong? Oh. Oh, *that*. Because she wasn't a child, after all. She wasn't going to sleep with him, but he had something, this waiter. Some freshness about him that reminded her of her past. She finished her steak, her peas and potatoes. She left a generous tip. Then she got in her car and drove to Hirschman's.

Nobody had removed the L-shaped arrow sign atop a stanchion that signaled the turn-off. The gothic lettering gave it a Sherwood Forest vibe. At the end of the road she reached a chain-link fence with a padlocked gate. It wasn't too hard to climb over. Clearly people had done it before her, while carrying six packs. All of the old buildings still stood, though windows had been broken. Graffiti scrawled in places. She found the indoor pool, which had been so magnificent once. Titan-sized, glittering and aquamarine. Big Mort took a personal pride in the fact that he could take his family to a place with a pool like that. Linda could smirk at the activities, the talent shows, the fleshy women and the balding men, but she couldn't deny her father the beauty of that pool. A moldering, empty ruin now.

Linda walked around the grounds, back behind the bunks where the kitchen staff had stayed, up along a path to a small clearing among the pines where she would go to fool around with Robert. She sat down on a log that had been worn smooth by all the boys and girls who had fumbled with each other here, summer after summer. And then, when it started to rain and it was getting too dark to see, she headed back to her car. She stuck herself in the driver's seat as the rain pelted down and she cried. She reached in her purse for the bottle of pills she had found in Flintwick's medicine cabinet and taken with her. *Just in case.* But she didn't have anything to wash them down with. She could cup enough rain in her hands, though, to take one of the pills. So why not. It would get her back to the lodge, where there was a glass and a sink and where she could easily swallow the rest.

Only one road, if you didn't count dirt lanes and old trails, would get you from Hirschman's back to the *Women in Love* lodge. It ran through the tiny town where Flintwick lived, becoming a main drag for a few blocks, the length maybe of two football fields. The rain had let up, leaving behind a wet sheen on the Victorians and two-story brick buildings, a bar on the corner with a neon sign in the window. Next to the bar was a gravel parking lot overrun with weeds, and the two pickup trucks that had pulled in there made the green GTO all the more noticeable. Jesse's car. Not his beloved 1967 silvery Corvette Stingray, still in their garage in California, but the one he'd been driving out here. She slowed when she saw the car. Maybe she should just go in and talk to Jesse, tell him she forgot her necklace at Flintwick's (Though why did it matter, at this bottle-of-pills point, if she had it or not?). This was a public place and that would keep her calm; despite how she might seem, she wasn't one for making a scene. Well, maybe in L.A., but not here, not now, not after the scene she'd already made in Flintwick's living room. But would he think she was crazy, showing up as if she'd followed him? Didn't he already think she was crazy?

She sat in her idling car, so immobilized by her thoughts that it took her a moment to notice that two people had walked out of the bar and were standing on the otherwise empty sidewalk. Two lovers, from the way they stood, his arms around her waist. A mist had risen in the night air, making the picture all the more romantic. She watched them in a kind of trance, even as she realized the woman was Marion and that Marion was leaning into the man who Linda didn't immediately recognize as her husband but rather as Jesse Parrish. They were leaning against the car in the parking lot when some instinct finally prompted Linda to step on the gas and disappear before they detected her.

She drove unthinkingly because her thoughts belonged to another Linda who wasn't even in this car but was somewhere else, maybe in Robert Rothman's car. Or Big Mort's. The streetlights of the town came to an end and the road turned back into the rural route that led to Flintwick's and, beyond, the *Women in Love* lodge. Marion and Jesse must have been behind her on this dark, lonely road that she knew so well. Everything was different shades of darkness: the trees lining the ravine to her left, the rock face that rose on her right. She pulled over to what could barely pass for a shoulder, got out of her car, and walked onto the blacktop, a thin fog encircling her legs. Something held her in place. She couldn't move and the headlights coming toward her grew brighter until they were blinding, the inverse of the pitch-black nights she had loved. All she could hear was the blaring of a horn, so much sound that it was almost no sound. The sensations were so extreme they became their opposites. It was that feeling of walking barefoot, as a child, on the asphalt driveway of the house in Mamaroneck, on the hottest day of summer; how it felt cold before it burned. She thought it would end this way. Hoped it would. But then the light vanished and the wailing stopped and she was still there in the road. No longer standing, though. She was down on the wet ground and pushed herself up. The guardrail that had been there a moment ago was torn away, and she stood in the empty space, looking out into the ravine, at what had once been a car. A marriage. A life.

fine like
hotels

∽

Lee, 2010

Linda shut her eyes and dropped her head, as if in prayer. Nobody ever taught Lee how to pray. It was something she'd only seen actors do until Big Mort's funeral. Her mother in black, standing and reciting words in Hebrew by rote. When Lee had asked her about it, Linda said it was the kaddish, as if everyone knew what it was. Like, *leave me alone, my father is gone, and I don't want to talk*. Not until later that afternoon—maybe when it occurred to her that Lee's father was gone, too—did Linda seek comfort in her daughter. At the house in Mamaroneck, she took Lee upstairs while the rest of the family gathered below, and they looked at photo albums. In the his-and-hers closets in the master bedroom they discovered a shoebox of yellowed newspaper clippings, ads that Big Mort had placed for his stores twenty and thirty years back. They seemed fairly generic to Lee, but they made Linda cry. How strange it was to see Linda supplicant. Stranger even than hearing Linda's story now, which Lee had somehow known all along. She had known it from Marion. She had known it since Flintwick's and that blooming that opened in her stomach and crept up the back of her neck when he told them how Linda showed up at his studio after Jesse died, how it felt like a theft.

She had known it, felt it, ever since then, but probably long before. Probably her whole life.

"And then what? They crashed and you just drove away?"

"Yes. I got back in my car and I drove away. I was in shock. Do you understand? I don't remember stopping at a pay phone, but I must have. The police received an anonymous call. All I remember is driving. I drove all the way back to Mamaroneck, to Big Mort and Bubbe's house. You were sleeping in my old twin bed with the white headboard, and you were sleeping so soundly. I remember the room smelled different with you in it. It smelled like applesauce muffins. I lay down on the carpet, as close to the bed as I could get, and I just listened to you breathing. You were so peaceful and perfect. I remember looking up as the sky got lighter through those white nylon sheers. I was about to lose it. I went downstairs so I wouldn't wake you. Big Mort never slept past five-thirty. He was sitting in his favorite chair in the den, and I came so close to telling him. He knew something was very wrong. I was shaking, and he held me and I told him I lost Jesse and I think he knew what happened, somehow. He must have put some version of it together when the police showed up that morning. They came to inform me of Jesse's death. They asked me questions, but they never really interrogated me and my father told them I had come home earlier than I had, that I left the lodge and was back before he turned in for the night. They knew Jesse was drunk and those roads were dark, with the fog and all the deer . . ."

Lee remembered that house, the room, those white nylon curtains like veils waiting for brides. Watching Big Mort and Bubbe play cards in their kitchen with the red countertop. Crazy Eights. Gin Rummy. Hearts. The crystal chandelier in the front hall. In the morning, when the sun came through, into the tear-shaped prisms and into your eyes. Dust beams slanting down. But the rest had always been hazy—what she and Linda were doing there. Where Linda went when it was just Lee and her grandparents. Big Mort's bearish arms. His big white teeth, which she realized only years later were dentures. Hadn't there been something formidable about him or something once-formidable that you could still detect, still feel in his presence? His power to make it go away, whatever *it* was, if it came to that. The gut feeling that Big Mort had covered for Linda in the way Lee instinctively knew that Linda would cover for her, if it came to that. An amoral protective gene. Linda the fixer.

"All you had to do was take care of Marion, right?"

"I went to see Marion in the hospital, yes, after the crash. But I went because I felt responsible, not because she was a loose end or whatever terrible thing you may be thinking. I sat by her bed every day and I told her everything I just told you. I couldn't help myself. I didn't know if she could hear me. It just spilled out. Once it was out of my system, I could straighten up, pull myself together, enough to get through the day, the week, the next week."

"Enough to buy Marion off and banish her."

"Banish? You're overestimating me. Even if I ever had those thoughts, I've never had that kind of influence. And I'd hardly call Big Sur banishment."

"But you *have* had those kind of thoughts."

"It was an accident, Lee. My god, it was an accident!" The quake in Linda's cry made Lee think of ancient pillars toppling. One summer, she had found a copy of the Bible at her grandparents' house, an easy-to-read edition that one of her cousins must have brought home from Hebrew school. The stories were as vivid and indelible as fairy tales. She thought of Samson now. Delilah over his hair with a knife. Linda was both of them, rolled into one. "He was my life," said Linda very quietly. "I'm so sorry. I can't tell you how sorry I am. I wish I had those tapes, those stupid fucking tapes, because I wish I could give you something more of him. You didn't get nearly enough."

But that was just it. Linda couldn't give her anything more of him. As though she were taking an inventory, Lee noticed something missing here among all the detail and revelation—the satisfaction, however small, however adulterated, that you might expect from someone asking your forgiveness. Linda was truly broken up. She was sorry for Lee. She just wasn't exactly guilty about it. Linda failed to ask for her daughter's forgiveness, Lee thought, not out of defiance or denial, but because Lee wasn't the one she needed forgiveness from. Only Jesse. It was always, ultimately, between Linda and Jesse. That impenetrability they had. *Hi, Jesse. Hi, Linda.* Linda had been living with her boyfriend, and Jesse cornered her in the kitchen and that was that. *I love you more than anything.* It didn't end, even when it was over. Even when Marion pulled him up off the floor at Flintwick's and took him upstairs, and Linda found herself with a bottle of pills at a deserted resort, and Lee was in her pajamas, in a small bedroom at the house in Mamaroneck, Bubbe and Big Mort reading her a story before kissing her good night. Lee could blame her mother for taking her father away from her, but she suspected deep down that Jesse wasn't hers to be taken, she never had the claim on him that Linda did. That maybe this is why it felt so sad and pathetic to be looking for some piece of him. It made her a misguided, humiliated Electra. And Jesse wasn't an innocent victim in all of this. If it had gone the other way, if Jesse hadn't swerved off the road, if he had hit Linda, if he had killed her, it would have been something he signed on for, part of the deal, their destructive dance. Marion was collateral damage, as was Lee. Was it any wonder she had felt so at home with Marion? Marion's familiar and relaxing loneliness, like a long bath.

Linda worked her fingers along the gold-hemmed edge of a colorful throw she'd picked up on a trip to India and reproduced for last fall's Linda West Home line. The look would be "exotic but fresh," as someone in Marketing put it. How Lee could have used someone in Marketing right about now, not to make sense of this situation but to package it, using words that no longer meant anything in order to sell it to her.

Lee drank her water down though it did little to wet her throat. How could it be possible—she gauged her own astonishment—that she felt for Linda's loss? Maybe it meant that her mother, not just her father, was something of a stranger, and Lee could swim in currents of sadness for strangers: people she watched on talk shows, people who posted pleading photocopied signs for their lost pets. So she felt for this woman she didn't know. But in a snap, as if a change in barometric pressure thinned the air around her, the cruelty inside pushed outward with greater force.

"It wasn't an accident, though. You walked out into the road."

"I didn't know what I was doing."

"You always know what you're doing." One of Linda's best and worst qualities, one that required, as Ellen Shelley might put it, a shit-ton of compartmentalization. Lee hadn't inherited that ability to hold herself together by splitting herself apart. But clearly she was good at keeping her own secrets.

Lee had the urge to fling her empty glass across the room, followed by the pitcher and the tray, to upturn the coffee table, but she only stood and took her glass to the kitchen sink where she rinsed it, dried it, and put it away.

"Lee," Linda called from the living room. "What are you doing?"

"I have to go," she said. She stood in the hall, under the arch.

"Go where?"

That was the question. She thought of Viv, in a taxi back from JFK, in her fluorescent-lit lobby, taking the paint-coated elevator up to her graciously proportioned prewar apartment, slipping off her shoes and walking quietly down the hallway, pulling back the duvet and getting into bed with Andy, kissing the back of his neck, holding him close to her. Lee caught sight of the pink sofa and wondered why it had never occurred to her to buy one for her own place. When she'd moved back to New York, she thought her small one-bedroom in Gramercy might be temporary. But a designer she was friendly with, a French woman who wore only a limited color palette of black, white, and gray, offered to set up Lee's place. She said it would be "sophisticated" and "classic" but still "lived in"—messy stacks of the right photography books— "and a little bit rocker." Lee said that sounded fine. And it was fine. Fine like a trendy, upscale hotel.

"I don't know where I'm going to go," said Lee. "I can't be here."

Bony hands, sunken, fragile, swimming eyes. Linda was no longer the woman she had been even moments ago. The one who had, more or less, sat down and said, "Let me tell you how it is, little girl." This woman couldn't tell her anything. This woman couldn't help her. This woman could only look on anxiously as her daughter walked out the door.

HE WAS TELLING her a story he would later recount on a late night talk show, involving his six-year-old daughter and a canoe. This is why she had come here, because it was like watching TV. Hypnotic. She knew the sex with him would be the same way and it was. She hadn't had to think or talk much, only smile when he told her how he missed the curve of her belly, grow wistful when he said he still thought about her all the time.

"When was the last time you saw your daughter?" she asked.

"A couple of months ago," said Jack.

"You should go see her."

"I know, but she's in school, in New York, and I'm here right now. I'll see her this summer."

"Yeah, but you should go sooner. Because you never know."

He didn't do anything as obvious as wince, but she could see she was depressing him. Reminding him of other depressing women again—neither of them wanted that.

"Sorry," she said. A deflated plastic lounge chair lay by the side of the pool at the house he had rented. Behind it rose a hedge wall of shiny deep green leaves. Hollyleaf cherry, she almost said aloud. The way she used to name the birds, sitting by the water with Viv and Andy. Instead, she pointed to the drooping lounger. "Hey, can you blow this up?"

"Sure. I'll blow, you watch."

It was a line from a movie he'd been in, delivered by an actress making the transition from child star to adult roles. She'd accomplished this rather successfully, too, the actress. So it was possible. But you almost always had to say things like that. Jack had been about ten years younger then, his face fuller, rosier, but he was aging well, looking weathered, leaner, more interesting, less like a puppy dog. What would his daughter think someday, maybe years from now, when she went back and watched his old movies? Would she think, *My dad was so beautiful once?*

a memory
you didn't know
you had

Viv, 2012

The package arrived on a Saturday a few weeks ago, and went in a pile that Andy placed on the table in the front hall. We have a front hall now, with a narrow window running the length of the front door, throwing a rectangle of sunlight on the floor, on a pair of little shoes. We have a jacaranda tree shedding purple flowers in our yard. We have a yard. We have a son, who pulled the padded envelope down and said, "mail darf" as he struggled in vain to open it.

"Maildarf," said Andy. "The parcel service of Middle Earth."

"Dada," said Leo, handing it to Andy.

"Can you take that over to Mama?" Andy asked. "Then I'll take you to the park."

"Mama," said Leo.

On the front was my name written in Lee's hand, with an Austin, Texas, postmark, no return address. It had been more than two years since I'd heard anything from her. When she came back to New York following the confrontation with her mother, we met up for dinner, though only after repeated attempts on my part to pin down a time and place. Already again, she was not quite contrite enough, and I was mildly aggrieved. But that disappeared when she showed up steadied by the kind of calm that a beta-blocking agent or benzodiazepine provides. That calm was reinforced over the course of the evening by several glasses of Malbec that I matched with mineral water. She told me what had happened with Linda. I asked what she was going to do. She'd already quit her job. There was no way she could keep working for her. *No, I meant, was she going to go to the police?* She didn't think so. Marion never had. What good would it do anybody now, Linda serving out a sentence, if it even came to that? The law seemed so far removed from what had happened—inadequate in a sense. Lee wasn't sure what was next. She thought she might travel for a while. *Still,* I thought. *Still, after everything. To be someone who can just quit a job and go traveling with no fixed return.* I envied her. That was as much as I knew.

The envelope contained a CD ("How old school," said Andy.) and a note for me. I knew, of course, what it must be and passed the disc to Andy. But I kept the note in my hand, not wanting to open it just yet. Some instinct told me I ought to be alone to read it. Whatever it contained belonged only to me, or someone I used to be.

"Should we play it?" Andy asked.

"You guys are all ready to go. Let's play it when you get back."

"The suspense isn't going to kill you?"

"I don't know. Maybe it'll be anticlimactic."

"Yeah. After all this time."

"But Flintwick always said it was really good. Music is the one thing you could trust him about. Marion also said it was great."

I felt I should stop talking, that Lee and Linda and Jesse, the Parrish Wests, were like an ex that you could bring up every once in a while, just enough to stoke a healthy jealousy, but no more. I had to have my limits.

"You guys go. I really have to get this stuff done. So we'll just listen to it tonight."

"Okay. Don't work too hard. We'll see you later."

I'm writing at all hours now for a new set of characters in a different town. Verona Crossing, Wisconsin, is located somewhere between Milwaukee and Chicago. Verona Crossing is populated with its own magnates, supermodels, law enforcement agents, restaurateurs, and a disgraced mayor currently having a second act as a highly regarded cocktail mixologist. When word of THATH's cancellation had come, Frank received an offer to work for one of the remaining L.A. soaps and suggested I go with him. "There's nothing for us here," he said of New York, as though it were time to leave the barren farm and hop a boxcar to a Hooverville. We had all seen the end coming. Andy thought we should do it. Pick up stakes, start again. His prospects were fine ("They have the Internet there.") and the change, he believed, would be good for us, for our family.

I want to compare it to a broken bone, what happened with Rodgers and coming clean with Andy. There had been a fracture and then I made the break complete. It could be fixed, it would heal, but we would have to immobilize it, work around it, learn to use other parts of our bodies in new ways. We would be able to walk again, and eventually there might not even be a limp. But still. There was a night, the end of a night, when I heard him come home to our apartment. I didn't know where he'd been. He must have sat in the dark, in the living room, for an hour before he came into our room, just as it was getting light out. I wasn't showing yet but I was already rounder, fuller. There was more of me in the bed. He lay down and put his body against mine, as if to make a seal between us. I wrapped my arms around me. There wasn't one moment: *I forgive you now.* I had hurt him, hurt us, and that never went away. It took root, but it didn't—allow me to switch metaphors—overrun or edge out everything else that could flourish between us.

Soon after we settled in to a home in Highland Park, Linda got in touch and invited me to lunch. I considered saying no out of loyalty to Lee and respect for her feelings. But I didn't know what Lee's feelings were—she was gone from my life again. What surprised me was how infrequently I thought about her. It wasn't an even exchange, Leo taking Lee's place in a trio. I only registered the similarity of their names months after Leo was born. If Andy did, he didn't say anything—we'd named him for Andy's grandfather. But Leo's presence demagnetized me to Lee's old pull, which isn't to say I didn't welcome the temporary quiet now, the shutting of the door, being left with Lee's letter. It's just to say I didn't miss her. Not like I used to. When I did things, I didn't wonder what Lee would think, whether she would approve. I went to see Linda not because she was a link to Lee, not because they were made out of the same stardust and I wanted to be in a haze of it once more. I decided to see Linda because while I had been so naïve so often, I knew what knowing Linda West could do for me out here. That long-ago night—the redwood deck, the pool, the movie director.

"Oh, Viv!" she gasped, clutching my shoulders, hands like hen claws. "You look *won*derful!"

"Breastfeeding," I exclaimed, matching her excitement. "It's the best diet ever."

"Yes, I have a dim memory of that." She pulled me in for a hug while the host, whom she called by name, patiently gave us a moment before leading us to our table—a slab of salvaged wood by a window of reclaimed glass. "You know, I did nurse Lee. For a little while anyway. Not that I'd ever get any credit for it." She raised her hands, palms toward me, as though surrendering to a judgment, a move I'd never seen her make. "So how is motherhood treating you?"

It was won*derful,* I said. Then she gave me her "Okay, for real, tell me, girlfriend" face. I quickly confessed to her how hard it had been, how unrelenting, especially at first. Sobbing in the shower, wondering how I would ever manage to leave the house again but not in an active, purposeful way, more in a mystified way: *I used to leave the house?* It was cold outside, a dirty New York winter. My body hurt. I wanted to convalesce. I had heard people say things like, "Parenthood is brutal but totally worth it." They made it sound like a particularly challenging workout and not like you had plunged to the bottom of a lake and grown gills and that the world beyond the watery light of the surface was no longer yours.

My maternity leave began just a few weeks before THATH's cancellation came down, so I had no work to return to, no old, familiar structure. I read a lot of essays written by women who hated playgrounds. I worried that my love was not unconditional. I worried that I worried. But then my heart would leap as I watched my son sleeping. It would somersault when I sat him in my lap and patted his back to burp him, which he met with a calm but alert look, like a curious sightseer, with his arms out and folded over each other like a genie. He broke my heart when he rested his little hand on my waist as I nursed him and when his cry grew faint, exhausted and trembling. Sometimes he looked like a turtle. Once, squinting and full-cheeked, he looked like Wallace Shawn. And when he smiled at me as if I lit up his whole world, it lit up mine.

I thought I had read enough baby-preparation books and seen enough diaper commercials to know what to expect: joy, aggravation, aggravated joy, joyous aggravation, lots of complaining about never having sex but not really caring because you were so tired and all you really wanted to do with that time was order takeout and watch TV. I expected to be changed in profound ways, though I didn't know what that would necessarily involve because these changes seemed to be so profound they rendered language inadequate. But I thought they would have to do with me and the baby, not me and Andy. If anything, they would exclude Andy and that's why we would have to remember to "prioritize our relationship" and I would have to remind myself that I was "not just a mom, but a woman!"

I hadn't expected mystery. Andy and I became mysterious to each other in a way I don't think we'd been since that very first time I'd heard his voice on the phone when I called about the room. I would watch him standing by the window holding our son and think of him as someone I wanted to get to know. I would wonder about him. A wonder that led to a want that lifted a spell. As though part of me had been asleep.

Somehow there was more space with three of us. It's too simple to say that this new space we found was where Lee used to be. But her absence could be as defining as her presence. It reminded me of that day I ran into Kirsten, on my own. How sure of herself she was with Lee out of the picture, this girl who had called us a planet and herself an ant. It also made me think of the way Frank had once swiftly absolved a character of insidious actions by attributing them to a brain tumor that merely had to be removed. Lee wasn't a brain tumor and I couldn't blame her for my being unfaithful to Andy. Nor could I simply excise the infidelity by not contacting Rodgers again. For a while, he became a kind of fantasy. I thought about him too much. I didn't go places he was bound to be, but on occasions where there might be some chance, however slight, of running into him, I made sure I looked good. On days when I just happened to look particularly good (pregnancy worked for me), days when Andy would compliment me, I regretted that I never ran into Rodgers. I didn't even try to reach out to Lee to talk about it. Instead I confided in new friends, women who had told me about similar confusions in their own lives and had trusted me to react sympathetically. Who understood fallibility. It wasn't Lee's fault. But she was a big part of it. Just as she had been a part of something for Andy that excluded me. Their attachment didn't involve me, and then it did, and I had to be there in order to be left out. I could get lost in the paradoxes. But maybe it wasn't that complicated. The old triangle fell apart. Andy and I created a new one.

I didn't tell Linda about the mystery, the wonder, the want. I took out my phone to show her a recent video of Leo, just under a year old then, laughing, and I could see her trying not to look bored. So I changed the subject.

We talked about her work. She had pulled back from the business and was considering selling the brand to a French conglomerate. We talked about L.A. *"This is where you need to be!"* She was excited for me, eager to help. This is how Linda enchanted you. How Lee did, too, in a quieter, steadier way. Their encouragement, their belief in you. It meant that you were unique, as special as they were, and you mattered. Linda had always treated me this way, and it felt generous, never strained. Until now. Now that she knew that I knew what she'd done. And what might I do with that knowledge? Obviously I'd done nothing with it yet. So what could she do for me to keep it that way? She didn't say this; she didn't have to. I suppose I could finally read between the lines. And maybe there had been something in it for her all along, an advantage in being kind to me.

"Have you heard from Lee lately?" Linda asked.

"No."

"Would you tell me if you had?"

"You'd probably get it out of me."

"Yes. I probably would."

Six months have passed since then, busy months in which I haven't

taken Linda up on any favors, but not because I've declined on principle. I'm keeping her in reserve. I'm sure there will come a time
when I'll need her, sooner rather than later, and more than once I've
thought about something Flintwick said—how Jesse would never
get his hands dirty. How that was the difference between him and
Jesse, between Jesse and Linda. It was the difference between Lee
and me. I had thought, hoped really, when we first became friends,
that Lee might corrupt me. But I'd been wrong about who she was,
and probably about who I was. Within her there was always something that wouldn't be compromised, that wasn't corrupt and wasn't
corrupting. I'm sure she didn't think so, but it was true. As soon as
Andy left with Leo, I sat down and read her note.

Dear Viv,

*I've forgotten how to write a letter. You were right, as usual, about
not hearing from me. I'm sorry it's been so long. I can't believe I
haven't met Leo. I like that name. I like thinking of your son as a
lionhearted boy. I hope you're doing well and I hope you're very happy
in L.A.*

*So, guess what turned up? I stopped looking after all of that
with Linda. But the short story is that a middle-aged divorcée in
Minneapolis moved into a new house, a house where Chris Valenti
used to live, and found the tapes in a box up in the attic. She had a
yard sale and this guy, a reel-to-reel recording enthusiast, happens to
see them next to a pile of old dishes, takes them home, and actually
knows what it is he's listening to. He gets in touch with Charlie
Flintwick, who gets in touch with me. Flintwick wants to remaster
and release them. Linda says it's up to me. Yes, I've talked to her.
Legally, it's up to her. But obviously legality never troubled her
much. It's strange, though, because when she put it to me, when she
said it was my choice, I thought at first that she was handing me a*

responsibility, the way she had given me a job. Like it might make me feel I was a part of things, but that ultimately she was merely delegating. Only she wasn't. She told me this was mine in a way that made it feel like an act of restitution. For so long I'd been telling myself that there couldn't really be any restitution because nothing was taken from me, nothing I ever really had. But I don't think that's true now. Because this does feel like mine. And if it's mine, it's yours too. And it's Andy's. When I think about it, maybe it really belongs to Andy more than anyone else.

    Some of the songs, you'll hear it, are kind of ragged. In a good way. I don't know if Jesse was able to get out exactly what he heard in his head. What I know is I don't have to try to understand it, it just wraps itself around you, all of that feeling. There's something familiar about it. Not that they sound just like his other songs. But it's more like they are a memory I didn't know I had. If that makes any sense. I'm glad they're here, these songs. I feel like they're on my side.

    Linda told me she saw you when we spoke on the phone. I'm not upset. Not really. I'm sure Linda can help you out there. I don't mean that it was mercenary of you or anything. I know you're not me and you don't have to feel about her whatever way I do. I don't even know how I feel about her these days.

    I should sign off, let you go listen and let my father have the last word. But, fuck it, call me selfish and sentimental, I want the last word. I don't have trouble meeting people. I meet them all the time and they usually want to know me. Or they think they do. I still have this ebb-and-flow thing with Jack, if you can believe it. (It has dawned on me that he is my Roy). I have friends, people who matter to me, but none of them matter the way that you did. When we were at Marion's that time, I had this thought that I could just stay there with her and never leave. An implausible scenario—impossible—but it became a feeling that was so real to me. It happens a lot—these feelings that have no form to take, no outlet, not even a name. What do you do with those feelings? Where do they go? I know I shouldn't dwell on them, and I try not to, but sometimes when I have no particular place to be and the sun is shining, I just drive and drive because I love what it reminds me of.

Lee

they could've
asked

∽

Lee, 1996

Viv said, "Let's do something sort of touristy." So Lee took what she thought of as the scenic route and drove them up along Mulholland Drive, winding east and down into the flats of Hollywood, along Franklin to Vermont and into Griffith Park. They parked by the Observatory, took in the requisite views of the city below, the ocean to the west, the Hollywood sign, and then they set out to walk along a fire road.

The trail was full, at first, with groups of hikers, charged with resolutions, to be fit, to be social in the new year. Neither Lee nor Viv minded the crowd. A welcome distraction in a way. It was day five in their seven-day stay here and though they weren't exactly tired of each other, they'd already grown accustomed to each other, to the sameness of the weather, the unchanging pace. Linda, her house, her pool, were no longer new to Viv. Neither were palm trees, celebrities, the first-rate fast food unique to this place.

Lee knew about a certain turnoff that led to an emptier stretch. More secluded, wilder. A bit more work for your legs. Too much talk would have left them winded so they stayed quiet as they climbed. Eventually the trees gave way to patches of scrubby chaparral. She'd once seen a coyote here on the way to the summit. This time, she saw a large mutt, with its owner, starting back down just as she and Viv reached the crest. There was no one else in sight. Only the two of them, standing silently in the sun for so long that it was almost a non sequitur when Viv said: "I used to be so scared of dogs."

"Why? Did something happen?"

"We never had pets. My dad was allergic. That was the story anyway. So I was never super comfortable around animals. And when I was in elementary school, at recess once, a black Labrador got onto the field. He was huge, at least he seemed so big to me at the time. I must have been six or seven. I have this memory of being out there with all these kids, no adults, and the dog bounding toward me. I didn't know that if you run, they think you're playing, that you want them to chase you. I was terrified and I just remember running around in a big circle and all the kids standing there and yelling but nobody doing anything to stop it and I didn't see any end to it. It felt like forever and then finally I fell. I want the story to be that the dog came to my side, licked my hand or something. But really he just ran past me, into another group of kids. And I was just there in the mud, in this light blue corduroy dress. Usually I wore, like, sweatsuits. But that day, I don't know why, I was wearing this dress and I thought my mom was going to be really upset to see it all dirty. But if she was, she didn't say anything. And I didn't mention anything about the dog. I never mentioned it to anyone really. Except you. Now."

"That sounds awful. The whole thing. But mostly that you were so alone."

"But I could've told my mom. I could've told anyone."

"They could've asked."

"True," said Viv. And she turned to Lee: asking.

What to tell her? Lee thought of what so often disturbed her lately: Andy and the last few months. Not as a sequence of events, not this happened, then this happened, then this and here's what it means. It was all still sensation for her. She didn't know how to explain that to Viv. But Viv didn't push for anything more. She just put her arms around Lee, a side hug, and kind of hung there, her chin on Lee's shoulder. Lee searched the skyline, the mountains, the basin of building after building, street upon street, that stretched out before them, the cluster of towers in downtown Los Angeles rising like a derelict Emerald City in the distance. How vast it seemed, but also, from up here, how shimmering and ephemeral. To steady herself, she held on to Viv, and soon enough they were breathing together, rising and falling, at the top of the trail.

Acknowledgments

Jesse Parrish is an imaginary, impossible combination of a number of much mythologized icons, but his background is particularly inspired by that of Gram Parsons and I drew on some details from the following biographies: *Twenty Thousand Roads: The Ballad of Gram Parsons and His Cosmic American Music* by David N. Meyer, *Gram Parsons: A Music Biography* by Sid Griffin, and *Hickory Wind: The Life and Times of Gram Parsons* by Ben Fong-Torres. I'm also indebted to the works of Eve Babitz, which, sadly, had been out of print until recently. A lot of what Andy knows about the Garden of Allah, and a good deal more about Los Angeles in the seventies, I learned from Babitz's wonderful *Slow Days, Fast Company; Eve's Hollywood;* and *Sex and Rage*. And I couldn't have conjured Elise Robin without some help from Pamela Des Barres's memoir *I'm With the Band*.

Huge thanks to Kate Garrick and Margaux Weisman. Kate, your vision and your unwavering belief mean the world to me. Margaux, you made this happen and your superb skills made it all the better. I've been so lucky to work with both of you. Thank you to everyone at William Morrow/HarperCollins who helped turn this into a reality, especially Katherine Turro, Maria Silva, Mumtaz Mustafa, and Julia Meltzer. Thanks also to Colin Farstad and Cathy Jacque. I'm so grateful to Lauren Acampora, Carlene Bauer, Sarah Bowlin, Stephanie Feldman, and Caroline Kepnes for all of your insight and encouragement. This book took shape over a number of years and it wouldn't really exist without the friendship of Alex Abramovich, Nida Alahmad, Kathleen Andersen, Jessica Berman Boatright, Coco Culhane, Jim Drain, Carrie Gabriel, Monica Khemsurov, Sam Lipsyte, Carole Obedin, Kelly Shimoda, Nicole Walker, and Rita Zilberman. Thank you to my friends and to my family, especially Renee Peppercorn, Phil Shapiro, Rebecca Shapiro, Reba and Hal McVey. And to the greatest of hearts, Lewis and Callum McVey.

P.S.

Insights,
Interviews
& More...

*

About the book

Read on

Reading Group Guide

1. The novel opens with news clippings about Lee's father, Jesse Parrish. Why do you think the author chose to do this? How does it set up the rest of the narrative?

2. Vivian says that her real life didn't begin until she met Lee. Do you think this is true? What defined her before she moved in with Lee and Andy? And how did she change once she met them?

3. In college, do you think that Lee is a good friend? Why or why not? Do you think that Vivian is a good friend to Lee?

4. The author includes a flashback in which Lee and Vivian attend another college classmate's wedding. What purpose does this scene serve? What do we learn about the characters?

5. Jesse Parrish takes on a mythic quality by virtue of the fact that he died so young. Why do you think we, as a culture, romanticize people that die before their time? Can you think of any real life examples?

6. If you were Vivian, would you go with Lee on her road trip? Why do you think Vivian decides to go? How does her marriage change over the course of the narrative?

7. Do you think of yourself as more of a Lee or a Vivian? Have you ever had a friendship that resembles theirs? What was the lasting effect of that relationship?

8. Lee and Vivian's parents and upbringings are presented in stark contrast. How do their backgrounds effect their choices?

9. What do you imagine the future holds for Lee and Vivian? When the book ends, it's unclear whether they will continue to foster a friendship. Do you think they will reconnect? ◝

An Interview with Deborah Shapiro, by Stephanie Feldman

Reprinted with permission from
Slice Magazine

Deborah Shapiro's debut novel, *The Sun in Your Eyes,* tells the story of Lee and Viv, two best friends who reunite after years of silence. Lee is looking for a partner in her search for the final recordings of her father, dead rock icon Jesse Parrish. Viv is looking for an escape from her soap opera writing job and her domestic life. Together they travel through Jesse's past, and their own, in search of a resolution to the bond they once shared.

Critics have lauded the book's portrait of female friendship, and through that friendship, Shapiro explores art and celebrity, parents and romantic partners, and what happens when you've already come of age but find you still have more road to travel.

Q: *Writing about music is notoriously challenging. Did you have any particular strategies or techniques for writing about Jesse Parrish's music, and Viv's connection to it?*

A: The thing that makes music so evocative—that makes us respond viscerally—is what makes it so difficult to get on the page. And language is its own kind of music, which I think is why a lot of writers can't listen to music while writing. It disrupts what you're trying to do sonically. So, I didn't really listen to anything while I was writing, but I had certain albums on repeat when I wasn't at the computer. There were a number of musicians I looked to in trying to shape Jesse into a character—Gram Parsons, Marc Bolan, Nick Drake, Tim Buckley. There's a critic in the book who describes Jesse as a "lesser, campier Neil Young" and I went down some YouTube rabbit holes watching clips of David Bowie on talk shows in the 70s. There's so much lore to draw on. It was harder to come up with Jesse's sound. But I kept going back to Big Star's *Third/Sister Lovers* record from 1974—this gorgeous record of falling apart—and I tried to write what I heard, more or less.

I also wanted to take into account the world around the music itself—not so much the industry, but the way listeners received it. I re-read work by Greil Marcus and Ellen Willis to get a feel for the way they describe music and performance, and how those descriptions become cultural commentary as well. And I wanted to explore the relationship between performers and fans, how intense and formative that worship can be. Lee connects to Jesse's music, or wants to connect to it, as his daughter. But Viv connects to it, much like me, as a fan. Andy, Viv and Lee's college roommate ▶

and obsessive audiophile, even more so.
Being a fan is basically this strange
one-sided relationship but it doesn't
seem that way when you're fifteen, alone
in your room with your headphones on,
listening to a song that both expresses
everything you're feeling and takes you
outside of yourself. Right?

**Q: *Critics have focused on the novel's
exploration of female friendship, but the
story also considers marriage and the
bonds between daughters and parents.
Did you begin with friendship, and find
yourself expanding your scope as you
wrote? How do these relationships
complement each other within the story?***

A: I did begin with friendship but it
quickly moved beyond that. Viv and Lee
don't exist in a vacuum. They each have
their own separate contexts that
influence their relationship—that draw
them together and pull them apart—and
I wanted to examine that. Each of them
envies and admires the other's family
and upbringing. Lee is drawn to Viv's
seemingly stable, level-headed parents
and Viv is taken with Linda, Lee's
over-the-top mother. And both women
learn about themselves as they learn
about their own families. With Lee, this
is more concrete, in that she actually
uncovers a secret that's essentially
affected the unfolding of her entire life.
But Viv also uncovers things about her
parents, not necessarily intentionally-

kept secrets, but the kinds of emotional discoveries or realizations that make you look at your family and yourself in a different light.

And there are lots of parallels and echoes and repetitions between the parents and children in this book. Lee, in particular, has such a conflicted connection to her mother. She can't stand her, but she can't escape her mother's sway, in ways large (working for Linda) and small (using the same luggage Linda swears by for travel).

Q: *So often we describe books as either character-driven or plot-driven. The* **Sun in Your Eyes** *is a character study, but also invokes a classic plot arc: the road trip. How did you marry these two approaches, or do you think plot vs. character is a false distinction?*

A: I think it is somewhat of a false distinction. Character *is* plot, of course. Any time a character makes a decision, or fails to make one—that's plot, in a way. As a reader, I tend to be more interested in characters, in their psychologies, their layers and nuances, and if this is revealed in skillful way, that's often enough "plot" for me. Still, as a writer, I wanted to use plot as a vehicle for exploring characters. I wanted to have some kind of engine for the story, and the "road trip" and the "quest" appealed to me—the "quest" especially, because it's never really ▶

about the about object in question, it's
about the search. In attempting to track
down Jesse's last recordings, what Lee
and Viv are really seeking is something
much more ineffable and unresolvable
about their relationship and themselves.
So, the lost tapes are something of a
MacGuffin. Finding them matters to Lee
but searching for them matters a great
deal more to her, not least because it
gives her a reason to insert herself back
in Viv's life.

But back to plot vs. character—there's
a moment at the end of the book, from
Lee's perspective, where she's prompted
for an explanation she can't articulate.
She can't say "this happened, then this
happened, then this happened and here's
what it all means. It was all still sensation
for her." I like a satisfying conclusion as
much as anybody, but I tend to like
narrative best when it becomes like
watching dance, especially one you've
seen before. What "happens" doesn't
really matter, or maybe you already
know what happens, but you're still
riveted by the movement and form and
feeling. It's why you can read great
fiction over and over.

**Q: Lee and Viv come from very different
backgrounds, and social class—
economic, cultural, ethnic—permeates
everything. We see it in the clothes they
wear, the houses they live in, and their
relationships with their parents. Was
this an inevitable part of describing**

*these women? Or did you have
particular goals in mind, and choose
particular writing strategies?*

A: It wasn't really until I went to college,
and then moved to New York City, that I
was exposed to certain gradations of
wealth and the signifiers of those
gradations. And that's something that
Viv, from her upper-middle class
suburban background, experiences when
she meets Lee. Viv notes that the
affluence she grew up around took the
shape of "remodeled kitchens and glitzy
bar mitzvahs." Lee's wealth, her
pedigree, is on a whole other level. She's
sort of bohemian royalty. Not only does
her family have money, they have
cultural capital, they have connections.
It allows her to move through the world
in a different way. And I was interested
in looking at those distinctions. So all of
those things—the way they dress, their
interior spaces—are signifiers I wanted
to decode. And that's something that
draws Viv to Lee, her fascination with
these signifiers. It's not money or flash
that interests Viv, but the kind of
glamour Lee has as a result of her social
class.

   There's a scene where Viv, looking for
a potential roommate situation, goes to
Lee's apartment for the first time and
sees a vase of flowers. It's not an
expensive arrangement, they're
wildflowers Lee must have picked, but
just the fact that she has these flowers ▶

both throws and delights Viv. It connotes some kind of aesthetic sophistication and leisure that Viv is only beginning to comprehend. She notes how her mother never bothered with flowers because they're frivolous. But it's their very frivolity that Lee is after and this is what charms Viv.

Details like this emerged fairly inevitably in the process of writing. But there were also certain decisions I made, like making Lee's mother, Linda, a fashion designer. It was a way of getting at some of those sartorial choices that give off a signal only to whoever is ready to pick up on it. You know, two people can both be wearing a black dress but because of the cut, the proportions, the fabric, their looks can be read entirely differently.

Q: *You've named Gram Parsons' music, Nicholas Mosley's novel* Accident, *and the William Eggleston photo that graces the hardcover edition of the book as some inspirations for this story. Do you find your inspiration mostly comes from other art? How does your experience as a listener, reader, and viewer inform your writing process?*

A: I'd say inspiration comes from art and life. But there's something transformative about experiencing good art or music or literature; it influences my writing process in that it generates a sense of possibility and usually makes me want to go create something myself. (Though it can also work the other way around, when something is so maddeningly great it just makes you think, *Why bother? It's all been done.* But I've usually been able to push through that.) The references to these experiences or certain works of art may not be direct or even noticeable in what I've written, but I like to think on some level the aesthetic traces are there.

Q: *The book employs both first- and third-person narration. How did you come to use these different points-of-view?*

A: The book is told mostly from Viv's first-person POV and Lee's close third-person POV. But there's also one section from Linda's perspective. I don't write particularly linearly and Linda's section came to me pretty early on, before I had figured out a way to work it in. I began writing this in first-person, from Viv's perspective, and one book I kept going back to was *The Great Gatsby,* where you have the narrator, Nick Carraway, telling you about this dazzling, deceptive, complicated world he gets involved in. He's in that world—so much that he almost disappears at times—but he's not really of it. I wanted Viv to be a little like Nick Carraway, but she didn't turn out that way. I couldn't make her disappear *enough.* At a certain point, I wanted to hear from Lee, not Lee via Viv. Lee isn't in her own head as much as Viv, so third-person seemed more fitting for her. She's closer to her emotions, in that she doesn't need to talk something through in order to understand how she feels about it, she doesn't need as much language around it the way Viv does. But she's also not as forthcoming about her emotions and experiences as Viv is. The slight distance of third-person, I think, works for her character in that way.

Q: *When you read the first chapter at your book launch, the audience laughed again and again. Did you consciously use humor to off-set the darker aspects of the book, or is it a natural part of your writing?*

A: It's not so much conscious—like, let's insert a joke here or this scene needs some levity — it's just the way I tend to think and how I relate. But there's also another kind of false distinction, between darkness and humor, and between seriousness and comedy. The notion that if something is comic it's lightweight, unless it's a social satire tackling Big Important Themes. Maybe the more helpful and true distinction is between solemnity and seriousness. Solemnity doesn't allow for the kind of irony that I think is an essential part of being human. But you can be serious and ironic. There are so many writers who do this expertly but I'm thinking specifically here of Robert Stone, who writes about the heaviest subject matter but he does it with such deft irony and shots of dark humor. The humor doesn't diminish the weight; it only adds to the depth. ∾

Deborah Shapiro's
The Sun in Your Eyes
Road Trip Playlist

"Come On Let's Go"—Broadcast
"September Gurls"—Big Star
"Alison"—Slowdive
"Tarifa"—Sharon Van Etten
"Can You Get to That"—Funkadelic
"Wakin on a Pretty Day"—Kurt Vile
"You Said Something"—PJ Harvey
"VCR"—The xx
"I Believe (When I Fall in Love It Will Be Forever)"—Stevie Wonder
"Regret"—New Order
"Sowing Seeds"—The Jesus and Mary Chain
"Two Step"—Throwing Muses